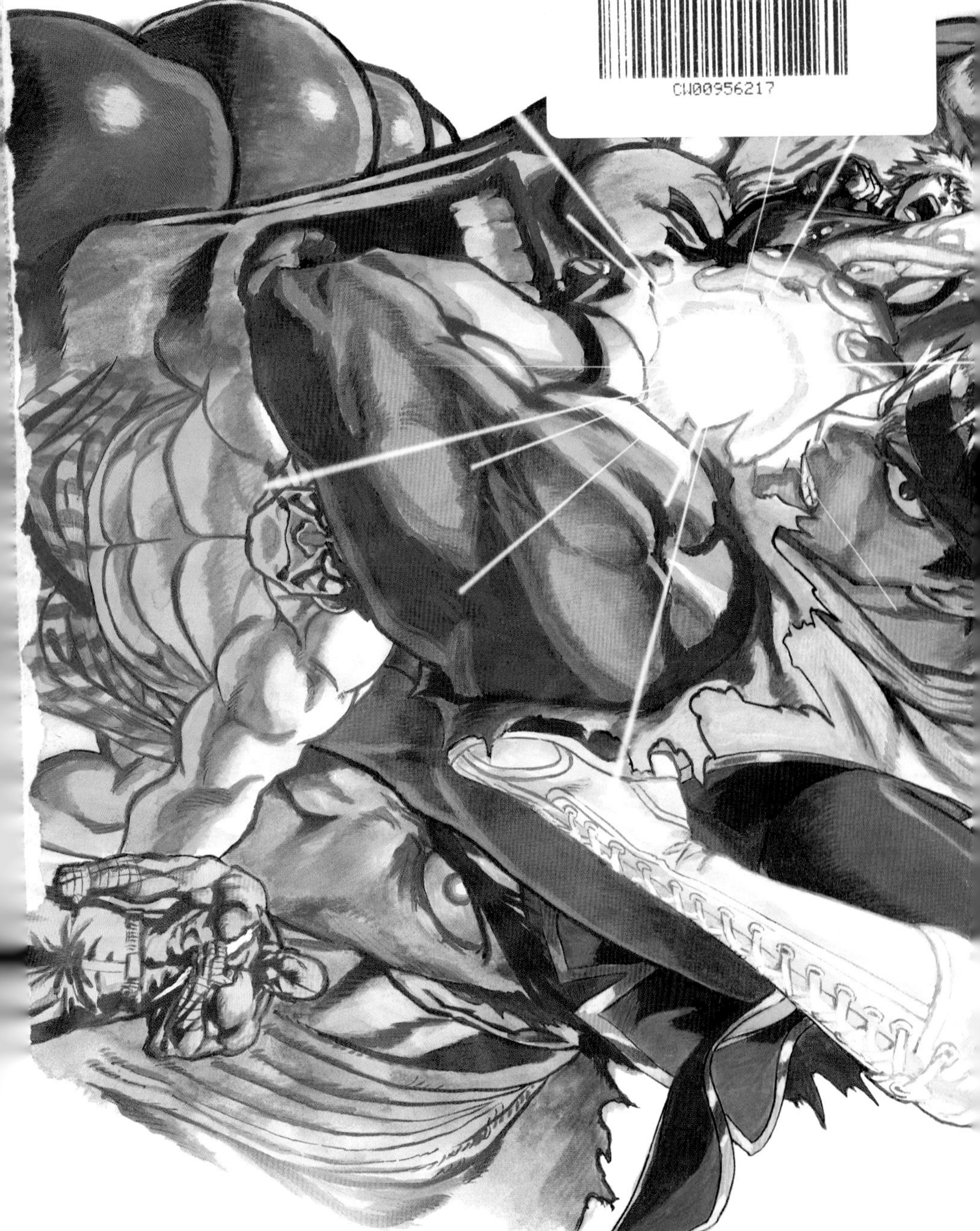

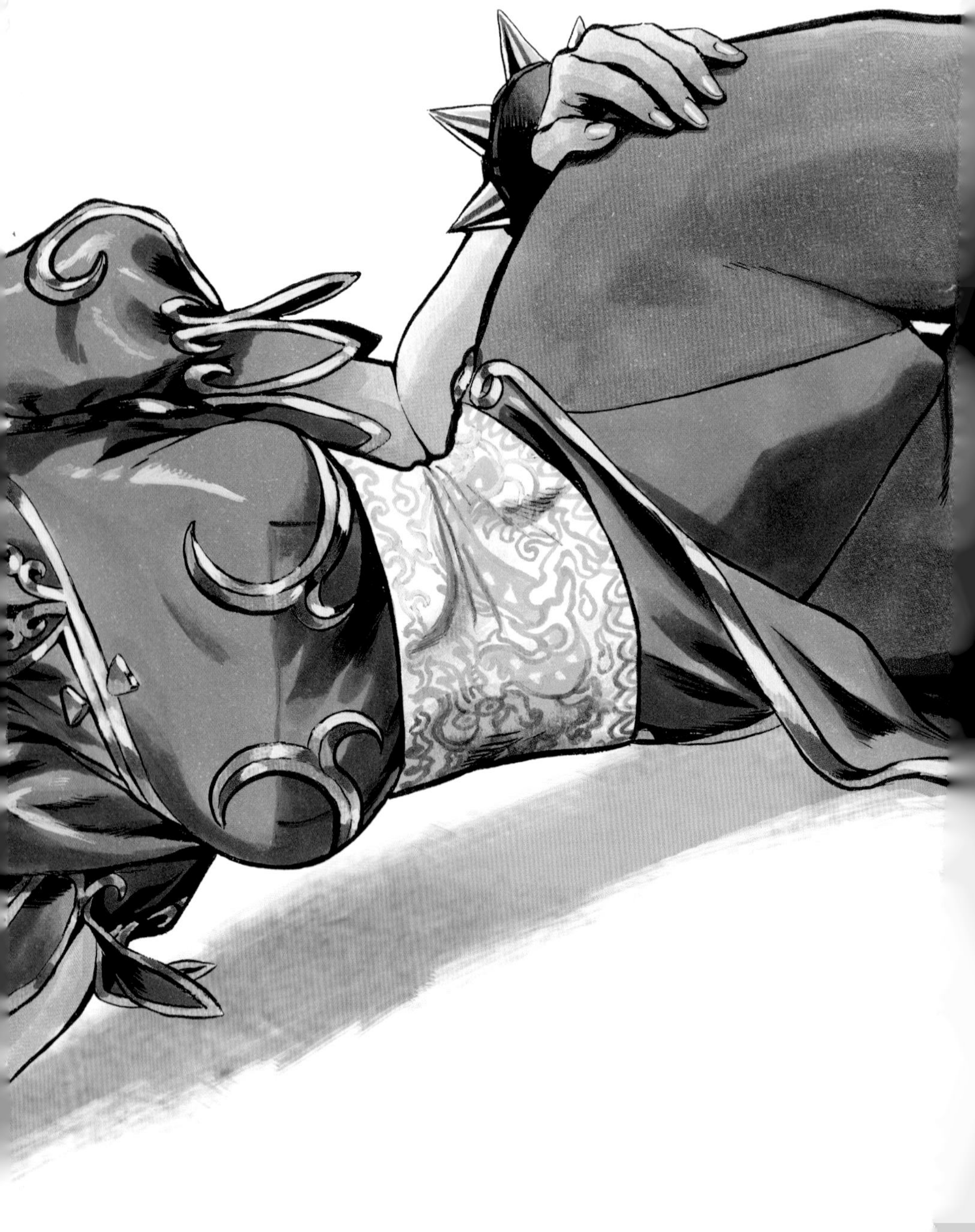

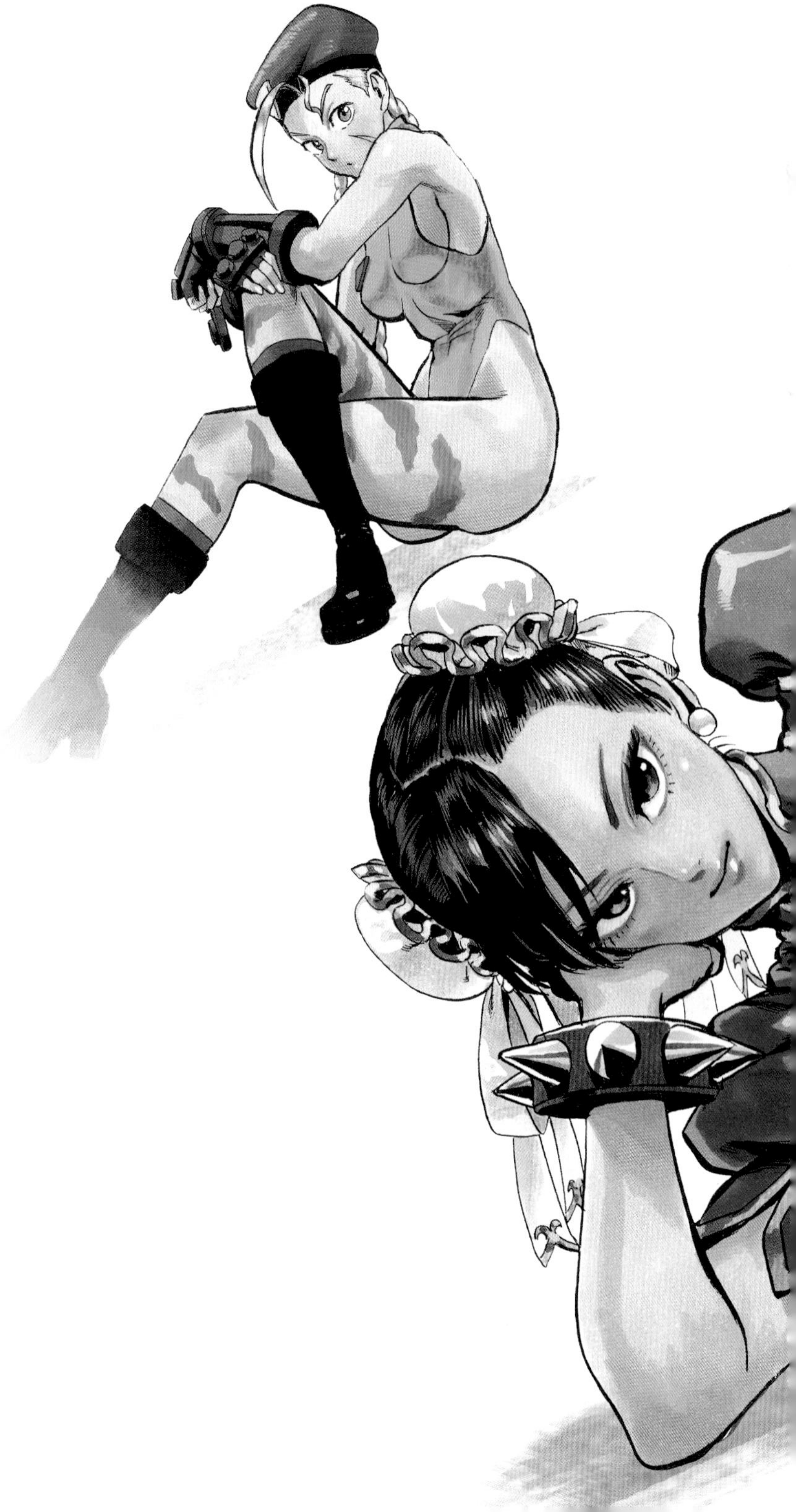

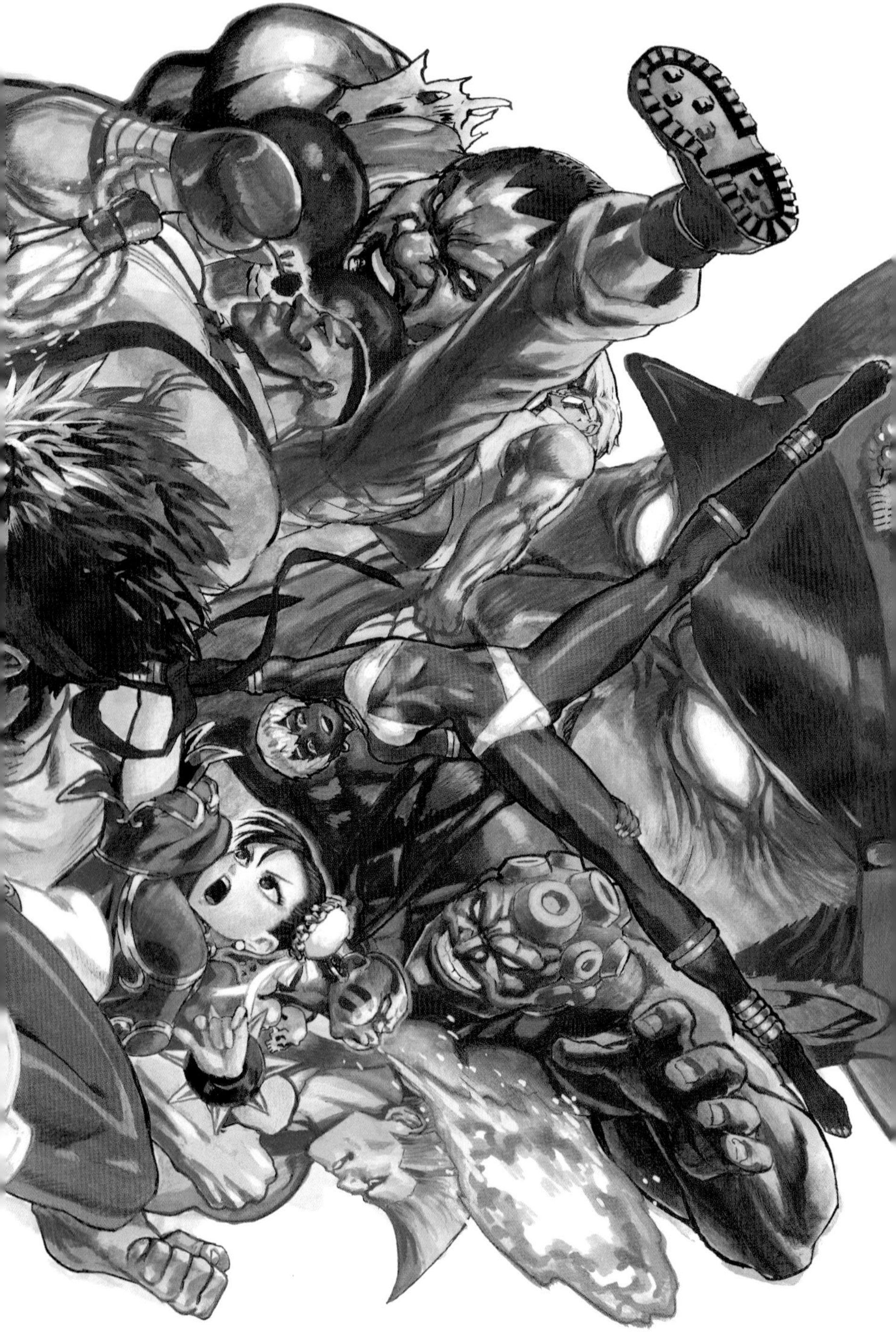

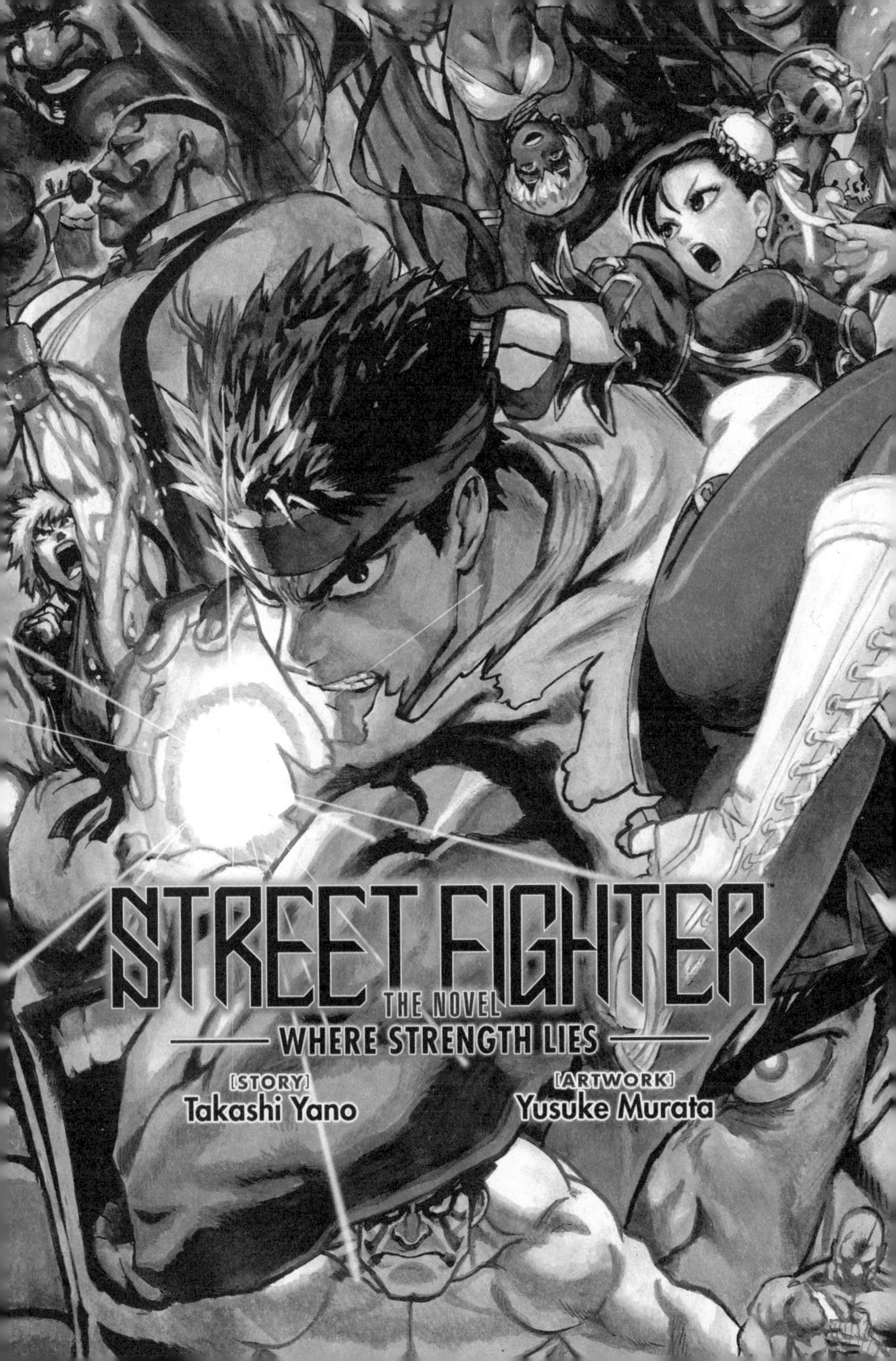
STREET FIGHTER
THE NOVEL
WHERE STRENGTH LIES
[STORY]
Takashi Yano
[ARTWORK]
Yusuke Murata

STREET FIGHTER
THE NOVEL

WHERE STRENGTH LIES

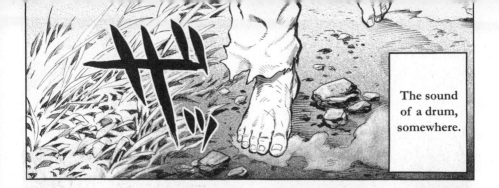

The sound of a drum, somewhere.

A great, massive drum.

ROUND 1
Roar of Bloodlust

It seemed
to
emanate
from
the black
clouds
that
blanketed
the earth.

ROUND 1
ROAR OF BLOODLUST

The sound of a drum, somewhere. A great, massive drum. Rumbling majestically, shaking the very darkness of the night. Like great peals of thunder, it seemed to emanate from the black clouds that blanketed the earth.

"But where's the sound coming from?" thought Ryu as he stared down the enemy standing before him.

Not a single tree dotted the landscape; just wasteland as far as the eye could see. The withered grass that gently brushed against Ryu's legs through his *dougi* uniform was the only small sign of life. Where could the unseen drummer possibly be, out here?

Nowhere.

Only two men stood—Ryu and the enemy.

"Your heart beats loud," murmured the enemy. Though the words were meant for him, it took Ryu a moment to realize. An encounter such as this was no time for talking, rare a chance as it was.

Master of the Fist, Kishin, Gouki...

The enemy had many nicknames, but how many could claim to have met the man? Those seeking strength, however, would inevitably come across his name in their travels.

Akuma...

Trained in the same school of martial arts as Ryu, and younger brother to Ryu's own master, Gouken.

Akuma's strength was awakened by bloodlust, leading him to

murder Gouken. If the master's fist was one of light, then his brother's represented the pinnacle of darkness. Akuma spoke once more.

"Your heart has been pounding for quite some time, now."

At the sound of the heavy, gravelly voice, Ryu could do nothing to stop the chills that ran up his spine. Every ounce of bloodlust that filled Akuma's being was poured into his voice, shaking the very atmosphere before reaching Ryu's ears. And from his ears, it crept into his body, as if a spreading infection. The voice was tinged with enough malice to cause such an illusion.

"Is that really my own heartbeat?" Ryu pondered as he reflected on Akuma's words. Who could believe that the incessant pounding was coming from within?

Nerves are inevitable before a fight, but when the heart beats fast, the body tenses. Learning to overcome those palpitations is just another necessary element of training.

Ryu could never mistake his own heartbeat for the sound of a drum.

If Akuma was correct, and the deafening sound was Ryu's heart—throbbing to near bursting—then perhaps his brain had just refused to accept the truth.

Because then he would be in no condition to fight.

"What do you seek?"

Akuma's words defiled Ryu's ears once again.

The enemy's arms hung loosely at his sides, his body undefended, as a red, mist-like substance flowed from him endlessly. It wafted off his swarthy skin and floated in place before rising to the heavens, as if Akuma's wickedness was melding with the darkness of the world.

The techniques used by Ryu and Akuma employed "*ki*"- an unseen energy that exists in all things. Those capable of wielding ki can amplify their own power- as well as that of nature and other people- and imbue it into their moves.

Theirs was a style originally created to kill. A nameless style. The red mist that oozed from Akuma was none other than his own ki.

Within all ki exists good and evil, light and dark, and there was no doubt which side of the spectrum Akuma's ki drew from. His was a ki formed from the desire to kill or maim the opponent beyond recognition.

"*Dark Hado*," or "killing intent."

That is what Ryu's teacher, Gouken, had called his brother's ki, fearing it.

"Answer me. Why do you fight?" shouted Akuma. His voice swelled like a gale, pushing against Ryu's body. Up until that point, Akuma's had stood nonchalantly, but now he planted his feet, as if to brace himself. With his right hand behind his head and his left at his solar plexus, Akuma didn't clench his fists but instead seemed to grip the very air, frozen in place. He stood tall; a Deva king statue , come to life.

Akuma's stance was one that Gouken had never once told Ryu about.

Little by little, the sound of the pounding drum subsided. Ryu purged his mind of idle thoughts, calming his racing heart. His body— chilled by the waves of Dark Hado—slowly but surely began to warm.

A desire to know...

That one thought was enough to rein in Ryu's racing heart. Had his master been unaware of the stance Akuma now struck? Or was it one used only by those with mastery over the Dark Hado?

He needed to know.

He would cross fists with the enemy and seek the answer directly.

Ryu's heart soared at the thought of the battle about to unfold with Akuma. Ever intrigued by strong fighters, Ryu was blinded to all else by his search for truth within combat. Once awakened to a potential opponent, all but the thought of clashing fists vanished from the world. This was what made Ryu, Ryu.

He slowly spread his arms to shoulder-width. Stepping forward with his right foot, he twisted his hips slightly, raising his face to meet Akuma's. His left fist rested near his chin, while his right froze near his stomach, jutting towards the enemy ever so slightly. In that pose, his body began to bounce rhythmically, starting at his knees and pulsing up through his hips and shoulders.

This was the stance Ryu had learned.

"You're asking me why I fight, huh?"

Akuma's lips curled upward at Ryu's reply, forming a fearless, wicked smile.

A sudden gust burst across the wasteland, buffeting Ryu's cheeks. The two trailing tails of his red headband fluttered aloft violently, like a pair of crimson dragons.

"I fight to seek those stronger than myself."

"What a fool…"

Ryu breathed deeply as Akuma murmured his reply.

Why the sudden breath? Because the demon was on the move.

No sooner had Akuma spoken that his right foot kicked off the earth. He closed the gap with mind-boggling force.

His right arm extended out of the Deva king pose.

Ryu hadn't noticed the moment when Akuma's right hand curled into a fist, but there it was. Ryu's own right hand rose from his abdomen up to his face as he pressed his elbow to his flank and stiffened his entire body.

Defense…

"Urgh!"

Akuma's grunt resounded just as his boulder-like fist crashed into Ryu's shoulder.

The force shook his bone to the marrow.

Ryu had thought his defense was solid, but now he was forced back, heels scraping into the earth. Even as he slid, though, he kept his eyes locked on Akuma.

The demon was already flying towards the heavens.

Arms once again locked like those of a statue, Akuma's right leg alone extended in Ryu's direction. His foot bent back at the ankle, forming a perfect chevron.

The blade of his foot.

After reaching the peak of his arc, Akuma's body began to descend rapidly, with all the weight of an iron mass. The jet-black demon let loose a bellow that shook the atmosphere as he hurtled downwards at Ryu.

Should he assume a defensive stance and wait for a chance to counterattack?

No…

Defense alone would not win the day.

Countless battles against fearsome foes had cultivated in Ryu primal fighting instincts that now awakened him. The earlier roaring of his heartbeat had long since subsided. His nerves were calm, and his body was loose.

This was how it always was.

Once a fight began, Ryu transformed into a beast. No more hesitation or indecision; overcoming the enemy before him was all that mattered.

Fight back!

Ryu psyched himself up.

Keeping his eyes trained on the flying demon, Ryu planted both feet, gripping the ground with all his might. Feeling the ki of the earth itself, he began to slowly twist his body. From toes, to elbows, to hips, to shoulders, to elbows, up to his hands, Ryu channeled every ounce of ki within himself.

When he could twist no more, Ryu released all the tension in his body at once and leapt.

"Shoryuken!"

With right arm extended— aiming to pierce the heavens themselves—Ryu flew straight at Akuma.

Flesh clashed against flesh in mid-air.

Ryu could feel the demon's kick connecting with his cheek, but he had already overcome the pain itself. Still, the force of it threatened to swat him against the earth. Ryu would not let it end there, however.

His right foot found Akuma's jaw.

He felt the impact in the bones of his foot, but only for an instant. Because without delay, the demon was sent skywards once more by Ryu's kick , soaring even higher than the peak of his earlier jump.

Simultaneous strikes.

As he hit the ground, Ryu recovered instantly with an *ukemi* rolling technique and righted himself.

"What the...?"

Ryu couldn't disguise the surprise in his voice.

Akuma should still have been airborne, but he now stood exactly where Ryu had initially come across him, before their fight began.

With arms dangling in a relaxed stance, Akuma angled towards Ryu, letting a faint smile curl his lips.

"Your fist is destined to face my own in a death match."

The imposing voice roared out across the nightscape. Ryu received the challenge in silence, locked in his battle stance.

Still facing Ryu, Akuma lazily raised his right hand, gripping the air. In place of gloves, his fists were wrapped by tight coils of rope, and Ryu instinctively knew that this was not meant to protect opponents but rather to guard the demon's own fists.

"Given your disposition, why have you not walked the same path as me?"

The sleeves of Akuma's dougi were in tatters, exposing his dark shoulders.

Ryu's dougi also lacked sleeves, leaving his arms bare from the shoulder down. It was in the colors of their respective dougi that the two fighters' outfits differed. Though washed-out and dirty, Ryu's garment remained white, while Akuma's was a deep black.

It was obvious at a glance that the demon's dougi had been dyed, as, strictly speaking, it wasn't uniformly black. Dark-red speckles stained the cloth. Could a once-white dougi have been dyed this dark by absorbing the blood of vanquished enemies?

Akuma himself was wreathed by the stench of blood.

"I have no need of the Dark Hado."

Ryu twisted his upper body, showing his back as he spoke. Keeping his hands out of Akuma's line of sight, he brought them together as if clasping as invisible orb. The ki he had channeled up through his feet earlier he now brought to rest in his *tanden*- a focal point for meditation located between the navel and groin.

The tanden is the place in the human body most capable of storing ki, and Ryu habitually amassed his ki there, to be released later in battle.

Among all the techniques of Ryu's style, this was the ultimate.

Ki traveled from his tanden to the rest of his body, flowing through his arms and coming to rest in the space between his palms. Multiple blue sparks rippled out from Ryu's body, crackling through the air.

Between his hands, a ball of lightning formed.

Ryu's eyes- trained on Akuma- now bulged wide.

"Hadoken!"

As he cried out, Ryu thrust his hands towards the demon.

The blue orb shot away, flying straight for the enemy.

"A fog shrouds your eyes..." murmured Akuma as he took a step and leapt forward, as if to confront the flying ball of energy head-on.

"I will clear it away for you."

A direct hit.

No...

The orb passed straight through Akuma. At that moment, it appeared to Ryu as though Akuma's body had split into multiple versions of himself. As the clones closed in on Ryu, they merged back into a single body.

"One instant, one thousand strikes."

Ryu heard the demon speak, and then...

Before he had a chance to think, Ryu's entire body was being hit by blows from head to toe.

Akuma struck countless times with every part of his body—hands, elbows, knees, legs, forehead, shoulders, back, hips—ravaging Ryu mercilessly.

Forget a counterattack; Ryu was helpless even to defend himself as his vision clouded over with a white haze.

It was unclear to him how long the assault lasted, but it ended abruptly, and Akuma's form came back into focus.

With both feet firmly planted and arms in the Deva king pose, he resembled something more than human.

Ryu, now released from the torrent of blows, could only manage to stand for an instant.

He suddenly felt drained.

By the time he registered the slight pain that came from his knees hitting the ground, his face was already in contact with the chilled earth.

"This is our style's ultimate technique, made only for those lacking even the barest respect for the sanctity of life. 'Shun Goku Satsu .'"

Akuma's callous words reached Ryu's ears as the latter actively commanded his lungs to breathe, just barely managing to remain conscious.

Shun Goku Satsu…

He had never heard of such a move before.

"Ours is a style meant only to annihilate, but your master, Gouken, denied that simple truth. He could only prattle on about how the clashing of fists leads to mutual understanding. About how that was the true meaning of battle. What nonsense."

Ryu felt something on his head. He only realized it was Akuma's foot when a single black leg of the enemy's dougi hazily came into view.

All his senses were numb. He had desperately been telling himself to stand, but his body wouldn't listen.

Instant defeat.

Never before had Ryu experienced such a crushing loss from an overwhelming gap in power.

An indescribable sense of regret racked his paralyzed body.

Heedless of Ryu's sorry state, Akuma gave a merciless taunt.

"When one learns the way of the fist from a misguided master, this is all that comes of it."

Misguided…?

No, wrong.

Ryu struggled violently to cry out in protest, but lacking the strength, he couldn't form the words.

His master had polished techniques meant to protect the weak. To communicate, fist-to-fist. And his master had chosen Ryu to inherit that will.

Akuma was the misguided one. The one who had strayed from the path.

Using these moves to *kill* was simply wrong.

"The Dark Hado lies at the heart of our style, and the path to the heavens is one of solitude. Only once all others have been slaughtered and suppressed can one claim the title of strongest. You and Gouken misread the essence of our style, taking it down the wrong path. While my journey will lead me to the heavens, yours has left you squirming in the dirt like an insect. Until you awaken to the power of the Dark Hado, you cannot defeat me."

As he spoke, Akuma's foot shifted left and right, shaking Ryu's head.

"It is for this reason that Gouken, your master, died by my hand."

Ryu felt utterly powerless, and Akuma's unfaltering words reverberated deep within his heart.

Died...

Yes, exactly.

The man grinding Ryu's face into the earth had murdered his master. This man was Ryu's nemesis, the object of his revenge.

Ryu felt a dim flame ignite in the deepest part of his soul. It was sparked by an emotion he had never felt before even once in all his past battles.

Rage.

This man had killed his master... An unforgivable act.

"Hmm...?" questioned Akuma before pressing his foot down harder, as if he had somehow sensed the change within Ryu.

"Are you planning to walk the same path as your master? Will you continue to preach those foolish, noble ideals as I send you to the pits of hell?"

"Shut up..."

Ryu spoke in a trance. He curved his abdomen—slack until a moment before—expanding his tanden and releasing its ki, which emerged from his mouth as a sound.

The deep growling was coming from within, Ryu realized. He clenched his teeth as hard as he could. Why was he able to do so when drained of every ounce of power?

"You fool. Gouken's fool of a disciple... Struggle!"

Akuma's voice was brimming with might.

"Struggle against me. Against the way of this world. Against your own lack of power. At the end of your struggles lies true strength."

"I thought I just told you to shut up," spoke Ryu, his hands gripping the ground. The nails of all ten fingers scraped the earth, biting into the dark red dirt.

Ryu slowly rose on trembling arms, lifting Akuma's leaden foot into the air.

"Rage. Show me your hatred."

There was a note of glee in the demon's voice as he spoke. His raised foot returned to the ground.

This man could not be forgiven...

Ryu's instincts roared.

As a boy, he had lived only to fight. To get stronger. Gouken had saved him and given him a life.

What is strength?

To the bloodthirsty beast of a child that Ryu once was, Gouken posed the question with a clear gaze, but behind those lucid eyes lay the blazing flames of passion. Baptized by that fire, Ryu could only hang his head in confusion.

The purpose of battle was not to crush one's enemy. Clashing fists could lead to understanding, allowing fighters to share their pain and suffering and to form true bonds of friendship. Gouken had used his own two fists to teach young Ryu these lessons and more.

He was a man worthy of emulation, and Ryu had received those teachings in order to become more like his master.

However, Gouken had vanished from the world one day.

No, he had been killed. Killed by the man standing before Ryu...

His master had passed before giving Ryu a clear answer to that question- "What is strength?"

So Ryu had wandered; he had roamed the earth, seeking opponents stronger than himself.

His journey had seen him through hundreds of battles, won him many friends, and brought him victory after hard-won victory. Every time, Ryu had become that much stronger, bringing him ever closer to the answer to his master's question.

The man staring down at him did *not* represent true strength. He had no reservations about slaughtering his enemies. He sought only pure victory, even if it meant leaving carnage in his wake. Such a man could never embody true strength.

The Dark Hado lay in direct opposition to the strength that Ryu sought.

Ryu spoke.

"I can never forgive you."

Arms now off the ground, Ryu rose slowly to his knees.

Akuma crossed his arms and stared at Ryu as a parent watching their child stand for the first time might, almost affectionately.

"Your forgiveness matters not. Let your fists speak for you," Akuma shouted as his own right fist roared upwards at Ryu's jaw. In boxing terms, the attack resembled an uppercut.

Light glowed in Ryu's eyes.

A crimson light…

Ryu himself hadn't yet realized that the Dark Hado shone out from his eyes; he only found himself mystified at how light his body felt. Moving like a feather on the breeze, he twisted his upper body away.

Akuma's fist sliced through the air.

Looking as though he meant to shatter the heavens in such an imposing stance, Akuma found his torso completely undefended for a short moment.

Ryu kicked off the ground with his right foot and began to rotate his body along its vertical axis.

Tatsumaki Senpukyaku.

A technique that sends the user spinning through the air while striking the opponent with an outstretched leg.

Ryu took advantage of the brief opening to land a blow to the demon's flank.

It was a solid hit.

Akuma grimaced in anguish as the force of the kick sent him to the ground. Without missing a beat, however, he struck the earth with both hands, performing an ukemi and righting himself.

"You won't get away…"

Ryu stopped spinning, landed, and continued his pursuit without delay.

One kick off the ground and he was airborne again, aiming a kick at Akuma's head, which was only just rising up again.

The demon blocked the attack by crossing both arms above him, but Ryu landed again and wasted no time with a follow-up. Ryu's left fist found its mark in Akuma's solar plexus.

The latter's body went rigid.

Still not enough…

This time it was Ryu's right fist that flew without a moment's hesitation. The ki flowed from his legs into his hips, and from his arms into his fists. Even after connecting with the enemy's jaw, Ryu's entire body continued to rise toward the heavens.

"Metsu Shoryuken!"

Akuma's body danced through the sky as he flew twice as high as Ryu had jumped. Naturally, Ryu was the first to land.

Throwing back his torso as he hung in the air, Akuma stiffened his body. With both arms and both legs extended straight out, he froze in place.

"Arrrrrgh!"

The crimson ki began to flow from Akuma's body while he bellowed. The streams coming from each of his arms forked at his fists, while additional torrents shot out from his legs, making six in total. It was as if six great serpents had exploded from his stomach, drenching Akuma in blood while somehow holding him aloft.

Ryu caught sight of a massive kanji character etched into the black clouds of the sky.

"天"- or "heaven."

The six crimson serpents that burst from Akuma had drawn the character overhead.

The demons's roar shook the darkness itself and then ceased, while the serpents slithered back into his body in a flash.

Still suspended with limbs outstretched, Akuma brought his gaze upon Ryu. His pupil-less eyes now glowed bright , and the surging flames of the Dark Hado burned across Akuma's entire body.

"Hmph!"

A grunt escaped the demon's clamped mouth. He began thrusting his arms repeatedly—left, right, left—as if to strike the grounded Ryu. From his open palms came flying balls of purple-tinged ki.

These were Hadoken attacks.

As a technique that requires the user to circulate ki from the tanden throughout the body, the Hadoken traditionally demanded a firm, grounded stance. But now Akuma was performing it while suspended in mid-air. Such a display of power would be impressive enough, but the demon was also managing to fire off the attacks from both hands, separately. Ryu had never encountered someone with such complete control over their ki, apart from his master, Gouken.

But being surprised would do him no good.

Ryu kicked off the ground in an effort to dodge the energy that sailed at his head. Akuma's Hadoken scraped the earth where Ryu had only just stood.

"Shit."

Ryu suddenly regretted his decision to leap away.

Akuma—floating in the sky only moments ago—was back on the ground. To make matters worse, he now stood at the spot Ryu was diving towards. In other words, Ryu was exposed and defenseless.

Beastlike fangs protruded past Akuma's dark, dry lips as he looked up and smiled.

"Messatsu …" murmured Akuma, drawing his right fist as far back as his navel in a stance resembling the start of a Shoryuken.

Ryu would be in real trouble if a Shoryuken connected with his rapidly descending body.

He couldn't let that happen…

He couldn't afford to die until he had killed this man…

"Kill." Ryu hadn't realized that such a concept was now in his mind. For better or worse, the overwhelming desire *not to lose* to Akuma wiped all else from this thoughts.

Remembering a technique of the enemy's he had witnessed earlier, Ryu brought his arms to the Deva king pose and extended his right leg. Forming that same chevron in the bend of his ankle, he poured all of his ki into the kick.

Ryu's body began to descend in a way unlike natural falling. As his leg sliced through the air and Akuma's Shoryuken continued to rise, Ryu aimed the kick at Akuma's face.

He felt the demon's flesh against the blade of his foot just as a dull pain exploded in his stomach, radiating out from Akuma's fist.

Just like the simultaneous strikes from before, but now reversed.

Ryu flew skywards, while Akuma hurtled towards the earth.

By the time he performed an ukemi and landed, Akuma had already tumbled across the dirt and started to right himself with slap to the ground.

Ryu charged.

He wasn't going to give the demon a chance to regain his composure.

Ryu's eyes–glaring at the struggling Akuma–traced a path through the air in crimson with their glowing light.

"Akumaaaa!"

His rage exploded in a roar, and Ryu realized that every hair on his body was standing on end.

His body felt surprisingly light. He had never imagined that giving into anger could feel quite this good. It was as if he suddenly broke free of shackles that had bound him until this point, and his heart felt an indescribable sense of liberation.

The roiling emotion propelled Ryu forward, ever forward.

The enemy was right before him.

Akuma slowly rose–arms slack at his sides–and jutted his chin out. An arrogant pose, as if to say, "Come at me."

Ryu didn't hesitate.

If death was what the enemy wanted, he would gladly give it to him.

His master's killer...

A hateful foe...

He couldn't forgive him…

He couldn't allow him to go on living…

"Messatsu…"

Pitch black ki began to ooze from Ryu's body as he slid into range of Akuma and brought down his bent right arm as low as his stomach.

"Shoryuken!"

Ryu's fist met Akuma's jaw, but he wasn't done, yet.

His elbow continued rising until it crunched against Akuma's throat. He used his forward momentum to drive his hipbone into Akuma's solar plexus. Finally, the same elbow smashed up into Akuma's chin.

Four separate hits from a single Shoryuken…

It was a move his mind never imagined possible, but now his body moved with a mind of its own.

Ryu touched down.

Once more he charged at the still upright Akuma before unleashing another Shoryuken. This one, too, included all four hits.

He didn't stop there.

A third Shoryuken.

The demon could take no more and was sent flying.

In the Deva king stance, Ryu waited for the enemy to descend.

Akuma crumpled like a great rotted tree as his face met the dirt.

Ryu watched the motionless enemy in silence, their positions from earlier now reversed.

Oddly enough, he felt none of the joy that typically came after defeating a powerful foe. The enemy lay prostrate, yet the rage within Ryu still controlled him.

Not yet…

It wasn't over yet…

The battle would end only when this man breathed his final breath.

"Get up," said Ryu, looking down at Akuma.

Splayed out on the ground, one of the demon's palms twitched. His fingers started to curl–starting with the pointer and ending with the pinky–until his fist closed around a wad of dark earth .

"Heheheheh…"

Still lying flat, Akuma let loose a bold laugh.

That was the moment when Ryu first felt joy during this fight.

Akuma wasn't down for the count yet, so their death match could go on. Ryu was on cloud nine at the thought of it.

The steam that rose from his body formed a black mist that enveloped him, but this wasn't the usual manifestation of his fighting spirit.

Death…

It was the Dark Hado, condensed; a thick, aura-like darkness that reeked of death.

"Fwahahahahahah."

Akuma's upper body rose as he slapped the ground with both hands. He stared up, his glowing red eyes fixed firmly on Ryu.

"Why not finish me off?"

Ryu couldn't answer. Wordlessly, he gazed down at the man, allowing Akuma to slowly get to his feet. The latter planted one knee in an effort to stand, but his body swayed violently. It took all of Akuma's prodigious strength to keep himself from staggering. After a great growl of an exhale, he spoke through his dry lips once more.

"Still not enough, then…?"

Akuma planted his feet, rubbed them against the ground several times, and bent down low. Ryu could sense the dark ki filling the demon's tanden.

"You've taken the first step towards enlightenment, but now you hesitate. How laughable. Why did you not crush my skull when you had the chance? Why not end my life?"

"Enough talk."

With nothing more to say, Ryu charged forward and was soon within range.

Putting all his strength into his right fist, he aimed directly at the demon's arrogant, leering face. The latter didn't even attempt to defend, so Ryu's fist smashed into Akuma's nose, like a great mallet striking a bell.

Akuma received the blow without flinching.

Ryu didn't stop there.

As his right hand pulled back, he launched a left hook at the side of the demon's head.

Looking like a statue of a Buddhist Arhat, Akuma raised his right arm to block Ryu's strike.

Their arms met in mid-air.

The demon grinned.

In that instant, it seemed to Ryu that Akuma's face was growing before his eyes. By the time he perceived the incoming headbutt, Ryu was blown back from the impact to his face.

Akuma was already in the air; there was no time to defend.

"Hmph."

The jet-black demon began to spin.

Tatsumaki Senpukyaku…

Before Ryu could jump away, a knee struck his undefended solar plexus. Akuma's spinning kick continued, striking Ryu with his extended right leg over and over.

Every hit was a solid one, sending shockwaves through the marrow of Ryu's bones.

Strangely, though, it didn't hurt.

Ryu felt only an odd sense of pleasure.

He had often delighted in fighting, but this feeling was one he had never experienced before.

This was, without a doubt, a death match. One destined to go on until one of the fighters was no more, involving nothing so heartwarming as "understanding" or "conciliation." Ryu was controlled by an absolute callousness that told him he *must* destroy this particular enemy.

And here he was, actually *enjoying* such a brutal battle.

No longer was Ryu thinking of revenge for his master or any such sense of duty. The barrage of kicks didn't even leave him an opening to breathe, and all he could think was how to perform the next counterattack.

Ryu's confidence told him that he couldn't be defeated; that was the extent of the power that now filled him.

Akuma's spinning slowed. He would soon land.

Just as what was likely the final kick connected with Ryu's flank , the demon's body began to drop.

A golden opportunity.

Ryu's mouth curled into an unearthly smile, his visage demon-esque.

"Die!" he roared, now in a trance.

Black mist poured from Ryu's open mouth.

He stomped down with his right foot as he closed in on Akuma. The latter was still in the process of landing, but Ryu leaned on him and raised his own right arm overhead.

His right hook traced an arc through the air as it closed in on the demon's face.

It connected, and he continued the assault.

Unable to defend against Ryu's attacks while trying to land, Akuma was smashed into the ground by blow after blow. Pinned between fists and earth, his head rattled around, side to side.

"Nuohhhh."

Ryu let loose a great bellow—not unlike one from his opponent—as he swung his right leg, aiming at a face now draped in crimson hair.

His foot smashed into Akuma's skull, sending the man flying.

Akuma's entire body, pinned to ground by Ryu's fists until a moment ago, was now kicked skyward. The gap between the two fighters widened as the demon spiraled through the air.

Ryu kicked off in pursuit.

Sent flying by the kick, Akuma still hadn't had a chance to counterattack.

As he leapt into the air, Ryu turned his back to the enemy. Glancing over his shoulder, he used the force of his spin to lash out with his left leg, delivering a solid blow to Akuma's own shoulder.

Akuma was once again airborne, juggled like a soccer ball.

Ryu did not pursue this time.

Instead, just as he landed, Ryu pulled back both arms, grasping an orb of air with his palms. Electricity began crackling between his hands. The sound grew more intense, sparking and burning well beyond critical mass.

The ball of flames had far surpassed the amount of ki that an average person is capable of producing, but still it rumbled and shook between Ryu's palms.

"Hadoken."

Akuma was about to spring off the ground, but now Ryu thrust both hands towards the enemy.

The flames danced.

The ball of red hellfire flew straight towards Akuma.

A direct hit.

The demon was alight.

Wreathed in flames of rage, Akuma flew backwards and used both arms to perform an ukemi. After flipping and regaining his footing, he gave a shout.

"Nuohhhhh!"

His cry sent tremors through the air, and the flames surrounding his Akuma's body were extinguished by the wave of Dark Hado he released.

"Yes! This is the death match I sought!" shouted Akuma with heretofore unheard joy in his voice. His crimson eyes glowed eerily.

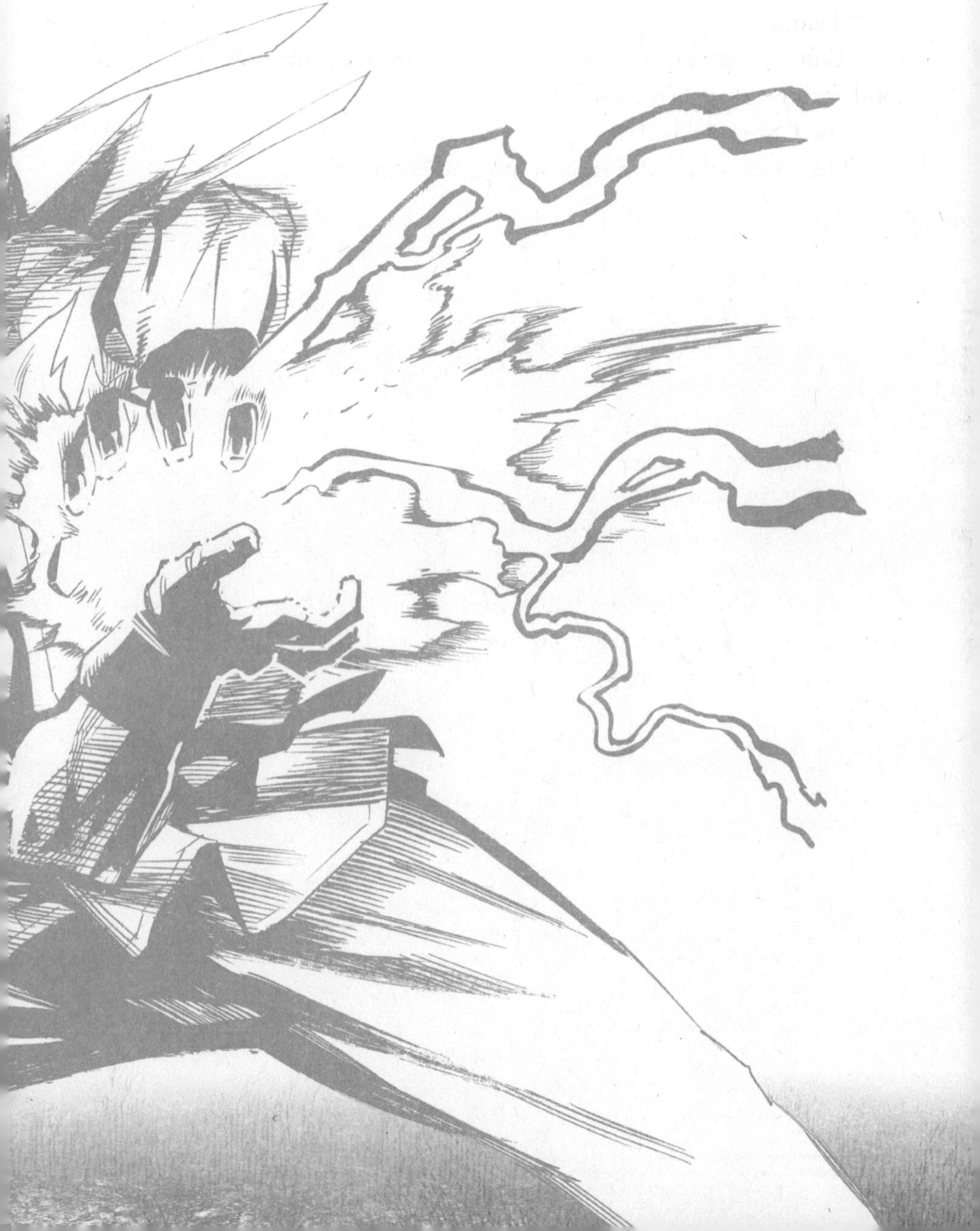

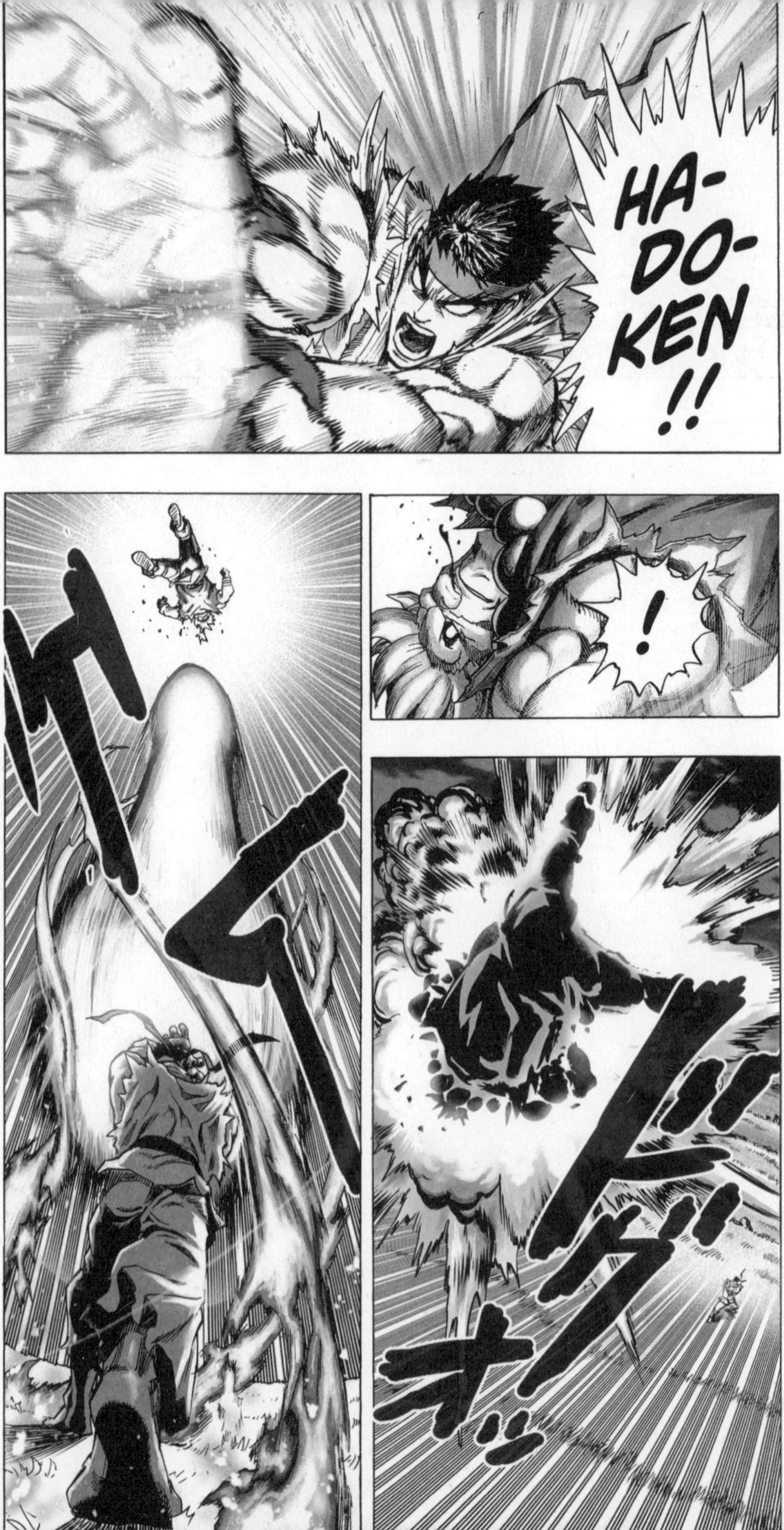
HA-
DO-
KEN
!!
!

NUO-OHH-HHH-!!

YES!

THIS IS THE DEATH MATCH I SOUGHT!

"If my eyes did not deceive me, then you are worthy of the Dark Hado's power."

"Shut up."

Ryu slowly stepped forward as he replied. Body feeling as light as a feather, he moved to close the gap at once.

"No more need for words. Now we let our fists do the talking, Ryu!"

This was the first time Akuma had spoken Ryu's name , and when he did, it sounded strangely intimate.

Ryu gave no answer.

He only kept walking straight towards Akuma.

There was no concept of "right" or "wrong," here. Ryu simply gave himself to the endless torrent of dark power that flowed from within. A force beyond good and evil now drove him, telling him what he must achieve.

Ryu struck forward with a simple and honest straight right, but behind the purity of Ryu's technique lay a swirl of ki, dyed the color of dusk.

Akuma stepped forward to meet the attack.

Each fighter's punch grazed the other's arm before smashing into their faces.

The grinding of flesh and bone was a wet and heavy sound—a sound Ryu heard through the rattling of his skull.

Neither the impact nor the pain could stop these two. They could think of nothing else but exchanging blows.

Another pair of simultaneous strikes.

And then a third.

Ryu's flank flinched just as Akuma's face did the same.

As if their very souls were resonating, the two fighters' bodies moved in sync.

Neither had any intention of defending; all that mattered was landing another punch on the enemy. Only the crunching sound of bone on flesh echoed out over the wasteland, through the night air.

The blood they shed was tossed about in the wind, wrapping them in a red haze. As their fists crossed paths over and over, they churned the suspended mist of blood, effectively forming it into a writhing, crimson beast.

"Yes, yes, Ryu! Hate me. I am the man who slayed your master. You could kill me one thousand times and still it would not be enough!"

"Shut up, shut up, shut up!"

Wicked smiles clung to the fighters' faces as they traded fists and words.

It was bloodlust–pure killing intent–that held command over the battlefield.

Ryu's left leg gave a violent shudder.

For an instant, he seemed to be on the verge of slipping out of consciousness, but he quickly brought himself back with a shake of his head.

An opening…

One Akuma did not overlook.

With Ryu leaning to the right ever so slightly, Akuma aimed a front kick that snuck past the inevitable path of Ryu's fist.

The hollowness in Ryu's eyes had implied a waning consciousness, but now they regained their light.

Akuma had fallen for it…

The near swoon was just an act. By presenting an obvious opening, Ryu had invited the battle-crazed Akuma to mount a vicious counterattack. Whatever sort of attack the invitation brought, Ryu could handle it just fine. After defending, he would have the perfect chance to retaliate.

Ordinarily, Ryu would never engage in such petty scheming. If winning demanded a false display of weakness, he would rather lose. That was the kind of man Ryu was.

However, his current mindset was hardly so pure.

Winning was everything…

No.

Killing this particular enemy was everything.

Akuma's front kick–determined to make its mark–flew towards Ryu's solar plexus.

Ryu managed to grab the incoming leg, and started twisting Akuma's ankle.

The demon knew full well that if he resisted, his ankle would break, so he instead twisted his body in the direction that Ryu started spinning.

Ryu released the leg, and Akuma spiraled in the air awkwardly.

"Die…" said Ryu as he let loose a strong right directly at Akuma's face.

The demon's spinning body was sent tumbling across the ground by the punch.

Ryu leapt.

The sharp blade of his right foot descended straight at Akuma.

The sensation of a cheekbone, cracking.

"Still not enough…"

Ryu grabbed the demon by his nape and stood him up.

Akuma tottered, on the verge of passing out. Ryu glared at him hatefully and started to amass ki in his tanden.

"Hadoken."

The ki—now a ball of flames—crashed into Akuma. Like a puppet without strings, the demon flew into the air and rolled across the ground. Perhaps the impact had brought him back to lucidity, because he now moved to lift his heavy body and stand.

He had no energy left to counter.

Ryu closed the gap instantly.

This would be the end…

Akuma's hollow eyes quivered, not fixed on any point in particular, as Ryu advanced within inches of the enemy and dropped down low.

He was preparing a Shoryuken.

At point-blank range, Ryu's body was level with Akuma's stomach. With the energy needed to resist already lost to him, even the mighty demon could not escape death should he receive the full force of a Shoryuken at this range.

The final blow.

Ryu felt his fist—brought low near his tanden—fill with ki.

Revenge for his master…

Ryu's eyes glowered at Akuma, but just as that word, "revenge," came to him, those eyes saw a vision. An old, bald man, with a long white beard and a mustache. The muscled arms that protruded from his ragged dougi were thicker even than Akuma's or Ryu's.

It was Ryu's master, Gouken.

The next to appear was a blond man.

An American garbed in red with a wide, lighthearted smile. A man who had trained under Gouken alongside Ryu.

"You really okay with your journey ending here, like this?"

The vision's voice rang out in Ryu's ears.

"Ken…"

Even in the process of unleashing a Shoryuken, Ryu couldn't help but utter the blond man's name.

A wave of nostalgia hit Ryu upon speaking the name in a trance, and his heart wavered. It was a pleasant feeling, like being awakened from a long dream by the sound of one's mother calling.

"Wh-what am I doing?"

Ryu's body abandoned the Shoryuken and went rigid.

Standing before him was an upright Akuma.

The demon's bruised and bloodied body was a mirror that reflected the terrible nature of its assailant.

"Did I do that?"

Ryu slowly stood up out of his low stance and reflexively stared at his own hands. Blood splatter had dyed his palms red—proof of his deeds.

He had been taken in by the Dark Hado…

The one thing he had tried so hard to avoid. But he had failed. Ryu's heart sunk.

"You would stop here, after coming so far?"

From above Ryu's hung head came the wicked voice.

Akuma…

The demon had regained consciousness and now looked down at Ryu.

Ryu leapt back to put some distance between them, but he couldn't bring himself to raise his arms and strike a stance.

He couldn't forgive himself for descending into darkness.

To hate, and to kill those he hated. That was not why Ryu had become a fighter. He sought understanding through battle, as well as the meaning of true strength.

Yet…

He did hate the man standing before him. Ryu wanted to kill him, so he had reached out for the Dark Hado. He was ashamed beyond words.

"Uohhhhhhhhh!"

The cry came from Akuma, who thrust both arms skyward, roaring towards the black clouds in the heavens.

Lowering his head to gaze at Ryu, the hateful demon spoke.

"Why did you not kill me?"

"I, I…"

Ryu couldn't answer. Had the Dark Hado retained its hold over him for a second longer, Akuma would surely be dead at this point.

Because the bloodlust was there, Ryu had no clear answer to the question.

"What gave you pause? What held you back? You have been chosen as one who can bear that ultimate solitude. Just like me… No, you are destined for even greater heights. With such potential, why do you reject the Dark Hado?"

The booming voice of the blood-splattered Deva king shook Ryu to his soul.

"You must have realized it, during our fight. That the Dark Hado is absolute truth, granted only to the strong. So why waver? Was it not strength you sought?"

"Not another damn word."

Ryu averted his eyes from Akuma, as if to reject him entirely. His hands did not curl into fists.

"Very well…" said Akuma, as bloodlust-imbued ki gushed from his body.

"My fists will rend your hesitation to shreds."

Just as Akuma moved to close the gap, he emitted a burst of pale ki. His body seemed to double in size, ripping apart his shirt and snapping the string of giant rosary beads. The beads should have fallen, but instead, they began to spin around Akuma in mid-air, as if they were loathe to part.

The pale figure could hardly be called human anymore. A single word passed through Ryu's mind.

Demon...

Ryu clenched his fists and struck a stance.

It was too late.

"Ashes to ashes..."

A mass of dark energy flew from Akuma's hands, striking Ryu in his solar plexus with a dull impact.

The demon didn't let up.

"Welcome to the gates of hell."

Another hit.

Another mass of energy- leagues more powerful than the previous one- pierced Ryu. The cruel ball of light passed straight through his body, emerging out of his back. As it did, the path of light formed a giant kanji character behind Ryu.

"Heaven!"

Ryu knew he had been contaminated by the energy that moved through his abdomen.

"Gah. Gahh..."

Ryu sunk to his knees. The demon—still clad in pale ki—turned his back and cast Ryu a sidelong glance.

Ryu's chest—caved in where he had been hit—heaved and shuddered. His thick, sinuous muscles had been pierced by the orb of Dark Hado, robbing him of the ability to recover.

That wasn't all.

The blood vessels that showed through the skin near the depression pumped blood so deeply red it resembled magma. The distended vessels rose from the caved-in area, spreading from Ryu's chest down to his abs.

The blood within glowed eerily with every breath Ryu took.

"I have infused you with my Dark Hado, which will now awaken your own. But know that mine is only the trigger. What drives you now has always been with you."

The demon spoke, watching Ryu over his shoulder and already

starting to walk away.

"Understand that the true death match will come when next we meet, Ryu. Remember this: I have spared your life tonight because I see that you are the only one who can give me the fight I seek."

The maddening, pale demon kept walking.

"W-wait…"

Ryu's utterance emerged with a red-hot burst of breath. His burning throat was desperate for moisture.

For blood…

He wanted red, glossy blood.

The power that flowed endlessly from his breast stripped Ryu of all consciousness.

"Gahhhh!" he screamed towards the heavens.

Before Ryu knew it, the black clouds replied with a clap of thunder and a sudden downpour.

Each icy drop that grazed his skin felt like a piercing dagger. It was as if his body–now raging like an inferno–instinctively rejected the cooling rain.

"I said wait…"

The color faded from Ryu's eyes, leaving them solid white just before they turned blood red.

Rage was all he felt, but not directed towards anyone in particular.

Simple, unceasing, explosive anger.

There was only one "strongest" in this world, and it was him.

He despised all living things, great and small.

"I am Ryu! I am true strength!"

His thrust his fists skyward as he roared. As if in response to his cry, six bolts of lightning flashed.

Splitting the black clouds, the lightning formed the character for "heaven" in the sky before fading.

As for what happened afterwards, Ryu's fate was unknown to all.

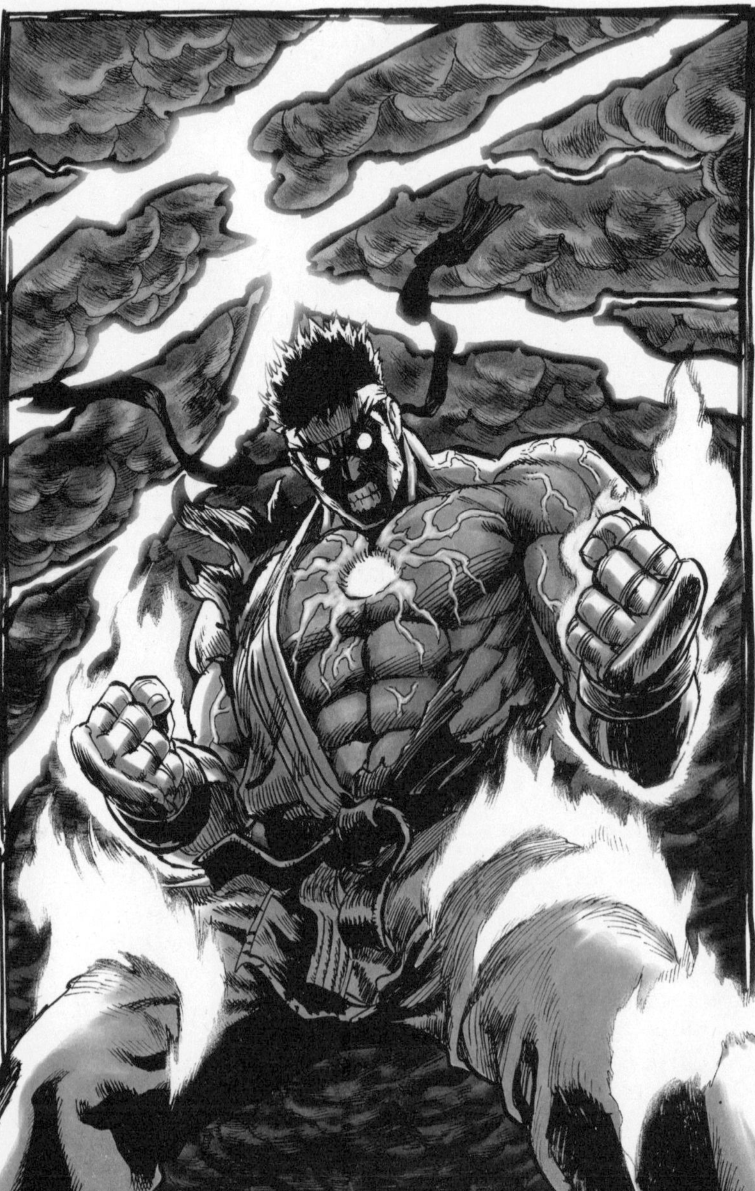

ROUND

2

春麗阿弗利加に至りて、白き髪の少女と邂逅（かいこう）す

RHYTHMIC
RENDEZVOUS

ROUND 2
RHYTHMIC RENDEZVOUS

"**Y**ou smell to me like a fresh wind ," said the girl with the dazzling smile.

Chun-Li returned the smile.

A gentle breeze blew past as their legs clashed high.

The opponent had blocked Chun-Li's kick with one of her own.

As they exchanged kicks, each stood perfectly rigid, locked in place.

One would never guess from their easygoing expressions alone that each was trying to kick the other. Rather, they smiled at one another gently, as if sharing an intimate moment.

The girl standing before Chun-Li was named Elena.

She had pure white hair cut short, and she wrapped her statuesque body with the skimpiest of white cloth garments, covering only her breasts and crotch. A risqué fashion choice, to be sure. Multi-colored rings hung around her arms, legs, and neck, giving her a distinctly tribal flair.

Chun-Li had come to Kenya on a job, because recently, strange rumors had been springing up all around the world.

An American soldier—or so they said—was attacking known Shadaloo associates, one after the other.

Witnesses were claiming to have seen a blond, blue-eyed man with a single, drooping lock of hair in front. There was one more thing. They said he was wearing thin-framed glasses.

Chun-Li had her suspicions.

In order to hunt down criminals across the globe, Chun-Li had become a detective with Interpol. She was now working on a certain case that consumed her life.

Shadaloo.

An organization of villains plotting world conquest. Though it might have sounded like something out of superhero comics, the danger represented by Shadaloo was real. Its reach extended to the militaries, industries, and economies of countries around the world.

Chun-Li's father was killed by Shadaloo, and it had been the hope of revenge that spurred Chun-li to become a detective and join Interpol.

Her life's mission was the destruction of Shadaloo.

However, she wasn't alone in that mission.

A certain righteous soldier had taken it upon himself to compile intel on Shadaloo and drag the organization's shadowy deeds into the light.

His name was Charlie—a renowned pilot in the United States Air Force.

He had somehow heard about Chun-Li's investigation into Shadaloo and asked if she would team up with him.

Shadaloo was a taboo subject within Interpol. To those out of the loop, it was passed off as some absurd fantasy, while those in the know even refused to utter the name.

Chun-Li didn't have a single ally in the agency, but despite being an outsider, Charlie was the first to join her cause

Then he died.

They said it was an accident during the test flight of a new fighter jet, but in truth, Shadaloo was to blame. Chun-Li later discovered a transfer of funds from Shadaloo to the company contracted by the air force to build the jet in question.

Shadaloo had killed Charlie.

Her former partner was an American soldier with drooping blond bangs, glasses, and a sleeveless life vest.

So could the rumored man actually be Charlie?

Chun-Li had come to Africa to determine the truth, because the soldier in question was spotted in Kenya in pursuit of one of Shadaloo's agents.

The soldier had departed, none the wiser to the agent's identity. Before leaving, though, he had had a friendly match against a girl who initially showed up to help him fight the enemy.

That girl was Elena, who now stood and faced Chun-Li.

Elena lowered her raised right leg to the ground smoothly, never breaking her smile at Chun-Li. Careful not to leave herself open, Chun-Li stared back while bringing down her own leg.

"Will you really tell me if I win?" questioned Chun-Li.

The hem of her blue China dress fluttered in the wind, and the white strings tying off her dual hair buns followed suit.

"Yes! I will tell you," answered Elena, her affable smile beaming widely across her face. The girl's whimsical personality was a perfect match for the torrid climate of her equatorial homeland , which filled Chun-Li's heart with an overwhelming sense of freedom.

Her body and mind danced at the lightheartedness of it all.

"I feel like I understand why your people love to dance."

"Will you not dance as well?"

"Once our fight is over."

"Very well."

Chun-Li checked her breathing and took a stance.

She placed her center of gravity slightly to the rear, while her left foot hung in front, toes barely grazing the ground. Both arms were level with her shoulders at a uniform height; her hands, open blades. Chun-Li pulled her chin in and sunk to half her normal height, pivoting her head to the left just enough to face her opponent straight-on.

A Chinese kenpo stance, drilled into her from a young age by her dearly departed father.

Elena, on the other hand, was not striking any stance at all. At least as far as Chun-Li could tell.

The position of her hips looked uncomfortable, like they were dropped a bit too low to qualify for a proper fighting stance. As her shoulders bobbed up and down to a set rhythm, her legs shifted open, closed, and open again to the same beat. Likewise, her arms bended and stretched in time.

To Chun-Li, it resembled a dance, plain and simple. Yet this was indeed Elena's fighting stance—the one from which she had launched those ferocious kicks, earlier

The black slaves of Brazil created the fighting style known as *capoeira*. Their hands were bound by fetters to keep them from escaping, so the moves they developed relied exclusively on kicks and other foot techniques.

This was Chun-Li's first fight against a capoeira user.

"Let's go," said Elena cheerfully as she danced forward to close the gap.

Chun-Li realized that she couldn't get careless.

The majority of fighting styles make use of techniques that exploit the opponent's ignorance of the style. An adept fighter employs feints and other unique moves to confound the complacent opponent and end the match with a single, decisive blow. If one is distracted by the flashy moves of an unknown style and then tries to counter based on what is *expected*, defeat is inevitable.

Chun-Li knew it was best *not* to move at times like this.

She stood still in her own stance and waited, watching to see how the girl would attack. Countering after the fact would be no problem, given the speed of her Chinese kenpo.

Elena closed in with regular, alternating steps, but nothing else about her movements could be called regular. Chun-Li couldn't for the life of her read when and where from the next kick might come.

A moment of laxness could be fatal.

"Ahah!"

The girl's carefree laughter sounded closer than Chun-Li expected, in a completely different spot than where her brain was imagining Elena should be, which meant that Elena must have sped up for an instant.

She was already at Chun-Li's chest.

Looking down, Chun-Li only saw a heel rushing up at her.

Upon seeing the sole of Elena's foot- caked with the dry red sand of Kenya—Chun-Li kicked her brain into high gear.

The girl's silver hair was lower to the ground than her feet.

She was unleashing these kicks by spinning around her hips, which acted as an axis.

An intense storm of kicks that made use of her whole body's centripetal force.

Not bad...

A faint smile crept onto Chun-Li's thin lips.

"Hah."

She leapt back two paces and grunted.

Elena's long, supple, brown legs were still rising. The girl's eyes were wide—as if in shock—as she confirmed Chun-Li's gaze on her and quickly moved to close the newly made gap.

As if in the middle of a cartwheel using only her legs, Elena moved into a somersault in order to land.

"Hahhh."

Letting out a deep breath, Chun-Li thrust her hands out in time with her steps. Had she decided to focus her tanden's ki into her palms at that moment, she could have shot an energy orb, but at this moment, she simply moved to strike Elena with open palms. She was timing the blow to connect with Elena's stomach just as the girl landed.

The spacing was right.

She couldn't miss.

Elena's right foot touched down, and Chun-Li's hands were already zooming forward.

A direct hit...or so she thought.

Her hands struck empty air.

No sooner had Elena landed than she was airborne once more.

The first kick was from her right. Then her left, and without an ounce of rigidity, Elena launched herself skyward again.

This was why one had to be cautious with unfamiliar fighting styles...

Chun-Li was too busy cursing her own carelessness to block the strong blow that smashed into her unguarded jaw. The pain wasn't bad, as she had tightened her core in anticipation. Still, it was a kick that made full use of Elena's centripetal force, so pain aside, the impact could not be ignored.

Such a hit was more than capable of flattening her against the ground, so Chun-Li took measures to avoid that by moving back, in the direction of the impact. She kicked off and somersaulted backwards into the air. After judging the timing while airborne, she gripped the earth in a handstand and opened her legs wide.

"Hahhhh…"

Gathering ki in her abdomen, Chun-Li began to twist the trunk of her body, winding up. She slapped her hands against the ground and poured all her energy into rotating out of the twist.

Chun-Li's body began spiraling through the air, moving forward.

"Spinning Bird Kick!"

Her legs followed the spinning of her body, turning into a storm of kicks.

She collided with Elena as the girl was landing from another cartwheel. Unable to cope with the barrage, Elena attempted to retreat, but her lithe body was hit over and over.

Each blow elicited a small yelp from Elena until she finally fell.

Chun-Li stopped spinning, bounced off her hands, flipped, and stood upright once more.

But by the time she found her stance again, Elena was already standing before her.

The girl was smiling…

She had just been grounded by dozens of kicks, but there she stood, beaming at Chun-Li. Staring down the enemy with eyes that sparkled like the starry night sky of Kenya , the unaffected girl didn't give off an iota of malice.

"So fun!" shouted Elena, unable to contain her excitement.

"I first thought you to be the refreshing winds that come before summer, but now you are as a tornado. How very strange."

Chun-Li couldn't tell if that was praise, but she was sure there was no ill-will behind the comment. The fact that the girl was so pure-hearted flustered her.

"Should we continue?" Chun-Li asked, reflexively.

Their bright, clear surroundings seemed ill-suited to battle. Some cool tea and pleasant conversation under the scorching Kenyan sun would have fit better.

"I want to know more about you."

"The unreserved appeal made Chun-Li blush unwittingly.

"I see…"

She tightened her face out of its relaxed state and tensed her body.

Elena's expression didn't change. Still smiling, she sank low and once again started bobbing in time.

First, the feint…

Chun-Li drew ki from the earth up through her feet and into her tanden. Adapting her body into a network for ki, she transferred the energy from tanden to torso, torso to shoulders, shoulders to arms. The faint, sparking sensation leapt from arms to palms.

Her open palms suddenly glowed bright. Lunging out of her twisted pose, Chun-Li thrust both hands towards Elena.

"Kikoken."

As she shouted, a pale blue ball flew from her glowing palms in Elena's direction.

"Eh?" came the surprised voice, several paces ahead.

Chun-Li broke into a run, moving towards Elena as if in pursuit of her own energy orb.

Her opponent was one with a constant rhythm. Not the type to tense up and defend against the attack.

So what *would* she do? The answer was obvious.

Meeting Chun-Li's exact expectations, Elena jumped high to dodge, straddling the ball and heading for Chun-Li.

Just as planned…

Chun-Li covered her mouth as she laughed to herself about how Elena's straightforward nature bordered on "adorable," but she soon composed herself and leapt up to meet Elena.

The rising Chun-Li and descending Elena clashed in mid-air.

Chun-Li wrapped her thin arms around the girl's neck, hooked her legs, and prepared for a throw.

"Gahh."

The usually lively voice cried out in pain as Chun-Li wrenched her arms around to throw Elena to the ground.

But just before Elena's head struck dirt, she thrust her hands behind her and spun backwards, avoiding most of the potential damage. She wore an expression of relief for a moment, but then Chun-Li landed and thrust out with a fully extended right leg.

The girl's own whip-like kick flew out to meet Chun-Li's, body reacting faster than mind. Chun-Li pulled her leg back, but it barely touched down before firing out again.

The second kick wouldn't be enough to end it either, though.

"Yah! Yah! Yah!"

Each cry was accompanied by a kick at Elena, with the kicking leg returning near Chun-Li's left thigh every time.

Even Chun-Li herself lost count of the kicks.

Hyakuretsukyaku…

An ultimate attack commonly known as the Lighting Kick.

Countless fighters had been brought to their knees by the continuous stream of high-speed kicks. And not just other women, of course. Men, too. In fact, probably more men than women, relatively speaking.

Chun-Li gradually sped up, each kick more intense than the last. In the end, her entire body was like a machine, operating solely to power these kicks. Once it reached that point, Chun-Li herself had a hard time stopping. It would go on until the enemy fell.

The speed of these kicks was enough to produce dozens of afterimages, so Chun-Li's view was obscured on all sides by the sight of her own outstretched leg.

But she knew Elena lay on the other side.

The pounding sensation traveling up through her foot told her as much.

When that feeling was gone, Elena would be defeated, but until that point, Chun-Li gave herself to the kicks.

"Yah! Yah!"

The kicking went on.

"Ahhhh!"

The elated, golden voice resounded from beyond the veil of kicks. It was clearly Elena but clearly *not* a scream of anguish.

Her building excitement had burst from her lips in joy; it was that sort of cry.

What was going on beyond the curtain of kicks? What was Elena doing?

Doubt crept into Chun-Li's heart.

Surely she had been hitting skin with each blow. That much was certain.

So why did Elena sound like she was having so much fun? Why hadn't the sheer volume of kicks brought her down?

No one had ever managed to endure Lightning Kick for this long, so Chun-Li was in uncharted territory.

How did the opponent remain standing after so many hits?

Fear dulled her judgment.

Thinking back on the fight, Chun-Li later knew that she should have stopped the Lightning Kick there and then. But hindsight is twenty-twenty, of course.

"Hyah, ho, yah!"

With a lively cry, Elena bounded over the veil.

"B-but how…?" muttered a dumbfounded Chun-Li.

Her shock was only natural, because she saw it all very clearly just as Elena leapt into vision.

Elena had been countering every kick of the barrage with a kick of her own, pitting foot against foot. She had then chosen a particularly high kick of Chun-Li's to use as a stepping stone, vaulting over the entire attack.

Elena was soaring over the Lightning Kick and descending towards Chun-Li, back arched.

At this point, Chun-Li's kicks were a runaway train that even she couldn't stop. She could only fight against the existing momentum, slowing the storm little by little, so stopping entirely would take several seconds.

She didn't have that kind of time.

Elena was already closing in.

With right and left legs split wide in a straight line, the white cloth covering her crotch flashed against her brown skin.

"You're practically nude …" mumbled Chun-Li in spite of herself. As she attempted to slow the kicks and switch to a defensive stance, her head was abruptly smashed sideways by the incoming attack.

Imminent defeat…

"Lynx Tail!" shouted Elena.

When she came to her senses, Chun-Li was airborne. Every time she tried to land, her body was assailed by blow after painful blow, creating a sensation of floating.

Elena was gripping the ground with both hands while gracefully spinning her spread legs about. Each sweep of a leg became a kick that knocked Chun-Li into the air, juggling her.

Chun-Li felt like the bounced ball of a performing circus seal.

She began to get angry.

"Listen, you…" she managed to mutter, feeling queasy as her field of vision seemingly spun in every direction at once.

She grew angrier every time she spotted Elena in the corner of her eye, grinning ear to ear like a child playing with her favorite toy.

"You've had your fun!"

Chun-Li launched a clumsy kick from mid-air, but it somehow connected with Elena's stomach.

The spinning stopped, and Chun-Li landed.

The two were still close enough to touch.

"Can you dodge this, I wonder?" asked Chun-Li gently, keeping her rage from showing on her face. At odds with these words was her body, which now moved swiftly and relentlessly towards her prey.

Another Lightning Kick.

The earlier mid-air kick had found its mark, so Elena was slow to react.

This time, Chun-Li felt a *different* fleshy sensation against her foot than earlier. The kicks were connecting with Elena's body.

Chun-Li almost pitied the girl.

"You'd have been better off falling to the last Lightning Kick…"

Her kicking leg suddenly changed course.

The final kick shot up towards the heavens, striking the girl's jaw from underneath.

"Kyahhh!"

Even the indefatigable Elena had to cry out in pain, but the protest went ignored.

Chun-Li followed her prey into the air, but she didn't kick off the ground with her legs to do it. Rather, she sprung up from a handstand and began spinning, legs spread wide.

It was the pose for Spinning Bird Kick, but with one difference; while Spinning Bird Kick moves the body forward, Chun-Li now flew straight up.

The airborne Elena began to fall, but she clashed with Chun-Li, rocketing back up.

"Ahhh…"

As if caught up in a typhoon, Elena rose again, the storm of kicks assailing her smooth, muscled body.

One particularly severe blow launched her up even higher, out of the gale.

The choreography was all under Chun-Li's control.

She stopped spinning and jumped again, in mid-air.

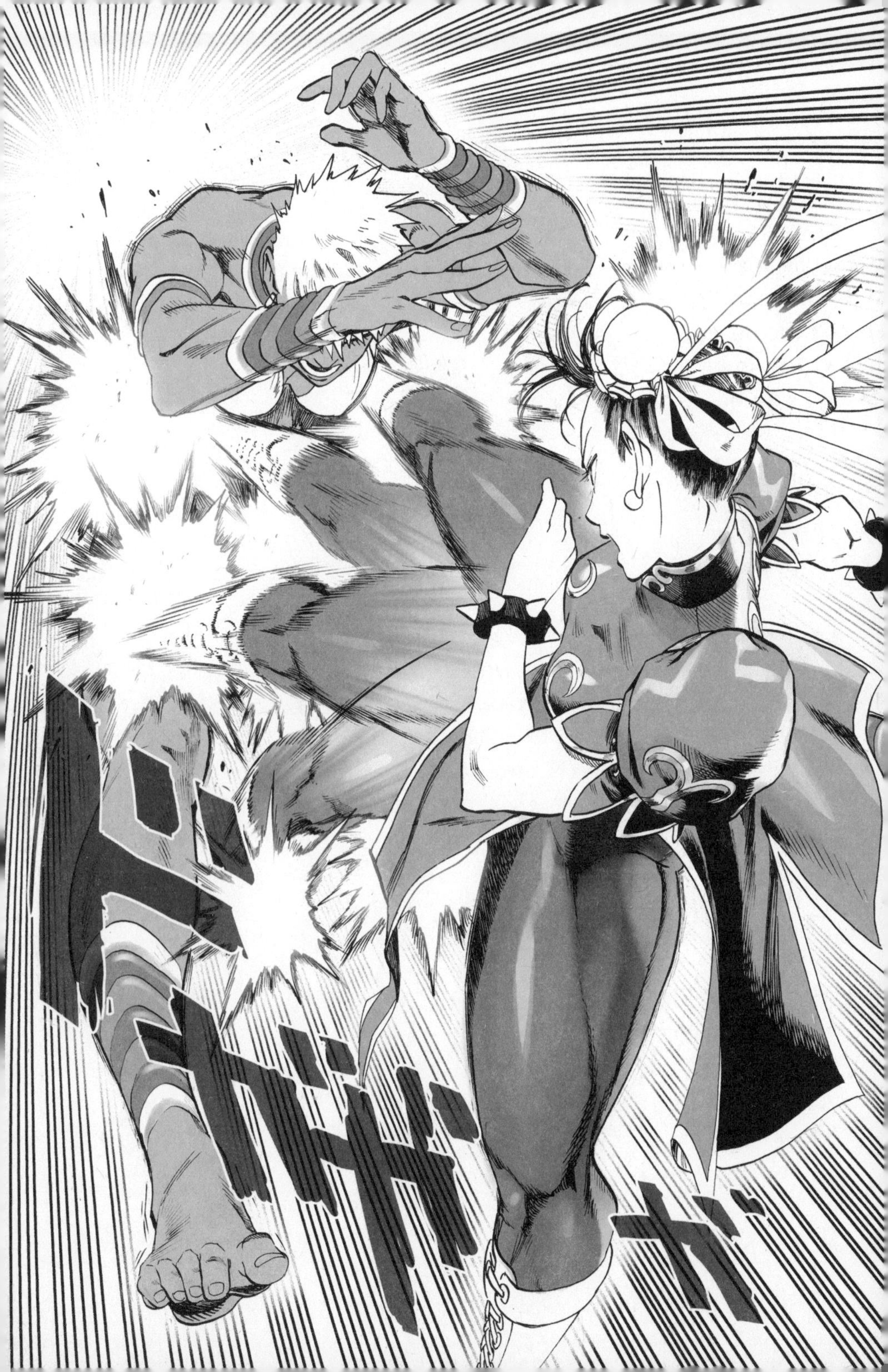
ドガガガガーガ

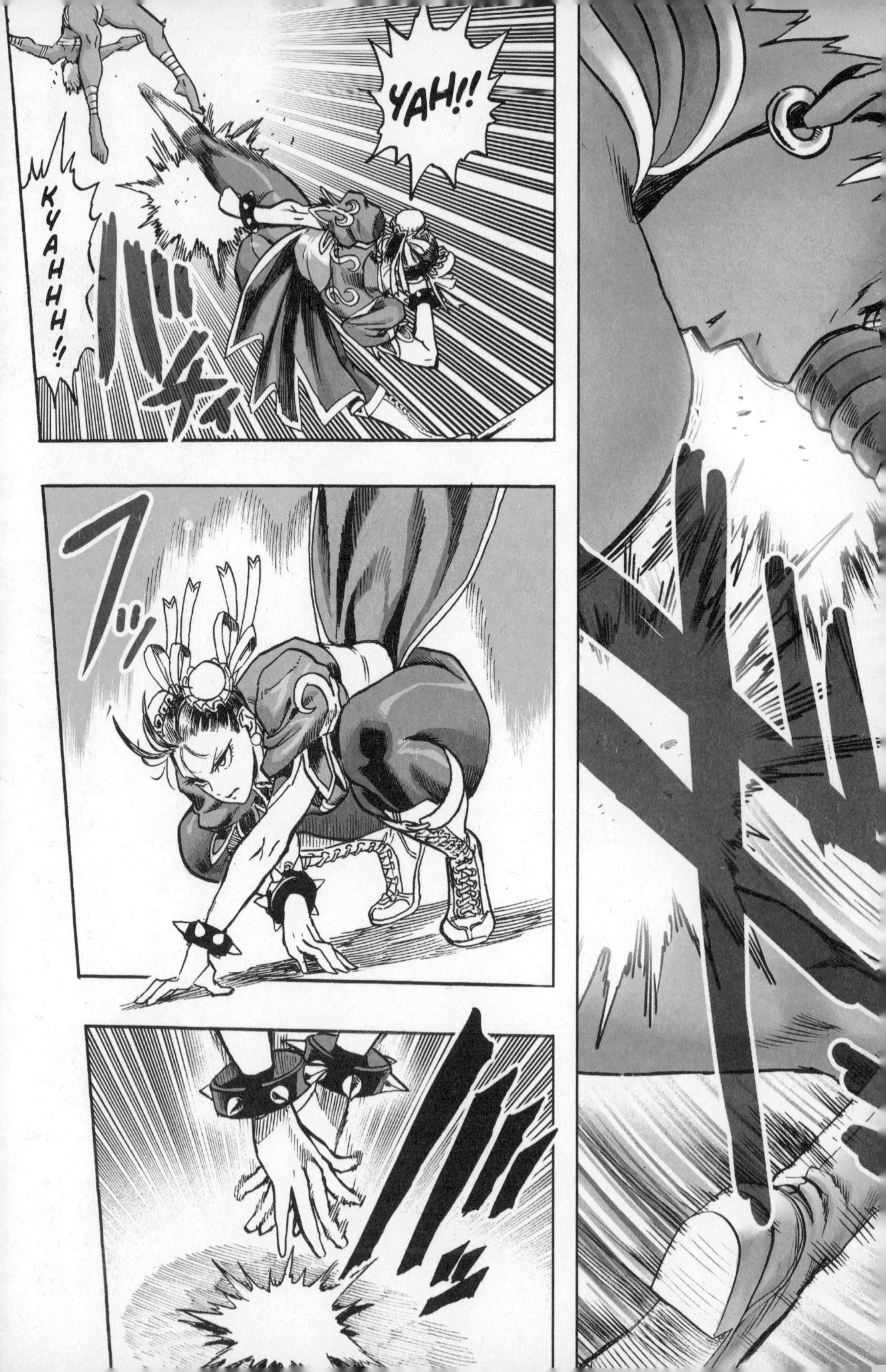
YAH!!
KYAHHHH!!

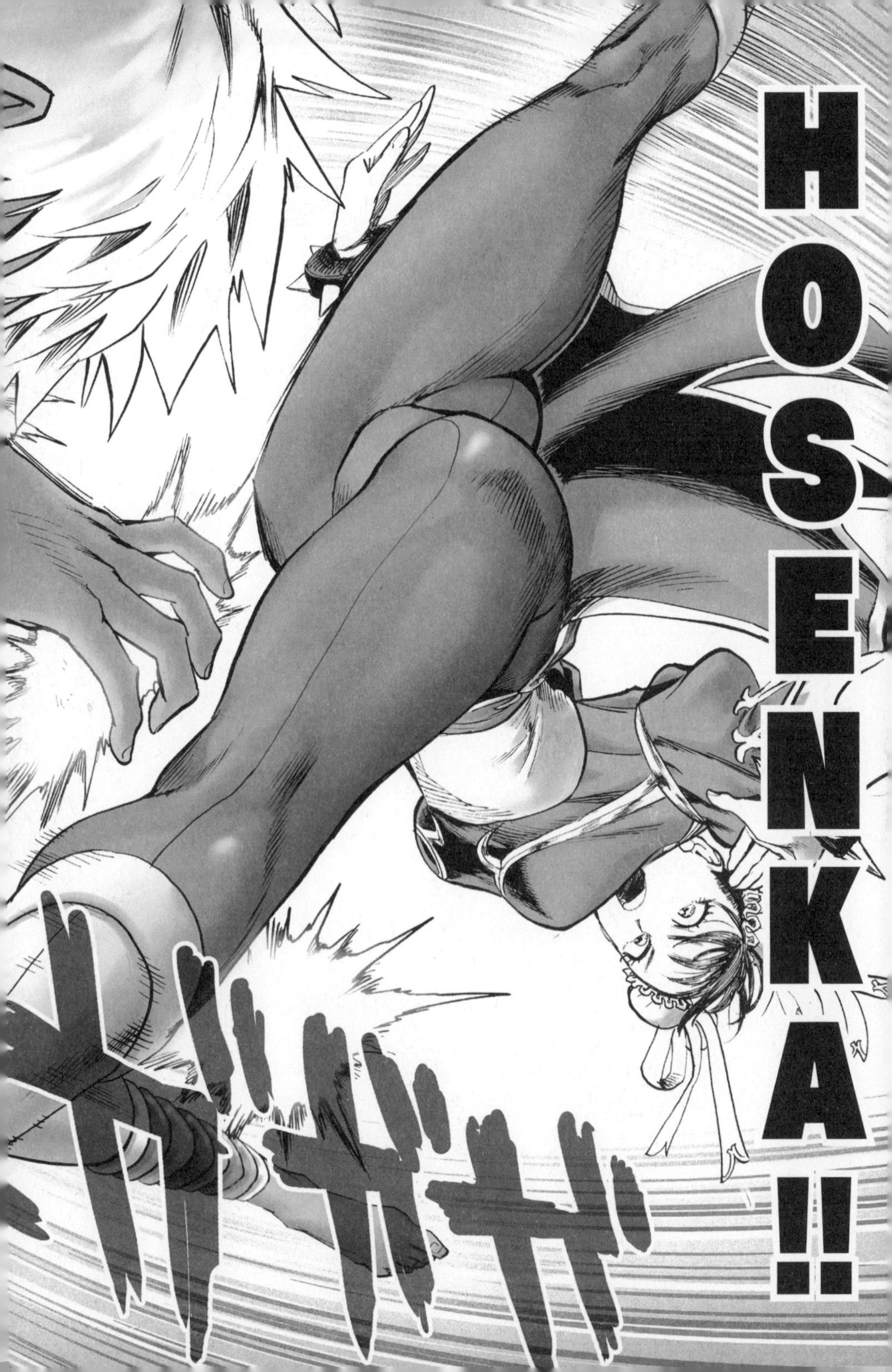
HOSENKA!!

Chun-Li clenched her body into a ball–knees against chest–and hurtled towards the defenseless Elena.

"Now!"

Judging the distance, she unfurled herself and thrust both legs upwards with all her strength, like a single spear.

A kick with every ounce of her power behind it.

Her white boots pierced Elena's back.

"Kyahhh!" screamed Elena as she spiraled towards the ground in a tailspin. Chun-Li glanced over her shoulder to see the girl fall before executing a perfect landing herself.

Hosenka...

Chun-Li had always specialized in kicking techniques, and this was an ultimate combo that utilized nothing but kicks.

No one could stand after taking those hits.

Elena fell with a thud, head first. Chun-Li worried that she might have killed the girl, so not for one second did she imagine that Elena could get back up.

Such was the confidence she had in her technique.

"Hahh..."

With a deep sigh, Chun-Li turned around.

"Eh...?"

She was nearly stunned speechless by the unbelievable sight.

Elena was standing.

"That move was wonderful!"

She stood with both arms thrust back, her body tilted slightly while looking at Chun-Li.

There was no sign of damage. Not a single bruise to indicate that a storm of kicks had just ravaged her.

The only explanation was that she must have somehow blocked or redirected every one of Chun-Li's kicks. But the continuous barrage left no time for that, with less than a second between each hit. Even then, the kicks were too irregular–nothing that human reflexes could cope with.

If Chun-Li's suspicions were correct, the girl standing before her had already become something more than human.

"Hey. By what name do you call that move?"

Chun-Li felt a pang of envy towards Elena, with her fiery eyes, asking the question as if nothing had happened.

The girl was a prodigy.

It wasn't as though she were lacking in effort either, though. Her strict father had no doubt trained her relentlessly in the art of capoeira.

But "effort" is all but worthless in the face of true talent.

Chun-Li knew that everyone always argued against that, saying that enough effort could overcome sheer talent. In reality though, the truly strong possessed talent. And beyond even *those* people were some that could make their feats look completely effortless.

Prodigies…

Those with innate ability.

Without a doubt, that was what this girl had.

She loved nothing more than facing off against strong opponents, and she couldn't help but enjoy any amount of training that would help her along her path.

Everything about fighting was a joy to Elena, so any fighter out there would be jealous of this girl and her gifts.

"Hey, did you hear me?" asked a frustrated Elena, puffing out her cheeks.

Chun-Li had landed with her back turned to Elena after the Hosenka, undefended. So why wasn't the girl attacking from behind now? If she had taken so little damage as to be able to stand, she could end the fight at once by striking at her apparently naïve opponent.

"Why?"

Chun-Li was mortified, her voice trembling. She kept her eyes cast down, preventing Elena from seeing the hot tears that now swelled at their corners.

"Why what?"

Elena didn't understand the question. After blinking the tears away, Chun-Li found the courage to look at Elena.

"Why didn't you attack when my back was turned?"

"That would not be very fun."

"N-not fun…?"

Elena had answered like it was the most obvious thing in the world, and she now stared at Chun-Li blankly.

"Don't you want to win?"

"Yes, I want to win!"

Elena's voice rang earnest, though a hint of childishness softened the declaration.

"So then why…?"

"Kicking you down from behind would not be winning," shot back Elena with self-assurance.

This girl was pure beyond words.

So many fighters in this world do whatever it takes to beat down the opponent, all in order to declare themselves winners. Chun-Li had faced no small number of such fighters, so the innocence of the girl who now stood before her was almost blinding.

When had *she* lost that pureness of heart?

It was as if her own heart was pricked by a thorn.

"You really remind me of him, you know."

"Him?"

Chun-Li closed her eyes without answering Elena's inquiry.

The figure that appeared in the darkness cast an intense gaze on Chun-Li.

He wore a headband of fiery red, and his sublime eyes sparkled beneath a pair of thick, black eyebrows.

Ryu…

A man who sought the greatest fighters in his pursuit of strength. He would face down one mighty opponent after another, never doubting his sense of justice and fair play. His faith in his own righteousness was pervasive.

Though their personalities differed, this girl resembled Ryu, Chun-Li thought.

The common element between them…

"Prodigy…" murmured Chun-Li, not at Elena or anyone in particular.

"I remind you of one called 'Prodigy'?"

"Pfft."

Chun-Li couldn't help but laugh. Elena took this as mocking, so she puffed her cheeks in anger.

Chun-Li bowed in apology, open palm before her face.

"I'm sorry. I didn't mean it that way."

"I find your words hard to understand."

"Elena…"

Chun-Li struck her fighting stance.

"I'm jealous of you."

"Why is that?" asked a confused Elena. Lured by Chun-Li's stance, the girl started bouncing to an unheard rhythm once again.

"Because you're strong."

Chun-Li charged, Elena smiling all the while.

"You really are incredible…"

As she spoke, Chun-Li clenched her right fist and moved to strike Elena's face, but the girl's head had already vanished from view as her body dipped down.

"Hah."

With a spirited battle cry, Elena spread her legs wide across the ground and begin to spin them around.

A sweep.

Elena's squat had forewarned Chun-Li of the incoming attack, so by the time the sweeping leg came around, Chun-Li was already jumping.

Twisting her body slightly, she pressed her left leg down in a kick. Yoshokyaku.

A white boot tip exploded against Elena's cheek as she tried to stand.

Chun-Li followed up by vaulting over Elena, grazing the back of her silver hair before landing, spinning around with a quick breath, and preparing for the next attack.

From a squatting position, she formed a blade with her right hand and thrusted out quickly. It was the fastest move she could use at nearly point-blank range. Like Lightning Kick, there was little force behind each strike, but it had the advantage of being too quick for the opponent to react in time.

Elena was only human, after all.

Prodigy or not, she couldn't break the laws of physics.

The flurry of chopping attacks caused Elena to stiffen.

Chun-Li stopped striking and channeled strength to her legs in order to stand. As she rose from the squat, her right foot left the ground.

A kick drove into the frozen Elena's face.

Just as the kicking leg touched down, Chun-Li drew ki from tanden to hands and launched another orb of light.

Kikoken.

Overwhelmed by the successive attacks, Elena couldn't dodge the direct hit to her stomach.

"Kyahhh."

The orb burst upon impact, sending tiny sparks leaping across the surface of Elena's body.

She leapt in the air, but the convulsions quickly grounded her, prostrate. Chun-Li breathed deeply and quietly looked down on her opponent.

She began to walk slowly while managing her breathing, never taking her eyes off Elena.

Chun-Li stopped a few paces away from the girl and spoke.

"I didn't think you'd let it end so soon."

Her voice was warm towards the motionless, grounded Elena. The girl's face had suggested that she wouldn't even be capable of a twitch for quite some time, but at Chun-Li's words, something snapped, and Elena lifted her head to look at Chun-Li.

"Eheh…"

Cheeks and nose covered in red earth, Elena smiled her innocent smile and pressed both hands against the ground, hard. The force lifted her entire body into a jump.

"Hup."

She managed to suppress the shock to her body upon landing from such a height, spreading both arms for balance before speaking, glee in her voice.

"It appears as though I remain undamaged, even from that attack. Yet, that strange orb made me lose all feeling!"

"It's called a Kikoken."

"Can I, too, produce such an attack?"

With this, Elena brought both palms to her side and thrust them at Chun-Li. Naturally, no energy sprang forth.

"I'm positive that you'd be able to."

"Truly?"

Elena gave a small hop, her whole body an expression of her joy.

"Yes. I can teach you."

"Do you promise?"

"But you have to beat me first."

"Understood!" answered Elena without a hint of hesitation.

"Beating me shouldn't be too hard for someone like you, right?"

The coyness was lost on Elena, so Chun-Li realized her comment was in poor taste.

Not that the girl even heard.

Her gaze–now more intense than before–pierced Chun-Li.

The instant Elena saw the Kikoken as a prize to be won, her eyes took on a new quality.

"You really are a child…" said Chun-Li, exasperated.

"Fighting you is so very fun, miss ."

"Right back at you."

Elena nodded, satisfied, but Chun-Li was already charging to close the gap.

A roundhouse kick.

Of course, Elena dodged the attack fluidly.

The instant Chun-Li's kicking leg landed, she struck out at Elena's face with her right fist.

The girl bent over backwards to dodge, transitioning into a backflip. Her legs stretched out as they flew, aiming for Chun-Li's chin.

Chun-Li's chest throbbed violently under her blue China dress as she adroitly considered how to best attack and defend.

She raised her left arm to guard against the kick and wondered how long it'd been since she experienced a fight this fun.

But Elena kept attacking.

The backflip opened a small gap between the fighters, but the girl immediately segued into a forward somersault.

As with the backflip, her legs became kicking blades, and this ferocious kick directed all of Elena's body weight at the crown of Chun-Li's head.

How to dodge this one?

A smile crept onto Chun-Li's face as she decided.

Just before the kick connected, she sprang backwards.

The hurricane of an attack sliced through the air, practically grazing the bridge of her nose.

"Yah!"

She launched a low kick at Elena, who had landed in a squat.

"Yahah."

With a brief laugh, Elena pressed both hands to ground, spread her legs, and began to spin. This was the same technique that had juggled Chun-Li earlier.

Chun-Li's low kick clashed explosively against one of Elena's legs, which skimmed across the ground. Intense pain shot up through their skins.

But that was no reason to stop.

Because a mere moment of hesitation could mean defeat where such high-speed exchanges were concerned. The first one to stop would lose, so as long as they both drew breath, the attacks would go on.

Leg pressed against leg in mid-air, but Elena didn't hold the position for long.

She spun backwards around her hips, withdrawing her kick as she stood.

"Yahhh!"

Chun-Li stepped one pace forward with her landing foot and kicked high with the opposite leg, aiming for Elena's face. One hit wouldn't be enough.

Another Lightning Kick barrage began, launching volley after volley, timed with short breaths.

The sensation Chun-Li felt against her foot was the same as earlier; Elena was countering every kick with one of her own.

"Your potential is honestly a little scary…"

Chun-Li was truly in awe of such innate ability, which she herself did not possess.

If she had been born with Elena's talents, what sort of life might she have led?

Chun-Li had been the one to decide to train her body and seek revenge against Shadaloo for her father's murder. She had opted to dedicate her life to her work as a detective with Interpol, gathering intel on international criminals so that she could one day kill Shadaloo's leader–Bison–with her own two feet.

None of it was because she actually enjoyed fighting, deep down.

In fact, the only fight she had ever enjoyed was the one against Ryu, when they were both competing in a fighting tournament hosted by Shadaloo.

That was where they first met.

Her goal had been to win the tournament and earn a face-to-face with Bison, so Ryu had been nothing but an obstacle to be overcome, at the time.

But he had beaten her soundly, and it had nothing to do with Bison or Shadaloo. Chun-Li hadn't been able to hold a candle to Ryu–a man who sought nothing but strength.

That fight had been the first time Chun-Li had felt true regret, a feeling she hadn't experienced since.

What is strength?

Chun-Li had never given the question much thought. The techniques she honed were simply tools of revenge.

But then Ryu had taught her that there was more to gain from battles than burdensome feelings like "hatred" or "resentment."

Chun-Li had changed, that day.

True strength.

That was what Chun-Li now hoped to achieve, and it wasn't something that could be reached while held back by a petty grudge. Her awakening to the nature of true strength had brought her that much closer to overcoming Bison.

She had come to believe that.

But now...

Compared to the girl before her eyes—one who reveled in every aspect of battle—Chun-Li was none so pure. That's why she was jealous and even a little angry.

"It's about time to end this," she said, slowing the speed of her kicks.

Elena's smiling face came into view beyond the thinning veil.

"I won't lose to you. No..."

Chun-Li's thin eyebrows angled downwards.

"I can't lose!"

The girl wouldn't be leaping over her again anytime soon.

Elena's purity was the reason she needed to be taught a lesson by her elder. She needed to learn that "fighting" is an act meant to hurt the opponent.

Feeling nothing but joy in the heat of battle was plain wrong, and innocent or not, everyone has the potential for malice. Elena just hadn't awoken to that potential yet, but that ignorance is reserved only for children who don't yet know the way of the world.

To grow up and somehow retain that innocence would be a crime, and Elena was old enough at this point. Chun-Li would have to show her the inherent evil behind harming others.

"Haaaaaaah..."

Chun-Li's every thought transformed into flames within.

She took a single step and planted her feet, pulling up energy from the earth.

She was suddenly very conscious of her status as a small piece of the greater planet, always connected to one another.

The ki began welling up inside her.

Elena's wild instincts took immediate note of the change to Chun-Li's being.

However...

"Too slow!"

Chun-Li–now clad in flashes of lightning–quietly wondered if Elena even heard her.

She raised her left leg a bit while spreading her arms and bringing them behind her.

"Amazing…" Chun-Li heard a wide-eyed Elena mutter.

Left foot stomped down and both hands pressed forward in Elena's direction.

Chun-Li was surrounded by a storm of ki, lightning, and wind, which all rushed towards her palms to create a ball of energy.

"Kikoken!"

It formed between her outstretched palms, swelling into something resembling a miniature sun. With a brilliant flash, it shot forward at Elena.

This wasn't something that could be dodged with a mere jump or backstep.

The orb connected just as Elena scrambled to strike a defensive stance, brushing past her arms and enveloping her entire body in light.

She began convulsing wordlessly before being blown back, as if trying to put some distance between Chun-Li and herself.

Elena slammed into the massive tree behind her, back first, and fell to the ground, motionless, save for occasional twitches upon the red earth. It was clear that this time, she would not be rising again soon.

Chun-Li walked slowly towards the still twitching Elena.

"Are you okay?" she asked, crouching down.

"I-I never knew such a thing was possible," replied the girl, shakily.

"That's because I never told you."

Chun-Li wore a distinctly *adult* smile.

"I really must thank you."

The tribe's chief–who happened to be Elena's father–bowed to Chun-Li.

"My daughter has come this far without ever tasting true defeat. As such, she never feared battle. By losing to you today, my Elena now knows fear."

"Elena is a strong one. I had no choice but to go all-out, honestly. My victory was, well… It could've gone either way."

"There is no 'luck' when it comes to battle. The stronger fighter always emerges victorious. Even when the outcome may seem arbitrary, one can be sure that it is the result of skill, or lack thereof. The weaker fighter can never win."

Chun-Li blushed and smiled at the man's words.

Luck does play a factor in every fight, in various ways, and the stronger fighter doesn't necessarily always win. She was sure that Elena's father knew that much, but still he had decided to voice his respect and admiration for her.

What a kind man…

Chun-Li was reminded of her own father.

"Chun-Li…"

Elena's voice came from behind her father. She limped forward while leaning on her brother's shoulder.

"You okay?" asked Chun-Li, once the girl was standing beside her father.

Elena nodded vigorously, the same smile plastered on her face as before the fight.

"That was fun. We ought to fight again sometime."

"Yes, of course."

"We must. So please come back to Kenya someday."

"It's a promise."

Chun-Li pointed her right pinky finger at Elena, causing the innocent girl to stare, eyes wide with confusion.

"In a certain land in the Far East, people make promises by linking pinkies. Then, whoever breaks the promise has to swallow one thousand needles."

"One *thousand?*" gasped Elena.

"I learned this from someone I lost to a long time ago. That way, I got another chance to fight him."

No matter how many times they fought, it always ended the same way, but Chun-Li didn't mention that part.

"Until next time, Elena. Be sure to get stronger by then."

Bright eyes welled up with tears against brown skin.

"You should really get out and see the world. It's full of plenty of other strong people. And I'm sure you would, well…"

"Just as she says," spoke Elena's father, without waiting for Chun-Li to finish.

"You must see the world if you are truly to find yourself. It is for your own sake."

"F-father…"

Elena paused a moment before nodding meekly. Then she turned to gaze at Chun-Li with renewed fire in her eyes.

"When next we meet, it may not be in Africa, but rather someplace else."

"That's what I'm hoping."

Elena reached for Chun-Li's outstretched pinky with her own.

"This is a promise…"

"Right."

Both smiled, surrounded by the red of the fiery Kenyan sunset.

This was the start of a long rivalry between these two.

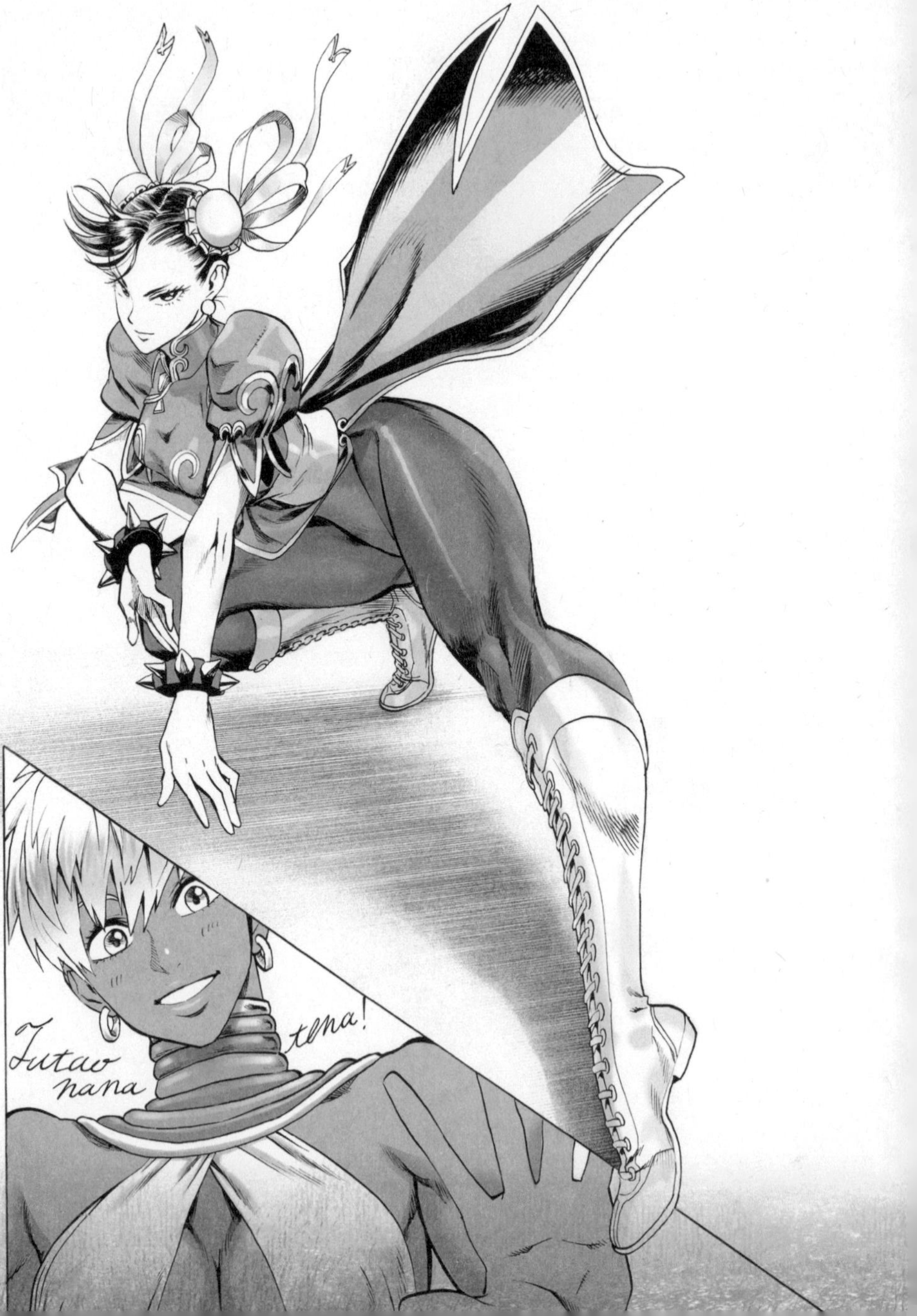
Tutao nana tena!

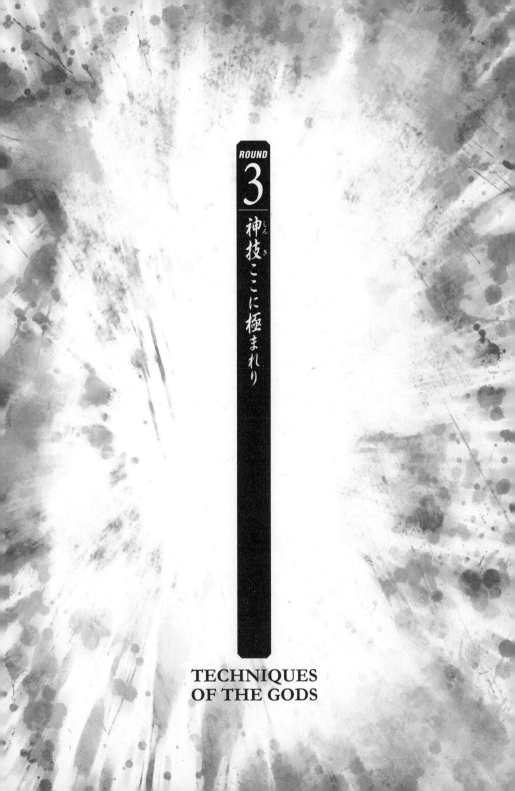

ROUND

3

神技ここに極まれり

TECHNIQUES
OF THE GODS

ROUND 3
TECHNIQUES
OF THE GODS

A single, plump index finger diligently applied the *kumadori* makeup. First, along the deep brow creases, then over the eyelids, inside to outside. Two more lines extended across each cheek, and finally, a pair of dabs at the downturned corners of the mouth, elongating the arc of the frown.

A pair of Daruma-like eyes beneath eyebrows thick as paintbrushes glowered at themselves, reflected in a mirror. The pupils flared with a rage intense enough to intimidate others on sight.

The man's jutting cheekbones gave his stern face a gargoyle-like quality, all topped off with a dignified ginkgo-leaf style topknot.

He was a sumo wrestler. A *rikishi*.

"Very well…"

Now finished applying the makeup, he spoke with satisfaction. His deep, bold voice shook the air of the still room.

This was Edmond Honda.

A ridiculous name for a rikishi, no doubt.

Using the Western "Edmond" for a sumo stage name was unthinkable. The extravagant makeup–clearly an homage to *kabuki* stagecraft tradition–didn't help either.

Above the standard loincloth he had tied a *yukata* robe that drooped below his waist, leaving his upper body naked. His exposed stomach, arms, and legs below the loincloth were swathed in a generous layer of fat.

But he was not *soft*.

That Honda's body was firm despite his girth was obvious at a glance. The sight of him might bring to mind a massive crag, standing tall and fighting back against the raging flow of a river.

Topknot, loincloth, yukata, and kabuki-style makeup…

Honda was a collection of stereotypes. The sort of man that a foreigner might picture when imagining "the Japanese."

<"Are you okay?"> said a man from behind Honda in English. The reflection in the mirror revealed him to be muscular and blond.

The honed body bulging from the dark green tank-top seemed to say, "Take a look at *this*." Round pieces of metal dangled from the silver chain around his neck.

Dogtags used to identify those killed in battle.

Honda turned around leisurely to face the man.

The windowless, Spartan room was no more than 100 square feet , with a mortar ceiling and walls painted white. Atop the cold floor sat a pair of unapologetically uninviting plastic couches.

The door–left open behind the man–also lacked a window.

<"Hey, sumo wrestler. You okay?"> asked the man again, raising his eyebrows high.

"I'm fine," replied Honda in Japanese.

He felt no need to speak in the foreigner's tongue. He was Japanese. If this other man wanted to speak in his own language, then so would Honda. This didn't come from a place of obstinacy; it was just Honda's style. Emotions speak louder than words, and if there were still a failure to communicate, fists would get the job done.

Or, in Honda's case, open palms.

People are fundamentally animals, so their hearts could speak to one another even where boorish conversation failed.

<"Steven!">

The voice came from beyond the door, and another figure appeared. This man was black, with a frame at least as burly as his friend's.

Both were soldiers with the American air force, assigned to the 1st Special Operations Wing unit (or 1st SOW for short) out of Hurlburt

Field, Florida.

The black man stared at Honda curiously, scanning him from head to toe several times before turning to the white man named Steven.

His gaze seemed to ask, "Is this dude really okay?"

Steven's eyebrows shrugged along with his shoulders , and the pair began speaking in quick English. Steven broke the silence.

<"Y'think this guy really knows the major?">

<"Not sure. But we know this sumo wrestler was chosen to face him, either way.">

<"I hear the major's the best close combat specialist in the whole air force. His hand-to-hand is insane. He's gonna tear this Japanese clown a new one, I say.">

Their less-than-polite conversation went on as they periodically glanced over at Honda.

Steven sighed as he spoke.

<"We rank-and-file don't get a ton of chances to see the major grapple. It's gonna suck when this fight is over before it even starts.">

<"Well, this guy'll probably manage to stay standing for a good five minutes.">

The black man turned to Honda and raised both fists into a boxing stance.

<"Good luck!"> he said, flashing his white teeth in a smile.

The man bowed deeply several times. Bowing not being a custom in the states, he must have thought it symbolized respect in Japanese culture.

Honda closed his eyes and brought a deep breath into the pit of his stomach. Exhaling slowly through his nose, he walked towards the two men.

He made straight for the door but stopped between them. Not turning to either one, Honda opened his drooping mouth to speak.

<"I'm fine. It won't go the way you're thinking, because I'm gonna win.">

He had understood their entire conversation, and his sardonic reply in English drove the point home. Ignoring the soldiers' wide-eyed stares,

Honda moved into the darkened hallway.

<"Long time no see, Honda.">

The American military man's easy tone was at odds with his grim expression.

With camo-print pants, high-laced boots, and a green tank-top, he was a soldier through and through. His bulging shoulder and back muscles gave him a square look, and one shoulder bore a tattoo of the stars and stripes- a clear expression of his patriotism.

But by far the most unforgettable aspect of the man was his hairstyle, which resembled what you might get if you pointed a paintbrush upright and cut straight through the middle of the bristles with a pair of scissors. He lacked eyebrows entirely, leaving a blank canvass of a forehead above his calm, soldier's eyes.

"How many years has it been, Guile?"

<"I don't exactly have the time to sit around keeping track of these things."> answered back Guile in a stiff, stony voice.

Both Honda and Guile spoke in their respective mother tongues. Their conversation was made possible by the fact that each had mastered the other's language, so even without bothering with the laborious task of translating, these two understood each other perfectly well.

They were friends who spoke with their fists. Whatever they might mean to communicate was told through the clashing of spirits.

"Which of us won our last bout? Do you recall?"

<"I did.">

"No, it was me."

Both wore the same faint smile.

They now stood on one of the runways at the 1st SOW base, where a number of soldiers had come to watch their fight.

The summer sun scorched the asphalt, making the area ripple with mirages. The runway's surface was hot enough to barbecue.

Even the oppressive heat wasn't enough to repel the spectators, though; they stood around with baited breath, waiting for the action to start.

None of this was authorized, of course.

It was an unofficial, unrecognized fight, organized by Guile's followers. Those same ardent supporters had invited Honda to the base and cleared this particular area of the runway of personnel, creating a space where the two fighters could go all-out.

Now, those hot-blooded American soldiers gathered around like small-time street punks hoping to catch a neighborhood brawl.

Naturally, there were no rules; the fight would go on until one fighter fell.

Their fights were always like that, whether they took place in a bathhouse in Japan, a wharf in America, or a temple in Thailand.

No matter where or when they fought, it was always pure combat with no need for rules.

This time was no different—just another in a long line of battles.

Honda was overjoyed at the prospect. He traveled the world, spreading the glory of sumo... It was that dream that had driven Honda from Japan ten odd years ago. Since then, he had met many brothers and sisters in arms via a series of trying battles.

Every fight showed him a new facet of his friends, allowing him to know them that much better.

This battle, too, was one meant to teach the fighters about each other.

Honda was nearly shaking with excitement.

<"Honda,"> said Guile, raising both fists near his jaw. He tilted forward, with a slight bend in his back. Nearly all of his weight was on his toes as he faced his opponent straight on.

This was Guile's stance.

Like a hawk eying its prey from high above, Guile pierced Honda with a sharp stare.

<"You're gonna see a new me, today.">

Honda scowled at Guile as the latter spoke, gradually dropping his hips and spreading his feet into a low, wide stance that supported his bulk. His arms were poised for the initial sumo charge, fists barely touching the ground in front of him.

"And what exactly is different today?"

<"I'll be coming at you to kill.">

The unsettling words escaped from the corner of Guile's mouth.

Guile wasn't usually the type to mention killing in the context of battle. He may have been a soldier, but he would never do anything to sully the dignity of a one-on-one fight.

But now he would be aiming to kill…?

A blazing heat ran up Honda's spine, from hip to nape.

<"Let's do this,"> muttered Guile.

The audience sensed the foreboding aura about their major and fell silent.

Guile's hips began to drop.

With right knee kinked at a ninety-degree angle, he bent his body nearly low enough for his left knee to graze the asphalt. The pose could have been considered a squat. Guile's rugged chin was brought close to his bent right knee, and he held up both fists on either side to protect it.

He was motionless.

For a moment, Honda was reminded of that famous sculpture. The one of the man resting his chin upon a fist.

Who was the artist? Modin?

Or maybe it was…

With a small shake of his head, Honda cleared his mind of extraneous thoughts.

<"Sonic Boom!">

Honda immediately regretted leaving himself open.

The instant he registered Guile's voice, a swirl of blue air was rushing towards him.

Sonic Boom…

One of Guile's trademark attacks.

He would draw both arms behind his back and swing them around with incredible speed, ripping through the air on either side of him and sending it forward. The vicious attack finished with the crossing of his fists in front of his face, which would produce a powerful soundwave. This move had the distinct advantage of being able to reach the opponent even at a distance.

It was already too late for Honda to dodge the Sonic Boom that now hurtled towards him. The swirl resembled a pair of dragons carving out a vacuum in the air and biting each other's tails. Or even the double *tomoe*–or comma design–found on many Japanese family crests. The circular blade spun furiously in Honda's direction at the speed of sound.

If dodging would do him no good, there was only one other option.

Honda crossed his muscular, fat-covered arms in front of his face.

The two serpents coiled around Honda's tree trunk-like arms, inflicting enough pain to make him think his skin was being rent apart. He could only wait for the vacuum blades to disperse.

The pain lessened, and Honda uncrossed his arms.

"Gahh."

He couldn't help but grunt.

Guile was already closing the gap, but how?

No time to think.

The opponent had entered an offensive stance.

In an instant, Guile vanished from the immobilized the Honda's vision.

Honda felt warmth across his back; something had wrapped around him.

A pair of arms.

The sumo wrestler's body was airborne, and the heavens and earth suddenly swapped positions with astounding speed.

The last thing he saw was the spectating soldiers, upside-down.

Honda went dizzy from the impact, and pain shot through his entire body like a bolt of lightning.

The arms released him, and his back was on fire. It was being baked.

The asphalt…

He was laid out on the ground.

"Guhh."

Honda came to senses after a moment of unconsciousness and

wasted no time lifting himself back into his stance.

With beastlike instincts, he scanned for Guile.

Only the crowd…

Guile was gone.

<"Honda,"> came a voice from behind.

He struck out with an open palm as he turned, but there was no satisfying *thud* of flesh on flesh. Only air.

Guile was there but far out of reach…

He held himself still in a crouch, scowling in Honda's direction.

<"That was just me saying 'hello'… *This time* it's for real.">

"Are we here to boast and bluff, or will you come at me like a man?"

Honda glared, arms drooping at his sides, as a single rivulet of blood trickled from his left nostril. He made no move to wipe it away, and he didn't break eye contact with Guile.

Letting his guard down for a moment would mean defeat. One instant of laxness and the Sonic Boom would tear his defenses to shreds.

Nevertheless …

<"Make a move, Honda,"> taunted Guile.

<"Us glaring at each other ain't much of a show.">

No victory could come from a prolonged stalemate.

Honda made his move.

"Dosei!"

The battle cry came from deep within his gut as he kicked off the ground.

Honda's bulk soared through the air, moving like a missile at Guile to deliver a headbutt.

Sumo Headbutt …

He'd named the attack himself.

<"Sonic…">

Guile's shout meant that a Sonic Boom was coming, just as Honda had predicted.

There was nothing to fear if he foresaw the attack; he could push past the impact and pain with strength of will alone.

Just as predicted, the Sonic Boom burst on the crown of Honda's head. His momentum slowed the moment he felt the pain, stopping his advance in mid-air.

Honda landed.

There was still quite a gap between the fighters, yet…

One massive step would be enough to reach Guile with a palm strike, so Honda brought his right foot forward.

Guile was already crouching again after releasing the last Sonic Boom, and Honda caught a flash of pale blue light in the soldier's eyes.

The sumo wrestler was advancing, just as Guile had hoped. Honda's single step was part of Guile's calculations, all to get his opponent to this spot. His right leg flew upwards, his blade-like foot ripping through the air and drawing a perfect arc through the rippling heat haze.

Flash Kick.

Another of Guile's signature attacks.

Honda couldn't help but smile, because now Guile had walked into *his* trap.

The step forward with his right foot was the bait, and the soldier had fallen for it fabulously.

During the duration of his Flash Kick, Guile was in mid-air, defenseless.

The match would be won just as he landed. Just as his feet touched down from the flip.

Honda gathered all his might and struck out with an open palm.

<"Not so fast!">

Guile's voice resounded just as Honda expected to feel flesh against his hand.

However…

What Honda actually felt was a pain like no other. As if his whole body were being cut in two, lengthwise, by a massive bladed object.

Could that have been the Flash Kick?

Nonsense…

Hadn't he dodged that?

Guile flew through the air.

There, again, was the trail in mid-air left by his foot.

Déjà vu…

Honda thought he must have been dreaming until he realized what had actually happened. Guile had landed and immediately launched a second Flash Kick.

A direct hit.

Honda's body was blown back violently and forced off the ground by the second kick.

Impossible. No…

This was really happening.

Attacking the enemy in an unguarded moment was part of the basics of fighting. Achieving victory through the impossible was at the heart of true battle.

In that sense, Guile's techniques had even more force behind them.

What an incredible man…

Honda thought as much the moment before his airborne body crashed down against the baking asphalt. Damage from falls was enhanced by Honda's size, and at over 300 pounds, a fall like this could be fatal.

Just as he felt his nape smack the ground, Honda curled his lower body in from stomach, to waist, to legs. His own thighs passed into view overhead–bringing his knees near his face–just before his body flipped over entirely , landing in splayed position like the 大 character.

From topknot-crowned head to toe, Honda's body was tingling and numb. Even the scorching asphalt only felt pleasantly warm. He was overcome by the urge to remain grounded.

"Is this really the time for that?" came a voice from within.

His own voice. Edmond Honda's.

He was the rikishi who had left Japan to bring sumo to the world.

All the eccentric costuming was for that purpose…

The kumadori makeup, the yukata, and even the ostentatious topknot were parts of his trial-and-error efforts to spread the glory of sumo.

The more famous Honda could become, the more effective his getup would be.

Westerners tended to be bad at distinguishing one East Asian from another , but they would have to recognize the fat man with the makeup and topknot as none other than Edmond Honda. A man who would step onto the world's stage and spread sumo to every corner of the earth.

This fight was but a single step of that process…

All for sumo's sake.

Why go to such lengths, though?

Because he believed that sumo was the strongest of all martial arts.

The rikishi's body- well-muscled by covered by a layer fat serving as armor- is unique in its ability to protect the fighter from the opponent's blows.

The sumo match- taking place in a sacred ring- is a rich spectacle developed over hundreds of years that pits wrestler against wrestler. A rikishi's arsenal includes open palm strikes, inside ankles sweeps, and a wealth of blunt attacks.

Honda believed that no other fighting style could claim superiority over sumo.

Sumo was strongest.

Sumo was supreme.

Sumo was truth.

This was why he could not lose.

"Arghhhh."

Power flowed into his still-numb palms.

A faint, electric tingling down Honda's spine caused his muscles to contract and expand.

<"Guess you're not ready to let it end there, Honda.">

The voice from overhead was so calm as to sound almost callous.

Coming at you to kill…

When Guile had said that before, it was no lie. It was only his warrior's pride that had kept him from finishing off the grounded Honda. The *soldier* in him would have gladly done so, but Guile was a warrior today. As long as his opponent had the energy left to stand, their fight would go on. For a battle between warriors continues until one fighter's will is completely broken.

Honda's will was plenty intact, and Guile knew that, so he waited.

The former began to stand, and the latter stared, fixated.

"Buwahhh!"

The wrestler was finally standing.

He dropped his hips, lowered his hands, and moved into his charging stance. Starting at the massive gut that spilled over his hanging yukata, a pair of red lines ran up over his chest and cheeks, one on each side.

Scars from the Flash Kicks.

Any halfhearted fighter would have been cut to ribbons, and even Honda's muscular body now bore more than just bruises. Close inspection would reveal a series tiny gashes. He only survived because of the unique armor protecting him–the combination of muscle and fat.

"Sorry to keep you waiting," he said to Guile, who had raised his fists to either side of his chin.

<"Round two, then.">

Guile's burst of speed was at odds with his disinterested tone.

He clenched his arms to his body as he moved. Refusing to break the stiff stance in his upper body, Guile was loose only from the waist down. His legs advanced at a quick tempo–left, right, left–almost as if he were sliding across the ground. It wasn't necessarily boxing footwork–a skill common to American fighters–but rather evidence of some military training that allowed him to advance smoothly and silently.

So smooth that it was nearly impossible to tell when either foot would move next. So adroit were his movements that he could have suddenly sprung in any direction without surprising anyone.

Unable to read the moves, Honda could only wait.

Even now, Guile's piercing gaze brought to mind that of a snake eying a frog with ill intent.

So Honda brought his lowered fists nearly close enough to cross and relaxed his shoulders. Taking even half a step forward could get him annihilated.

He waited…

Guile suddenly turned his back to the wrestler, preparing to spin his body.

It was coming.

Guile peered at his opponent over his own shoulder.

The attack would be aimed at Honda's face. But what sort of attack?

A bent right elbow appeared from beyond Guile's spinning back, and as it sliced through the air between the fighters, the arm extended, revealing a fist.

A backfist.

Honda crossed his arms in defense just before Guile's attack crashed into his upper arm with tremendous force.

Guile had vanished from view, and Honda found his body jumping into the air with a mind of its own.

Something even deeper than instinct had helped him read Guile's next move. Honda thought to himself that if such a thing as superpowers existed in the world, then the snap judgments employed by warriors in the heat of vicious battle should surely qualify.

Such was the subconscious nature of his reaction.

It was short hop, bringing him only slightly off the ground.

Guile's left leg carved a path straight through the small gap between Honda's soles and the asphalt beneath.

The wrestler landed.

No time to take a breath.

This particular kick of Guile's came with a certain unbreakable habit.

Honda jumped again, still breathless.

Where Guile's left leg had just been, his right now traced the same arc, barely skimming across the ground.

Of course it did.

When performing these leg sweeps, Guile *always* made it a double.

Even if one defended against the first, the second would finish the job. The goal was to bring the enemy down no matter what, but once one caught onto this trend, avoiding both hits was a simple matter.

Honda was airborne. He hadn't jumped straight up, though, but rather towards Guile.

Guile was below, launching the second sweep, defenseless, his right leg still engaged in the kick.

A counterattack against Honda at this moment was impossible.

A relaxed smile emerged at the corners of his red, painted mouth. The white teeth barely visible between his lips were clenched so tightly they might have cracked from the pressure.

"Dosei."

Honda thrust downwards with a palm strike accelerated by gravity.

Looking up, Guile clicked his tongue.

The heel of Honda's palm exploded against Guile's rugged cheekbones. A shockwave rippled from cheeks, to nose, to eyelids, to lips, momentarily warping Guile's entire face.

Honda felt the asphalt's heat under his feet, but his palm still pressed against his opponent's face.

Guile's tanktop-clad upper body began to bend backwards, succumbing to the force. His right leg–bent in a crouch–couldn't endure the pressure exerted by Honda's palm and began to bend at the ankle. As the right leg went, his left cracked.

Even with Guile smashed into the ground, looking up, the palm still rested on his face.

Honda felt a dull cracking sensation travel up through his hand.

The asphalt? Or maybe Guile's skull?

No time for thinking- only action.

The wrestler removed his hand and let both arms drop, waiting for Guile to stand.

No…

Because he wouldn't just be getting up leisurely.

Honda dropped his hips lower than before and began amassing ki in his tanden, between navel and groin. A charge at an opponent in the wrestling ring could never win the day without a generous supply of ki in the tanden.

"Haaa…"

He let out a slow breath and stared at the fallen Guile.

Honda realized that the last successful hit against the soldier was in fact the first of his that had connected since their fight began.

The sounds of the audience suddenly reached Honda. None of the spectators could believe that this fat clown had knocked down Guile.

Perfect…

The more unthinkable his eventual victory seemed, the greater the upset. When he finally beat Guile, the men watching would understand the splendor of sumo.

"Come now. Get up."

Honda lowered his bulk and waited.

He saw the shoulder with the American flag tattoo twitch. The meticulously cut blond hair shifted slightly, back and forth. Guile placed both hands on the asphalt and rose.

"Hah…"

With a grunt, Honda thrust an open palm at the air.

"Hah, hah…"

Another thrust. Then two in a row.

The shadow boxing continued.

Still thrusting, Honda inched towards Guile. His soles felt the baking earth as each palm shot out.

A trembling Guile forced his head up and rose shakily. A pair of blue eyes glowed out from his bloodstained face.

<"Shit…"> muttered Guile with a sigh.

Yes…

Just as Honda knew all about Guile's habits, so too was Guile familiar with Honda's current movements.

The palm strikes at the air while slowly advancing. Guile knew better than anyone present what was coming, and it took all he had to attempt to strike a defensive stance.

Too late.

Honda was in range, and he had laid all the groundwork.

"Hah!"

Every ounce of power within him went into the next thrust. One intended to actually strike Guile.

But not just a single hit. No.

This barrage wasn't so lenient as to stop after two or three hits, either.

Alternating between left and right, it was at least as ferocious as a rush, in boxing.

The assault left Guile not even a moment to breath or come to his senses. The arms he had raised in defense were easily smacked away, leaving him bolt upright and vulnerable to the merciless stream of blows.

<"Noooooo!">

<"Damn, fat man!">

The crowd was losing it.

Good.

The more shocked, the better.

"What do you think of my sumo…?"

Honda's utterance was cut short by a sudden blow to his face. Something had hit him. Or shot at him, rather.

It wasn't a blunt strike, though; the pain he felt was a *cutting* sort.

Sonic Boom.

The palm flurry stopped, and Guile stood before him.

When did the soldier manage to target him?

No time to ask questions.

It was obvious that Guile must have found an instant to guard and retaliate.

Honda had messed up, but regret in the moment would do him no good, because his opponent was already readying his next attack- a swift kick at Honda's right thigh.

No need to defend. He would take the hit and keep on fighting, because faltering here could only lead to defeat.

Honda had finally taken control over the flow of battle, but Guile had somehow reclaimed the initiative.

Whether on offense or defense, keep on pushing back .

That was at the heart of sumo.

"I won't retreat."

Ignoring the sharp pain on his thigh, Honda pressed forward.

Serpentine veins bulged out from Guile's bloodstained forehead.

Having finished the kick, the soldier now moved to bring down his left arm on Honda's crown like a hammer.

The wrestler raised his head ever so slightly to meet Guile's fist.

The strike connected where Honda's skull was thickest–at his forehead- producing a dry thud.

It was minimal defense, but still defense.

By taking the hit on the forehead, Honda rendered Guile's feint of a hook as useless as a bladeless knife.

The gap between them was as small as it had ever been.

Perfect for a throw…

It was at this distance that the merits of sumo could really shine.

Guile thrust up a knee in an attempt to put some space between them, but Honda wrapped his arms around the soldier in an embrace. The camo-clad right leg–now raised and bent at the knee–was pinned.

Honda reached behind and gripped Guile's belt, while the latter's arms rested atop the former's shoulders.

A *morozashi* grab.

In the ring, this move had never failed to win Honda the match.

Moving as if to carry Guile away, Honda lifted the soldier until his left foot raised off the ground. With his waist gripped tight, Guile's back was forced into a curve.

Honda suddenly felt himself suffocating.

Hot blood poured from his nostrils, and he wondered what had happened.

His nose was crushed.

In his confusion, Honda found himself staring at Guile's head as it moved towards his own with astounding speed.

A headbutt had broken his nose.

And more were coming as long as he maintained the grab.

Honda's left hand began to slip from the belt as the flurry of headbutts continued, allowing Guile's left foot to touch back down.

The perfect form of the grab was long since ruined.

But of course. Because this wasn't sumo.

It was a street fight…

Getting the opponent in a morozashi grab hardly guaranteed victory, here. Not in a battle without rules. Not when headbutts constituted fair play.

Honda was the one in danger if he didn't release the grab.

Pulling his hands away from the belt, he pushed against Guile's chest.

The soldier staggered only briefly before rushing forward again.

Honda took the opportunity to regain some semblance of a stance. There was no time to worry about his nosebleed, but the charging stance was essential.

The two fighters once again drew near.

With fists raised to attack, Guile's eyes shone with unshakable killing intent.

Honda couldn't let himself back down, though. He knew that from the start, because he truly believed in the strength of sumo.

Drawing closer silently like a snake in the grass, Guile spread his arms as far apart as he could.

A Sonic Boom was coming.

By the time Guile's fists pointed straight behind him, coils of air already swirled through the heat haze.

Honda somehow knew that this attack would be nothing like the earlier ones.

<"Sonic..."> shouted Guile.

The arms came hurtling around either side of Guile's thick chest, bringing with them a transparent scythe blade through the haze.

The two men were nearly close enough to touch, so a direct hit at this range wouldn't end well.

Slipping up could mean death.

However...

Honda would never leap back in retreat.

To triumph *after* taking the opponent's strongest attack head-on and surviving—that would be a true victory.

A smile came to Honda's face.

<"Hurricane!">

The energized blade of air loosed by Guile's fists flew towards Honda. Several times larger than the earlier attacks, this one resembled a small tornado.

A tornado...

A vision of a certain man suddenly appeared in Honda's mind. A man wearing a red headband and a dougi with ripped sleeves. One always seeking the strong while also embodying strength, himself. Always looking to the future, sight never clouded.

It was Ryu...

Another Japanese fighter, like Honda.

"Tornado," or *tatsumaki* in Japanese, was part of one of Ryu's attack names, which is why Honda was feeling nostalgic despite the urgency of his situation.

Even now, was Ryu out there, somewhere, fighting in search of strength?

Without a doubt.

Honda had to keep winning his own battles if he wanted to keep up with Ryu.

He couldn't fall, here.

Snapping out of his trip down memory lane, Honda saw Guile's vacuum tornado coming for at his throat.

"Dooooosei!" came his battle cry, deep from within.

Honda raised both arms high above his head and swung downward, aiming to crush the tornado with between his open palms.

A shrill, piercing noise rang out, reverberating through Honda's palms. It felt less like a sound and more like a physical shockwave, causing the spectators to cover their ears in distress.

Kashiwade...

It's a Japanese tradition to bring one's hands together like that while praying at Shinto shrines. The act is considered a divine one, as it expresses respect and gratitude towards the gods.

Rikishi are fighters with a strong connection to the gods of Japan. Once a sumo wrestler reaches *yokozuna* rank, he is said to be a living god, in fact. The belt worn by those yokozuna serves the same role as the *shimenawa* rope commonly seen at shrines.

By imbuing his kashiwade motion with his very soul, Honda channeled the gods in that instant. Naturally it would take a superhuman body to destroy a manmade tornado.

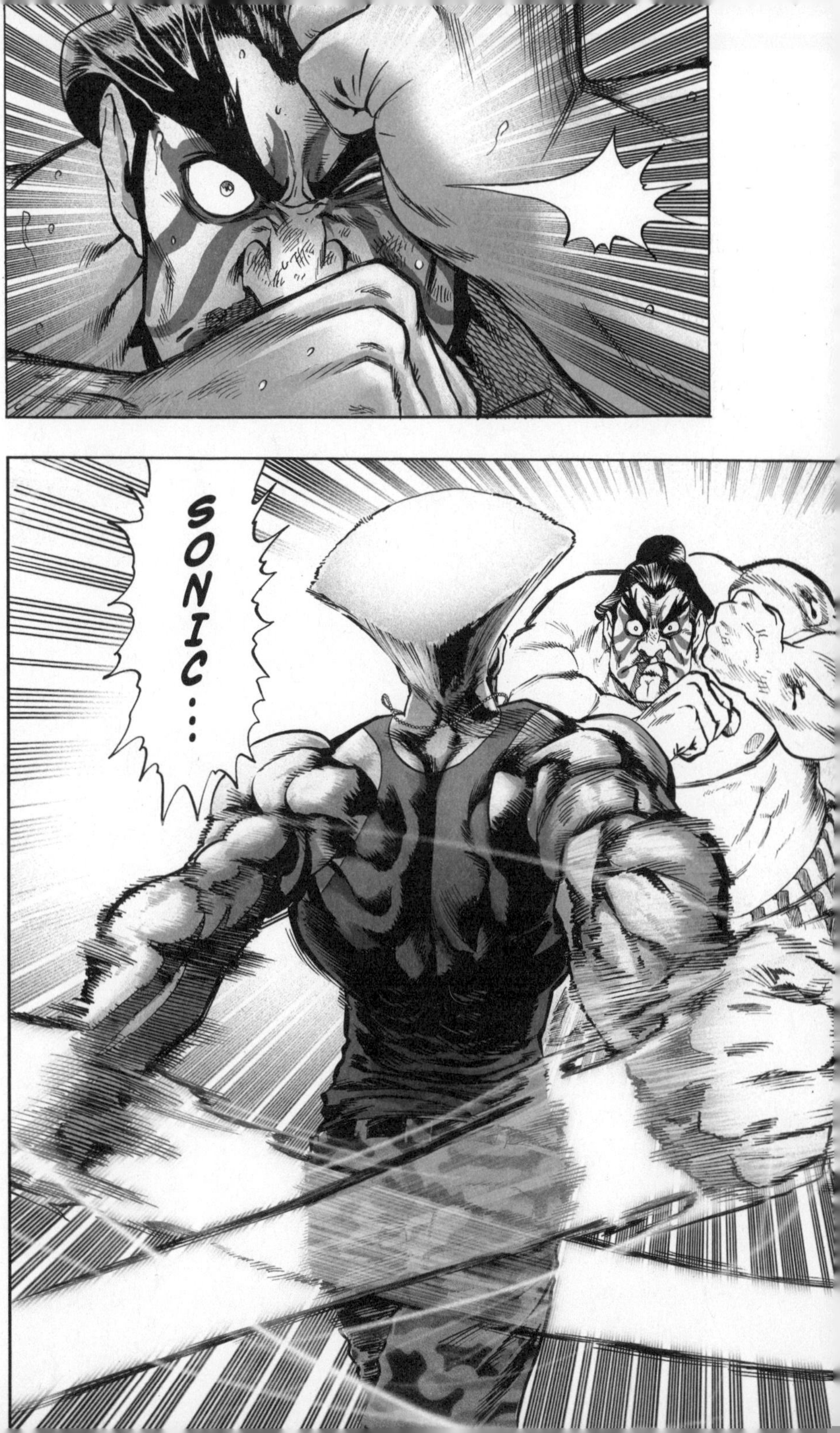
SONIC...

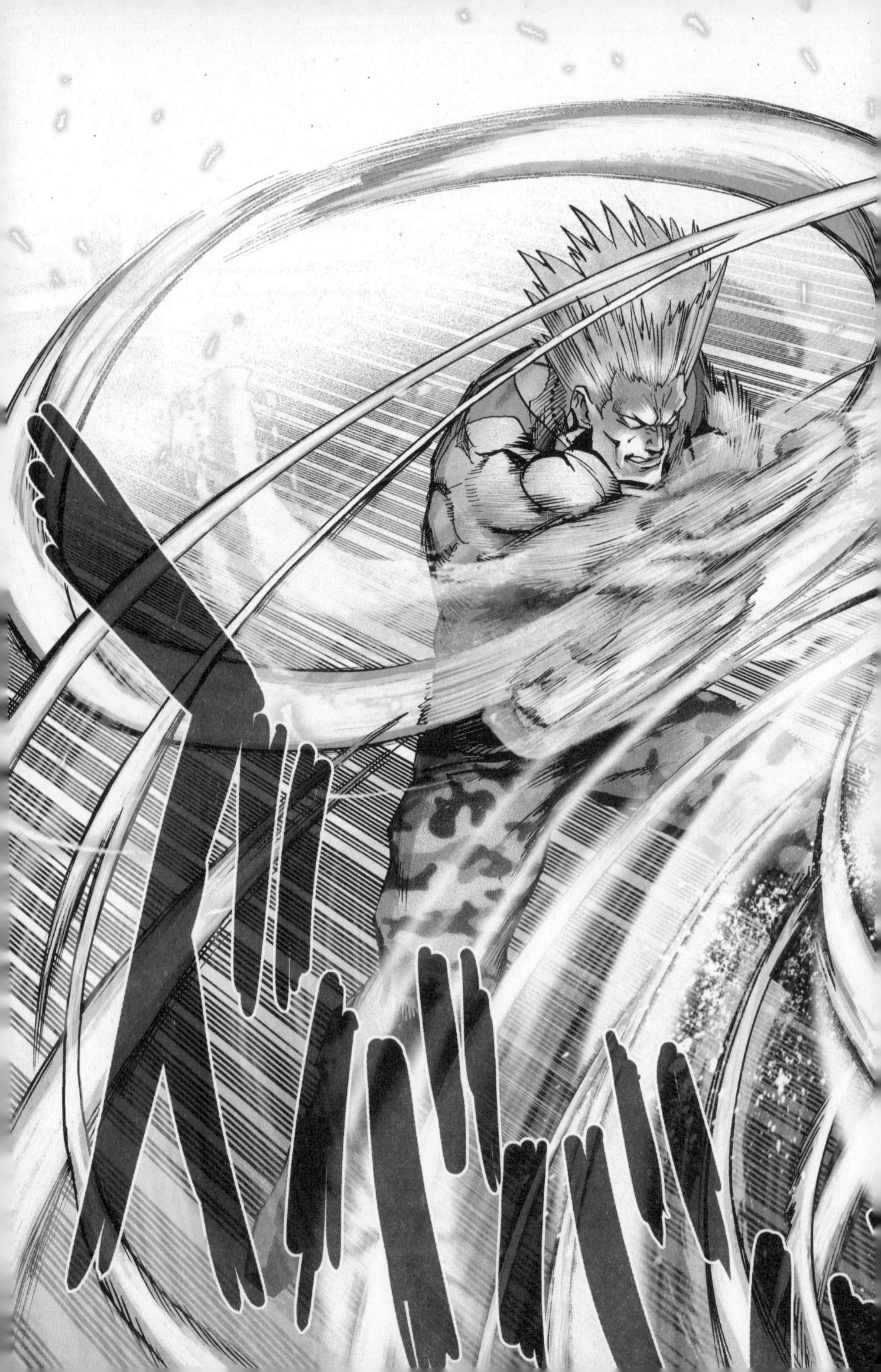

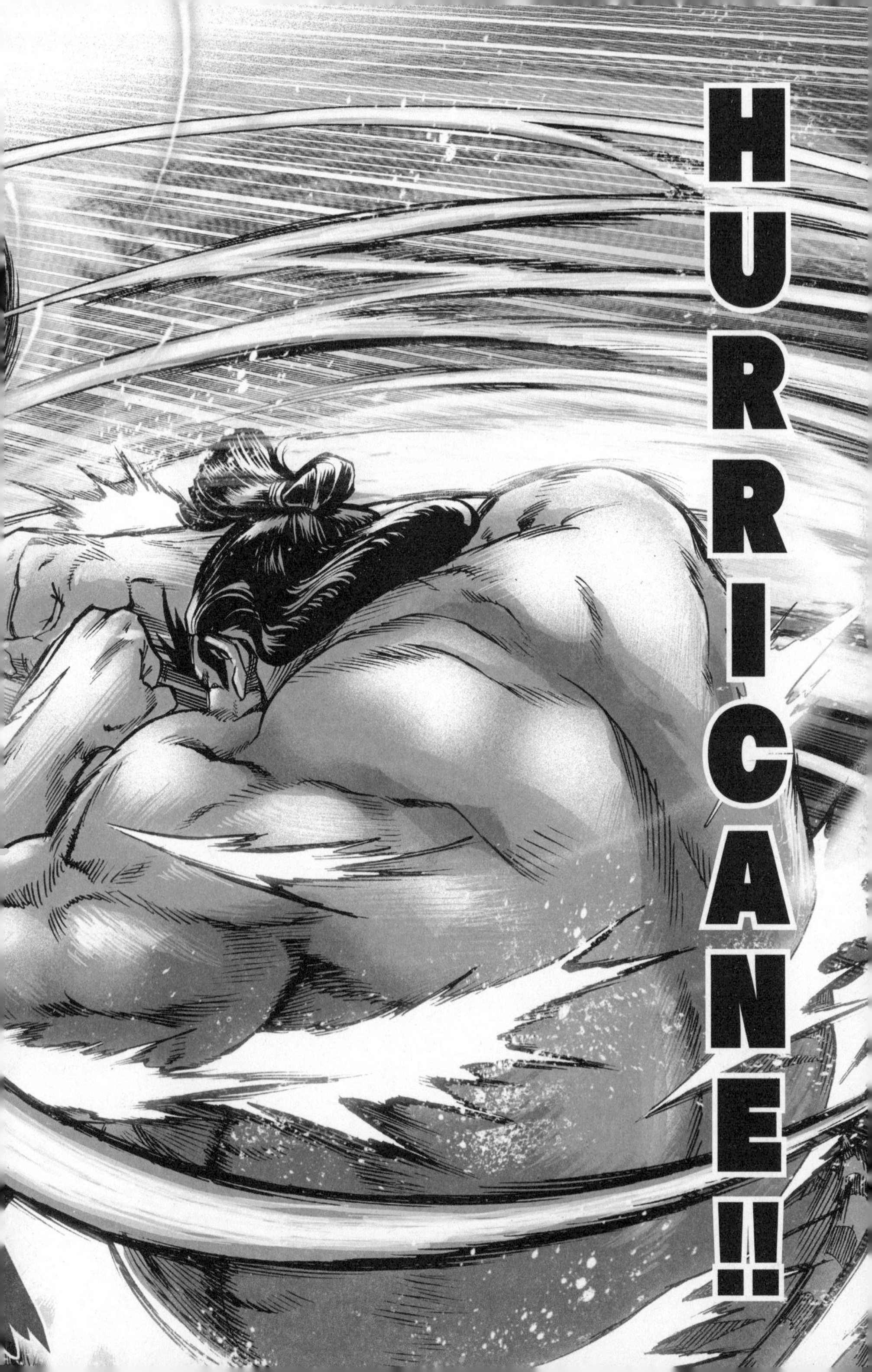
HURRICANE!!

Honda separated his numbed, tingling hands.

Several paces away stood Guile–hesitant to believe what he had just seen, yet still standing bravely, invigorated by that very act.

"Come at me."

Honda spread his arms wide. Facing Guile, he dropped his hips and stretched his arms, hands, and fingers high, as would a yokozuna entering the ring.

They had better be watching.

For this was the Japanese art of sumo.

Honda's thoughts were directed at the watching soldiers, who now stood awestruck.

Guile dropped into a squat.

Both fighters realized this exchange would be the final one, and in the end, there was only one technique Guile could choose to rely on.

Flash Kick…

Guile's square jaw flapped as he muttered something, but in the same instant, his downcast eyes looked up and flashed, piercing Honda.

It was clear that the soldier was building up power in his core. The energy flowed from stomach to hips and toes, and from navel to upper body.

As the power surged, Guile leapt. His entire body was gearing up for a final, deadly attack.

Guile's right leg rose towards Honda's stomach like a sweeping knife. No, not a knife; the kick would be as sharp as a Japanese *katana*.

<"I can't lose to you.">

Honda stepped into the kick, making no effort to dodge. It would only wound him deeper at closer range, but even knowing that didn't stop him.

The wrestler pushed past the kick's impact and rushed at Guile. Just as he grabbed his opponent, a military issue boot smashed into his chin. However, the arc of the kick was cut off there. Guile's momentum ceased, as the grab kept him from rising any higher.

In the *sabaori*–or "forward force down" –position, Honda tightened his grip.

The knee of Guile's kicking leg was practically brushing against his own shoulder.

Honda held his opponent tight in the embrace and began to bend over backwards. The traditional suplex was a bit too violent to serve as a clincher in the sumo ring, but this was a street fight.

Guile's head crashed into the asphalt.

Honda hadn't held back. He didn't have that luxury.

A part of him knew the attack might kill Guile, but he wasn't so naïve as to let that thought turn into hesitation.

The details weren't important, here. What mattered is that Guile's body was driven into the hard ground. Both fighters remained in that bent position for a moment before collapsing.

When Honda rose his head, he saw that Guile was unconscious, the whites of his eyes rolled back.

<"Take care of yourself."> said a young, enthusiastic soldier as he gripped Honda's hand with force. The wrestler accepted the handshake and nodded in return, a bit embarrassed.

At a distance, a bruised Guile watched the crowd of soldiers in amazement.

American men tend to have a simple respect for the strong , so by beating Guile, Honda was worthy of their respect.

Between the handshakes and autograph requests, Honda didn't have time to wipe away his kumadori makeup. Before he knew it, the helicopter assigned to carry him away had arrived.

Despite the organized quality of the event, their fight hadn't been approved by Guile's air force superiors. If Honda didn't depart the base soon, he would likely be imprisoned, while Guile and the other soldiers would receive some sort of punishment. The helmeted, sunglasses-wearing pilot approached Guile for a signature and mentioned that they'd better get the show on the road.

The wall of soldiers parted, and Guile stepped calmly through the opening, arms crossed.

<"So you're leaving? Just like that?">

Guile's right eye bulged wide, while his left was shut tight, making it hard to tell exactly what emotion he was trying to express.

"No choice, it seems," replied Honda gravely.

<"Even if you're not gonna be caught here, I can't promise they won't arrest you the second that chopper lands.">

"We'll deal with that when it happens."

<"I might've lost this time, but...>

Guile uncrossed his arms. The arm with the flag tattoo slowly extended towards Honda and the bumpy hand—unmistakable as a warrior's—unclenched gently. A friendly smile unbefitting a major in the air force rose on Guile's face.

<"Looking forward to our next fight.">

"As am I."

The rikishi's massive hand enveloped the soldier's. Muscles bulged in both of their upper arms.

<"I won't lose, next time.">

"I suspect it will be another victory for me."

<"Watch yourself, out there.">

"Mhm."

The two men smiled at one another, sharing a moment of mutual recognition.

It was for that moment that Honda fought.

He had gotten to know Guile that much better, and now Guile knew a bit more about Honda.

The many fights to come would only serve to strengthen both of them, and at the ends of their chosen paths, they might bump into each other again.

It was clear what Honda had to do.

Just keep moving forward.

Whether on offense or defense, keep on pushing.

"I'd better be off."

Honda released Guile's hand and moved towards the helicopter in silence.

He boarded the aircraft without looking back and closed the door slowly. The harsh whirring of the propellers started up, and Honda was airborne.

Looking over the shrinking base, the wrestler lowered his gaze and spotted Guile- now a mere pinpoint and the only one left on the airstrip.

"Until next time…" said Honda, though his friend was already far out of earshot.

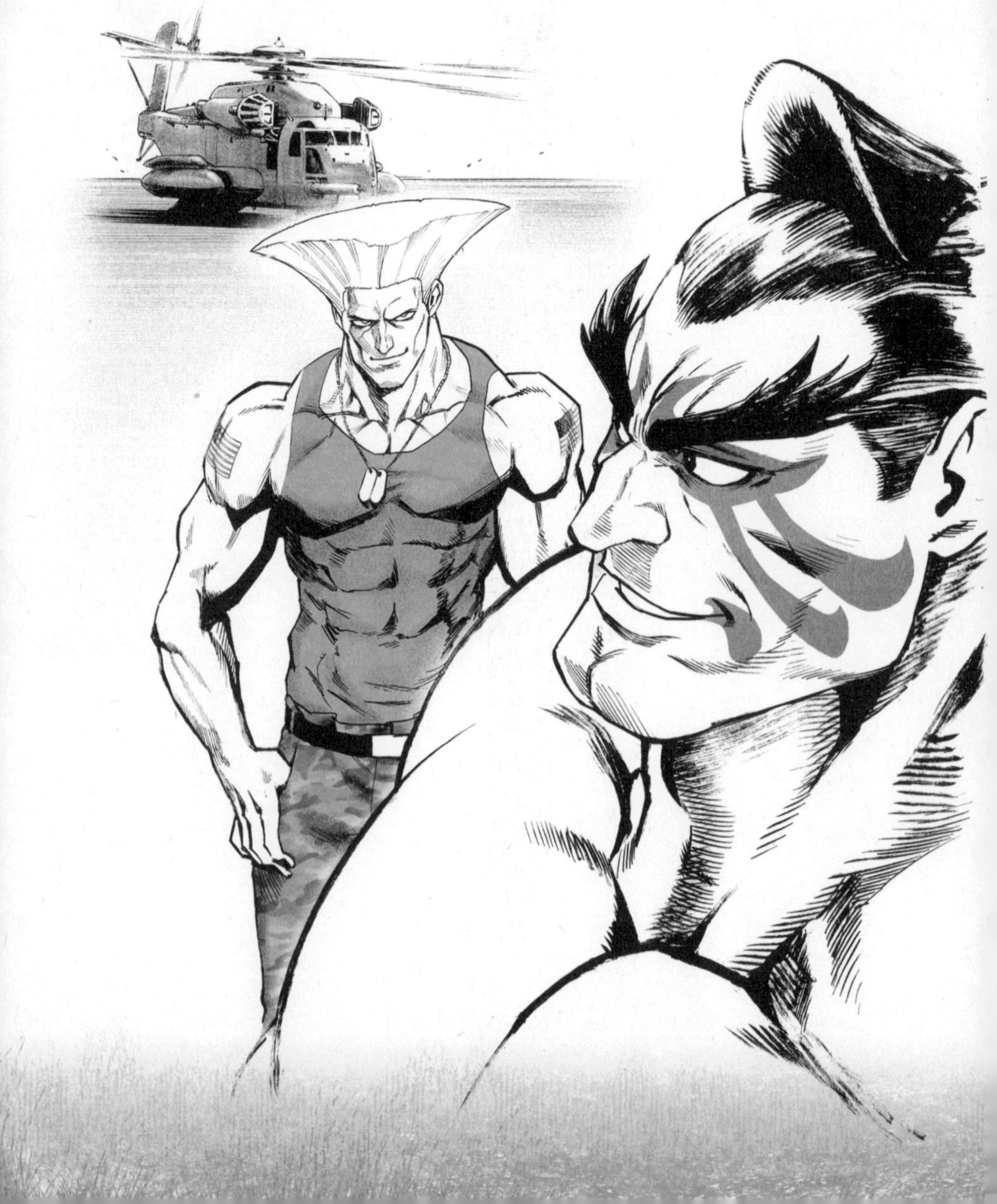

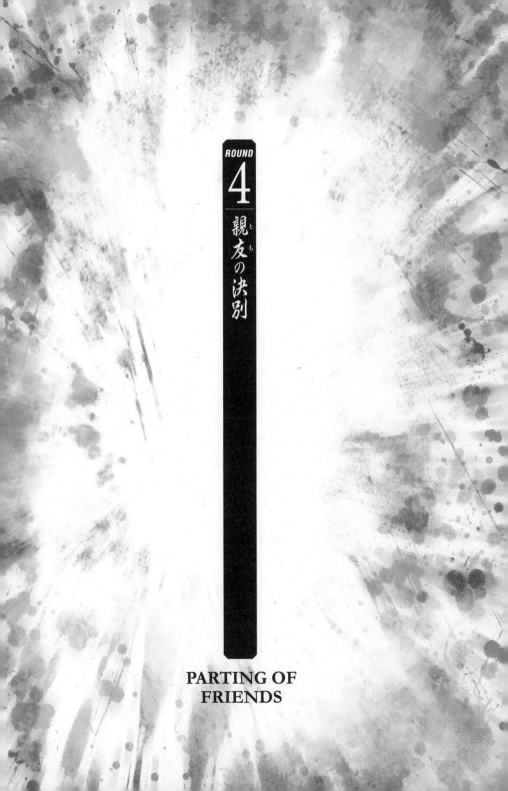

ROUND

4

親友(とも)の決別

PARTING OF
FRIENDS

ROUND 4
PARTING OF FRIENDS

"**A**-are you really…?"
He couldn't finish his sentence.

Ken Masters was dumbstruck by the sight of his friend looking nothing like he remembered.

"And who are you?" fired back the man at the frozen Ken.

Ken didn't believe his own ears. That voice couldn't really be *his*.

He had expected a voice clear and unhesitating, full of integrity, but the tone he heard gave him the complete opposite impression. It was bitter, gravelly, and with a strange, halting nature. The sort of growl one might expect from a vengeful spirit on a moonless night.

The once-white dougi–an expression of the man's purity–was stained black, and a gaping cavity marred his exposed chest. Deep within the dark hole, his red muscles twitched in time with his pulse.

Eyes that once burned with aspiration now shone blood red, and the rows of teeth that peered from behind his smile were clenched nearly to the cracking point.

"Is that really you, Ryu…?"

Voice shaking, Ken finally managed to utter his friend's name. The man glared, motionless, not raising so much as an eyebrow.

Ryu tilted forward slightly and raised one hand to the cavity in his chest, as if in pain. The gloves he wore were torn, with threads sticking out here and there. The blood that clung to and crusted over the stuffing gave Ken some idea of how many foes Ryu had beaten down in recent days.

"I finally found you, but now…"

The search had not been an easy one.

It had been about a month since Ken had first heard the rumors that Ryu had vanished.

Ken's family was one of the richest in America. Upon hearing the name "Masters," the smile that might arise on most people's faces would be one tinged with jealousy.

And now, Ken was the head of the family. With connections to just about every industry imaginable, the Masters' collective interests earned more in a day than a person could spend in a lifetime.

Naturally, Ken led a busy life.

Taking off an entire month from work would normally be unthinkable, but Ryu was an irreplaceable friend, so the search for him took priority.

Ken had been born to a Japanese father and a half-Japanese, half-American mother. The Masters family and its wealth had come by way of Ken's grandfather on his mother's side. The family business fell to Ken because the last head–his uncle–never produced an heir.

Up until that point, Ken had been a fighter. Even now, the name "Ken Masters" was a legendary one among fighting circles.

Though born and raised in Japan, Ken had traveled to America to hone his skills, and he had made a point of joining and winning every martial arts tournament he could find. The nature of the contest didn't matter; he would win every one.

In fact, Ken's uncle had first learned of his nephew when he had witnessed him triumph at a certain tournament.

The secret behind all the victories was Ken's fighting style. The one he had learned in Japan, before traveling to America. The one developed from assassination techniques used in Japan since ancient times.

His master's name was Gouken.

The larger-than-life man had taken those assassination techniques and raised them to an art form, but his stubbornness had kept him from taking on disciples without good reason. Ken's arrival had been an unpleasant surprise, but the old master had been forced to train the zealous boy.

Gouken had one other disciple.

The sincere and straight-laced Ryu. Or at least that had been Ken's first impression of him.

Ken had respected his master and spent day after brutal day toiling and training, and Ryu had always been at his side.

The quest to become stronger...

That was Ryu's purpose in life, and at one point or another, he had infected Ken with that same drive. The two became friends.

How long had it been since then?

When Gouken had been vanquished by his own brother, Ken left for America, where he had accepted his destiny as part of the Masters clan as well as everything that came with that.

Meanwhile, Ryu had never changed tack, simply continuing down the path of martial arts.

Ken had been green with envy.

Part of him wished his could live Ryu's life, wandering one wasteland or another in search of strong fighters. But he also knew that was a dream that would never be realized at this point.

He had his family. His wife. His child.

With so many things worth protecting, Ryu's freewheeling lifestyle was not in the cards for Ken.

Still, Ken's impulses had led him out to the streets now and then. He could relieve a bit of that tension by crossing fists with other prideful fighters. It had worked for him, as a compromise.

Even so...

Ken had remained envious towards Ryu, whom he considered both friend and rival. Ken looked back fondly on the days when he and Ryu had polished their skills together in pursuit of strength. Those had been the best days of his life.

That was why Ken couldn't accept the Ryu he was seeing, now.

"Looks like you've become everything you hated."

Though tinged with geniality, Ken's words didn't seem to reach his friend. Ryu simply stood, glaring with furrowed brows, as a raw, putrid miasma rose from his entire body.

The Dark Hado…

Ken suddenly remembered wh at Gouken had told his two disciples before their forced parting.

Given their roots in assassination, Gouken's techniques could easily lead a fighter astray to a place of deep darkness. If one were to seek only power with no regard for the lives or deaths of others, then the ki flowing from one's tanden would lose all purity. Body and mind would be overcome by bloodlust, eventually bringing about a complete loss of self.

Instead of the usual ki, a fighter ruled by such bloodlust would produce the Dark Hado.

Gouken's younger brother, Akuma, had experienced just that when the allure of power became too great to resist.

Ken had never met a person possessed by the Dark Hado before, but upon seeing the sinister coils of jet black and crimson ki that flowed from Ryu, he instinctively knew that this was what Gouken had warned them against.

More than anyone, Ryu was obsessed with the notion of "strength," so he made an easy target for the Dark Hado.

"Those who pursue strength without second thought cannot escape the darkness…"

Gouken's parting words pierced Ken anew and echoed within his mind.

"Hmm?"

Ryu's right eyebrow twitched, and his eyes–continuously red from pupil to sclera–stayed fixed on Ken.

"I remember."

The words sounded as if they had traveled from the depths of hell to reach Ken's ears.

"So it's you."

"Ryu."

"You know my name, yes. And your name is…"

The corners of Ryu's mouth curled up in an eerie smile.

"…Ken."

"Yeah. Your friend, Ken."

Ken felt hot tears well up at the corners of his eyes, but he fought to hold them back. Staring at Ryu, he spoke again.

"You remember me, Ryu?"

"You fool."

"What'd you say?" Ken asked his friend, whose smile had turned scornful. Ryu let loose a beastlike laugh and began to bounce his shoulders in rhythm.

"It's laughable how you cling to old ties."

"*Old* ties…?"

Every word Ryu spoke was more unbelievable than the last, and with each utterance, Ken felt his heart drop.

"You're already a relic of my past. A chance meeting between us now is utterly meaningless, so why do you appear before me?"

"I'm here to save you."

"*Save* me?" spat Ryu with another sneering laugh.

"You're under no obligation to 'save' me, nor do I need saving."

"You seriously mean that?"

"I have nothing more to say to a fool who questions every word."

The Dark Hado enveloping Ryu grew thicker.

Black mist wrapped around his clenched fists, and his tattered gloves squeaked with tension.

"I'm not here to fight you. Not the way you are now."

Ken and Ryu's friendship had been forged through countless battles, and every time, each would learn something new about the other, deepening their mutual respect.

Ken always wanted Ryu to be in proper, peak condition for their fights, so the Ryu that stood before him now wasn't someone he wanted to face.

"If you mean to deny me, then do so."

Ryu's feet gripped the earth. One fist rose to his jaw and the other to his chest.

His fighting stance.

The two fighters stood in a back alley in a nameless village somewhere in Eastern Europe. They had the place to themselves; not a single villager walked the streets. The stage was set, and there would be no one to interfere.

Still…

"I really don't wanna fight you like this," shouted Ken.

His words never reached his friend, though, which became clear when Ryu kicked off the ground in a vicious attempt to close the gap.

Ken struck his own stance at once. The stance Gouken had taught him…

One forged through endless training alongside Ryu. One that Ken had made his own.

A right hook came flying.

Ken raised his left hand to protect his face, and the punch dug into his upper arm.

"Nngh."

A strained breath escaped from Ken's mouth.

The punch was heavier than any he had felt before, and it made him shudder.

All within a fraction of a second.

A sudden blow to his nose cut off all thought. It took the intense pain that followed to make Ken realize he'd been hit.

Ryu's right arm had snaked through Ken's defenses in order to hit with the elbow, which now vanished from view.

An elbow strike…

No sooner had Ken formed the thought than his stomach was suddenly and violently shaken.

Ryu's left fist had lashed out as soon as his right arm pulled back, driving deep into Ken's red dougi.

Ken's breath was cut short.

"Tatsumaki…" muttered Ryu heartlessly, at point-blank range.

A Senpukyaku kick was coming.

Ken understood that much, but he couldn't react in time. Ryu's brutally heavy blows had rendered his body stiff.

It was clear that Ryu didn't hesitate in the slightest as he attacked.

A person will almost always hold back when striking another. The extent to which they do so will vary from situation to situation, but fear of the opponent and fear of killing the opponent will stay one's hand on a subconscious level. It's essentially impossible to hit another with one's full strength.

The exception to this rule is, of course, when the aim is to kill. Once that potential death is no longer a concern, all hesitation is dispelled.

Such was the nature of Ryu's attacks.

Fists ruled by bloodlust know no restraint, which meant that the force behind Ryu's blows was unlike any Ken had ever experienced.

"...Senpukyaku."

As the cold word left Ryu's mouth, his body rose from the ground almost gently. He stopped in mid-air, began to spin, and extended a kinked leg that proceeded to bludgeon Ken without mercy.

Ken fell, unable to withstand the blows.

He pressed his hand into the ground in an attempt to stand, but a weight suddenly fell upon his bent back, pressing him into the earth.

Ryu's right leg.

As heavy and solid as a cudgel, the leg kept Ken from budging an inch despite his every effort to stand.

"Why don't I break your spine? Perhaps that would keep you from running that mouth ever again."

"Stop it."

Ken immediately regretted his futile plea.

Ryu was now a demon overcome by bloodlust; he was in no state to honor any such request. As if to affirm Ken's thoughts, the pinning foot drove into his back with even greater force.

Ken's bones began to grind within.

"You don't want to fight me? Don't make me laugh," came Ryu's voice from above, just barely drowning out the creaking of Ken's bones.

"Nothing but the lowly prattle of a powerless insect writhing in the dirt."

"That how you really feel, huh?"

"You continue to talk nonsense, even now? There is a point when perseverance turns to stupidity," continued the callous Ryu, assaulting everything Ken held dear.

"You're a true friend and the best rival I'll ever have. Me dying won't change that."

"You've never stopped looking for something to cling to in your pathetic life. That is why you cannot beat me. In the end, you're reduced to a worm struggling under my foot. Friend? Rival? Ridiculous."

Ken asked himself if this could really be the Ryu he knew.

Was the pure-hearted Ryu who sought strength really gone?

If so...then who was this man?

"Now die."

The pressure on Ken's back intensified.

"I..."

Ken turned to look at Ryu through tear-filled eyes.

"Did I really have you pegged all wrong?"

"Are those your last words?"

"Not a chance."

Power filled Ken's body, and he knew exactly where it came from.

Anger.

The anger at having been betrayed by his best friend was what gave him strength.

Ken's life until this point had been relatively free of discouragement and setbacks, but now, every word that came from Ryu's lips sparked an uncontrollable anger within Ken. Every hateful roar fanned the flames of rage in Ken's chest.

And now, those flames filled his feet as they bit into the earth.

"Ohh..." came Ryu's disdainful voice from above. His right leg began to rise.

"I can't forgive you for this," said Ken as he slowly righted himself.

Ken couldn't submit to such an evil force. His sense of justice wouldn't let him back down from an opponent driven by the Dark Hado.

Ryu removed his leg from Ken's back.

With one final push, Ken found his footing.

"You fool," muttered Ryu, already in an offensive stance.

The two fighters were close enough to feel each other's breath.

Ryu drew both hands back, clutching an invisible ball of air.

The Hadoken.

Ken wouldn't survive a direct hit at this range, and mounting a simple defense would hardly be enough.

All thoughts vanished as he cleared his mind.

Ki flowed to Ken's right fist as it dropped near his waist, and it was suddenly afire, the blaze a manifestation of his spirit and rage.

The fire gave off no heat, though.

Sparks began to gather between Ryu's palms, eventually forming a ball of light that seemed to swell to near bursting. All he had to do now was to thrust both hands at Ken.

Waiting for that wasn't an option.

Ken bent his elbow in as far is it could go and then released.

"Shoryuken."

He flew, the extended fist wreathed in flame, like a crimson dragon dancing towards the heavens.

Ryu's Hadoken stance was shattered as the fiery uppercut drove into his jaw.

"Tch."

Ryu made a point of clicking his tongue leisurely as he flew.

Too shallow…

The feedback in Ken's own fist told him that much.

He landed, but Ryu was still airborne, so Ken crouched again and let loose with another Shoryuken.

This one crashed squarely into Ryu's back.

Though his body had begun to fall, it was now thrust skywards once more. Ken landed first, again.

"Still not enough…" he said to Ryu, whose body now curved backwards in the air.

A third Shoryuken.

It bored into Ryu's forehead as he came down in a tailspin, the strike from below sending his body spinning end over end before crashing into the earth.

Ken touched down an instant later, and he maintained his stance, eyes trained on Ryu.

His friend's limbs were splayed and his body motionless, but his red eyes remained open, staring at the starry night sky.

"Heheheheh."

A bold laugh.

A cloud of dust whirled about Ryu where he lay, and the black-garbed demon rose.

"Why stay your hand?" he asked, without a hint of emotion.

"You might have evaded death today had you finished me off."

"Yeah, but that would mean actually killing you."

Despite the beating he had just taken, Ryu appeared completely unharmed. Perhaps being ruled by rage and bloodlust had dulled his sense of pain? Or maybe he had somehow rendered the attacks harmless at the last second? But no- Ken's fist wa s still feeling it. He had definitely struck Ryu. So how was his friend unfazed and upright again?

If this was the strength that the Dark Hado offered, then it was no wonder that Akuma had succumb. And now, Ryu was also in that power's grip...

"How did you stand when I was bearing down on you?" asked Ryu, presenting his clenched fists as if to make a show of it.

How *did* Ken stand?

He had been in a daze. The desire not to lose transformed into anger with him and gave him strength. Ryu's betrayal had lit that fire.

"It was the Dark Hado."

For a moment, Ken couldn't process what Ryu said.

When the implication of his friend's words hit him, however, he understood fully the rage that had overtaken him. The power that came with it was granted by the Dark Hado.

"Leave your burdensome emotions behind and give in to the strength, for that is the road to greatness. I finally understand that truth, Ken... In that sense, perhaps we are more alike than I thought."

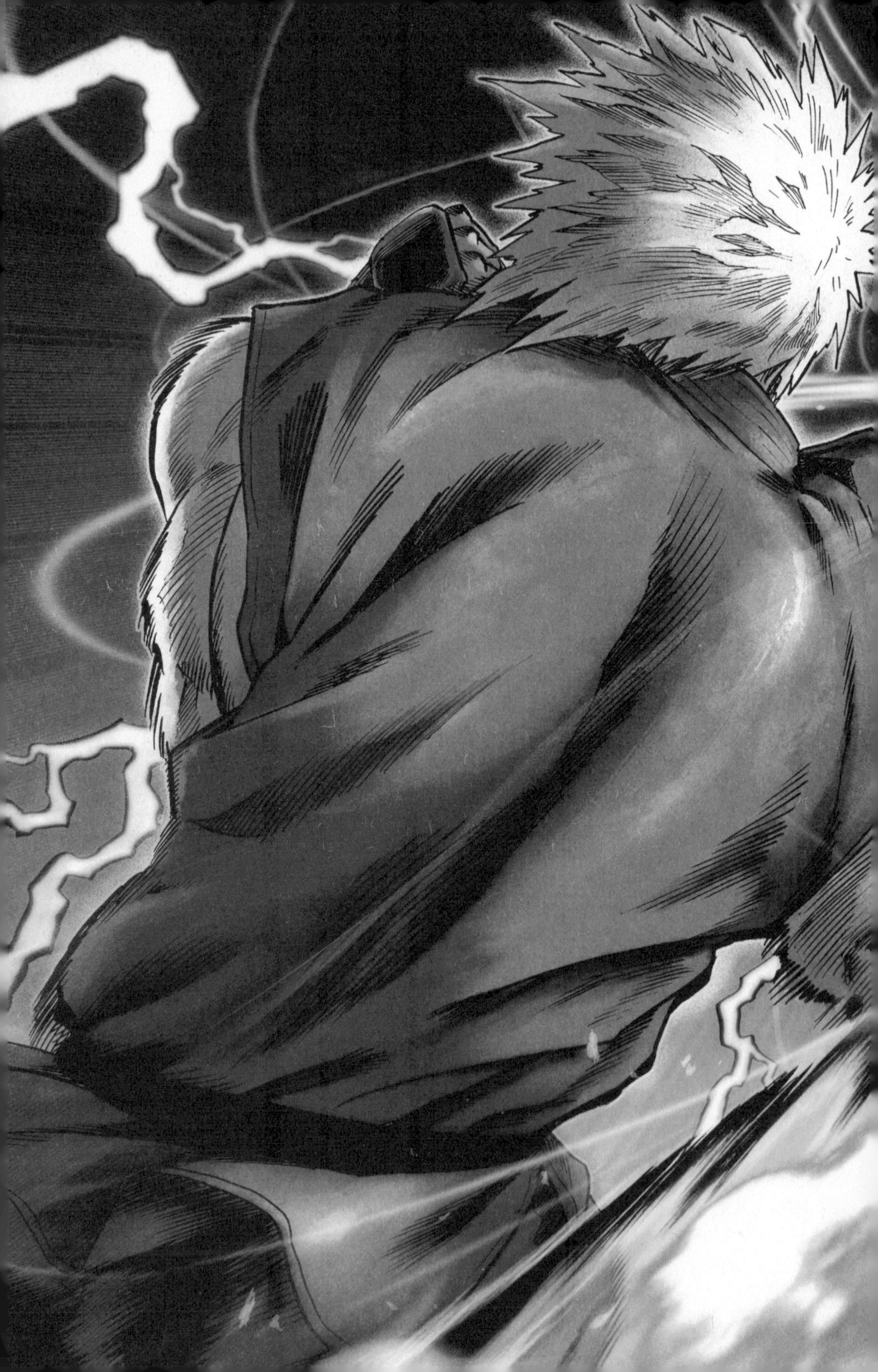

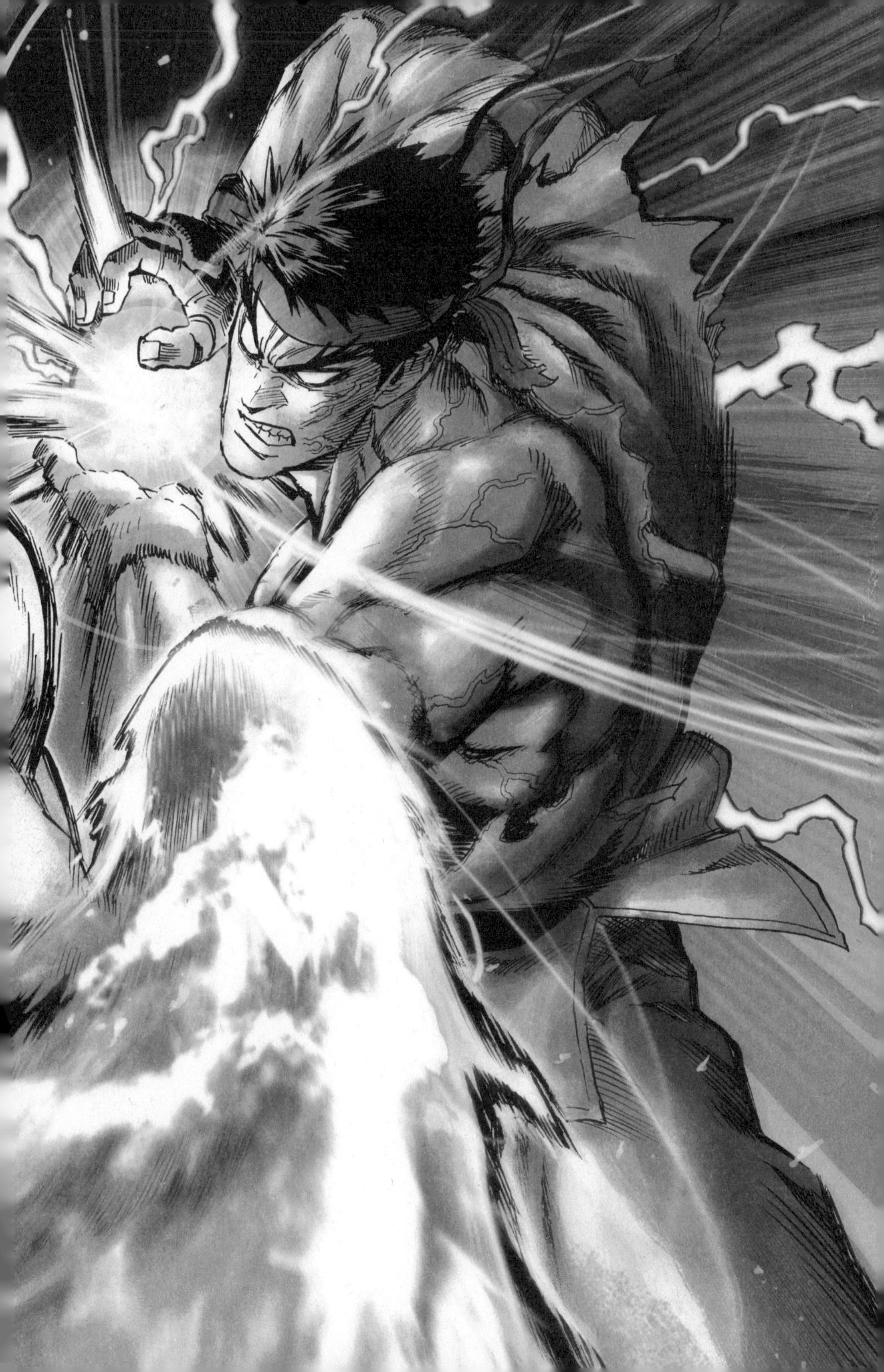

SHORYUKEN!!

TOO SHALLOW.

TCH...

"Shut up," shouted Ken in rage.

Ryu's smile was a gleeful one.

"Yes, good. That anger *is* the Dark Hado. Fighting to resist the rage and bloodlust is paradoxical, no? Come to your senses, Ken."

Ryu was talkative now, filled with self-satisfaction. With every word he uttered, Ken's image of his friend shattered anew.

Ken wondered to himself what the right thing to do was.

He understood that this man wasn't the Ryu he once knew, and tears began to pour from his eyes.

"Kill, kill, and kill again… Kill until you're the sole, strongest survivor upon this earth…"

The tears came every time Ryu spoke.

"What's left for you then?"

"Once every last man is defeated, there will only remain the gods in heaven, ripe for the slaughtering."

"You can't seriously be saying that."

Ryu didn't answer. He was drunk on the Dark Hado, with that fearless smile plastered across his face.

"You chose the wrong path, Ryu…"

Ken closed his eyes, cutting off the flow of tears. He cast his gaze downwards for a moment before clenching his fists and staring at Ryu once again.

"My friend has lost his way, so I've gotta risk my life to save him."

"Risk your life…? Your choice of words foreshadows your fate, Ken."

Ryu struck a stance.

"You've always been like that–spouting pretty-sounding nonsense. You say you walked away from the world of fighting for your precious family. For your 'loved ones,' but that's not it. Not really."

Ryu's red eyes flashed eerily.

"In truth, you finally realized that no amount of training would ever allow you to defeat me. So you turned away from me with one excuse or another about the things that needed *protecting*."

"Shut up…"

Rage rushed back to fill Ken's heart.

"Even now, you drone on with that nonsense as you prepare to face me, but deep inside, you know that you've gotten weak, yes? You cannot die so long as there are those in your life that need to be protected, but your unwillingness to die makes you fear true battle. Such a fighter could never be strong. Do you hear me, Ken…?"

Black mist poured from Ryu's mouth as he rambled. The dark ki surrounded his face, transforming his visage into something demonic.

"I have never once thought of you as friend nor rival."

Something in Ken snapped. He couldn't hold back the sigh that emerged, nor the words that followed.

"Enough…"

Ken's earlier rage was gone, replaced by an iciness in his heart. The despair over a man he once considered a friend turned to self-derision. He realized how pathetic he must have always sounded, going on and on about being friends and rivals.

"It's nothing but bloodlust that's making you fight now, and there's no way I'm gonna let myself lose to someone like that."

"So even your reason for fighting is a worthless platitude? How hard you try, never getting anywhere. And while you march in place, I walk the path towards true strength. A path leading to heights you will never reach."

"Enough talk. Let's go."

"As you wish."

Ryu was on the move.

Ken leapt forward, desperately telling his own heart to know no fear.

The two fighters stopped once within range, braced their legs, and swung out with right fists in sync.

Both fists struck the other man on the left cheek.

Simultaneous blows.

However, there was an apparent difference in force between the two attacks.

No matter how well he had psyched himself up, Ken refused to give in to the wickedness of the Dark Hado, so his blows could never match the brutality that powered Ryu's. The difference was less subconscious, more instinctive, and there was nothing Ken could do about it.

Both fighters were blown backwards.

Ken brought his upper body back up to prepare for the next attack, but Ryu had already composed himself and launched a kick with his left leg towards Ken's face.

Ken raised his right arm to defend, and the resulting crunch resounded through his muscles.

"No big deal."

An arm or two was a small price to pay if it meant defeating this opponent.

He felt the ki well up deep in his stomach and lashed out to punch Ryu in the face.

Next would be a right leg kick at mid-height.

The kick's arc was bringing it straight towards Ryu's flank.

It whipped out in a spin as Ken twisted his body, hitting the still fazed Ryu.

"Not done yet."

The kicking leg touched down, and Ken readied his body to unleash a second kick, this time with his left. As it sliced through the air before connecting with Ryu, the leg burst into flames. Like with the earlier Shoryuken, the fire was a pure manifestation of Ken's own fighting spirit.

The second was a spinning back kick, which meant that Ken had to turn his back to Ryu for an instant. His left heel came flying around at full speed.

A direct hit.

No...

Ryu was smiling. His left knee was raised high to meet his left elbow, and between the two was Ken's foot, trapped as if between a pair of fangs.

It wouldn't budge.

"You're always, always..."

Ryu raised his right arm high.

"...full of openings."

As he spoke, the raised hand descended on the trapped leg. It smashed down where shin met knee, sinking deep into the red dougi.

"Guwahhhh."

The leg was free, but Ken knew it would all be over if he fell now, and that knowledge kept him going. His left leg had lost all feeling below the knee, so he tried to brace himself in an attempt to revive it. Still, he was forced to take 90% of his weight on his right leg.

Ken glared at Ryu, a cold sweat forming on his forehead.

There was nothing to be done about the pain that wracked his body. The more he tried to endure, the more his wounds screamed back in protest.

It was no use.

The pain threatened to break Ken's will, his body screaming to surrender.

Ryu would show no mercy.

A fist flew at Ken, still struggling to conquer his pain. A vicious attack aimed at his face that he could neither dodge nor defend against. The shockwave spread through his body, forcing his numb left leg to buckle.

Desperately, he endured.

Another hit.

He endured.

And then another.

Still, he endured.

"Even with no options left, you play the role of the petulant child. Just what I would expect from a spoiled brat who never knew hardship."

As he spoke, Ryu seemed almost indifferent. Like a mere bystander to the mechanical volley of punches he brought down on Ken. The latter's fists remained raised in his stance out of a futile sense of duty, while each blow smashed his body to one side or the other.

Ken's beaten eyelids began to swell, and his vision grew dim. Once the eyelids split and blood started to flow, what little he could still see would soon be clouded by a wave of red.

He had lost all feeling in his jaw—now numb from the beating.

Every part of his face was swelling, as if his head were an inflating balloon.

This would end in his death...

Ken reflected on that fact hazily.

His own death was almost an amusing prospect, like something happening to someone else. The storm of blows had rendered even his thoughts limp and relaxed.

"Stubborn, aren't you?" murmured Ryu, his fists still flying. He was truly aiming to send his lifelong friend to the gates of hell.

Ken asked himself why he hadn't fallen yet.

He didn't know. All he knew was that he couldn't fall.

Obstinacy...

Obstinacy towards what purpose, though? No way to say.

He wasn't the type of man to fall here.

Not the type of man to die like this.

He hated the thought of letting this relentless, grinning demon get his way.

Just like a younger brother resisting his older sibling. He might never measure up, but he would keep resisting, sobbing all the while, just to keep his tormenter from having that satisfaction. It was that sort of obstinacy.

His defeat was at hand, but Ken couldn't accept it.

His was a willpower that lies in the heart of every man from the day he's born.

A man's core...

It was a pure and simple thought that now kept Ken standing, and it had always been this way with Ryu.

The desire *not to lose* to this man.

The desire to surpass him.

Just as Ken always longed to triumph over Ryu, he imagined that Ryu felt the same way about him. They had spent years together sharing meals and lodging, all the while in pursuit of that elusive "strength."

That was no dream. No illusion. The time they spent together was real.

Ken could only think that the Ryu standing before him, rather, was a fiction of some sort.

"How long're you gonna keep sleeping, Ryu?" muttered Ken through bruised, puffy lips. Ryu's incoming fist hesitated for an instant before continuing on its path.

"Master's gonna be pissed if you don't wake up soon."

Ken couldn't keep himself from speaking, as if in a daze.

"It seems your spirit is already well on its way to the pits of hell."

Ken heard his friend's voice clearly, the clarity of it forcing him to realize that this was, indeed, reality. His vision was completely clouded over.

Black and red speckles danced across the inside of Ken's eyelids, and on that dim screen appeared an image of himself as a boy.

He and Ryu were in the middle of a furious sparring session.

Next, he was enduring austere training from his master.

It was a moment of calm that brought him the briefest respite.

Ken longed for those days and everything that came with them.

Knowing they were lost forever, he felt his heart tighten.

"Come on, man. Open your damn eyes already…"

Upon hearing his own voice, Ken realized he was crying.

He had never wept in the midst of any other battle, but this was the second time during this fight. Ken was struck into silence.

If he had the luxury of crying, then he could certainly find the will to struggle.

The state of his body didn't matter anymore; he would keep on fighting even if reduced to nothing more than a head.

Such was the way of the warrior.

"No matter what happens, you'll always be my friend. You get that, Ryu…?"

"Silence!" screamed Ryu in a far higher-pitched voice than before. A particular heavy punch came flying at Ken.

The blow to his face sent him spinning through the air horizontally. He skidded and rolled across the ground, putting distance between himself and Ryu, whom he stared at through the last pinpoint of vision available to him.

He had shaken Ryu.

The demon was still filled with bloodlust and resentment, but a flicker of *something* rocked his heart, and Ken felt it.

It was there, somewhere deep...

Part of his Ryu's old self- the part that sought strength so earnestly.

"I see, now..."

Ken staggered to his feet, but Ryu had already vanished from Ken's still hazy view.

He looked up suddenly.

There.

Plummeting, with foot blade poised to strike and a frenzied look on his face .

"I'm gonna *make* you remember..." whispered Ken to the glaring Ryu.

Ken curled his body inward.

"Shoryuken."

He flew with right fist extended, and the two clashed in mid-air.

Ken was the first to land.

Staring at the sky through swollen eyes, he spotted Ryu still airborne– back curled like a shrimp .

Ken had won the clash...

He psyched himself up again and prepared for a follow-up attack. Eyes still trained on the falling Ryu, Ken pulled both palms back.

He grit his teeth and cupped the familiar ball of air. The sparks of the Hadoken began to crackle in the space between his hands.

Such was his focus that for a moment, he lost sight of his friend. When he spotted him again, Ryu was floating in mid-air, striking a stance, arms pulled behind his back.

Like Ken, Ryu was clutching an orb of air, but his soon burst into flames.

Ryu's demonic, blood red eyes pierced Ken, and a grin of pure killing intent adorned his face.

Ken angled up to face his friend , but it was too late.

The fireball flew.

"Hadoken."

Ken's panicked cry came as he thrust both arms towards the blazing mass. The two attacks collided and produced a brilliant flash. The shockwave smashed into Ken just as his vision went white. He was now completely blinded.

The white quickly faded to black, in which concrete images began to appear, but Ken could still only see bits and pieces of the world through his swollen eyelids.

A strange silence…

Ryu was gone.

Ken peered at the sky through his restricted vision and then lowered his gaze to the earth, searching for his friend.

The narrow alley was a dead end, so the search wasn't a long one.

Ryu had really vanished. Ken couldn't feel his presence at all.

Had their entire fight been a dream?

No. The pain that wracked Ken's body was proof enough.

So why was Ryu gone?

"Ryu…"

With right fist to chest, Ken called out his friend's name.

The cool night air caressed his swollen, burning face.

"What am I supposed to do?"

His best friend in the world was now a murderous demon, and no amount of sweet sentiment could bring him back. Ryu's sudden disappearance may have just been his fickle way of ending things for good.

Was there any reason left to pursue?

Had they ever really been friends and rivals? Doubt crept into Ken's heart.

Maybe Ryu's cruel words during the fight betrayed true feelings he had harbored all along. Maybe Ryu had already given up on Ken, who had been unable to fully commit to the path of a martial artist. Worst of all, maybe there had been hidden scorn behind Ryu's smile every time

Ken spoke of friendship and rivalry.

There was no way to be sure…

The thought brought Ken grief.

No matter how hard he trained, Ryu was always two steps ahead, moving at a pace Ken couldn't maintain. Unable to accept that, though, maybe Ken had fooled himself with talk of earnest rivalry. It wasn't unthinkable, and now Ken couldn't be certain of anything.

An oppressive weight fell upon his shoulders.

"I'm such a dope…"

"Indeed you are."

Ken had believed he was talking to himself, but now a voice came from behind. One he knew.

It was Ryu.

Shudders ran up Ken's spine.

There was no time to turn and look.

A foot smashed into the back of his knee, causing his otherwise firmly planted left leg to buckle, and an instep connected with the side of his now tilted head. By the time Ken processed the spinning kick that had hit him, he was grounded.

The sole of Ryu's foot crunched down on Ken's head as he struggled in the dirt.

"Amateur… Amateur, amateur, amateur," came a merciless voice. With every whisper of "amateur," the foot rose and came down again on Ken's head. Pinned between the foot and the hard ground, his skull gave off a dull thud with every stomp.

"You relax as soon as the enemy vanishes…? So very telling of your limits, Ken. A man like you is 100 years too early to face me."

"You don't really mean that."

"Fool."

Just as Ken felt Ryu's foot leave his head, he was rocked by a blow to the gut. The ferocious kick sent him flying in a curled mass, but one of Ryu's thick arms lashed out to grab Ken by the nape of the neck, leaving him dangling in the air, still bent over in pain.

The two were face-to-face.

"You've always been such an eyesore…"

As he spoke, Ryu drove his left fist into the still dangling Ken's stomach .

The pained groan came with a spray of blood, which soaked the demon's forehead.

Though quickly losing consciousness, Ken saw the dark blood cling to the tightly tied headband before it dripped down onto Ryu's face.

He didn't have the energy to resist any longer.

"What a nuisance you've been, like a lost puppy who can't take a hint…"

Foul miasma flowed from Ryu's mouth with every word and assaulted Ken's senses.

The impact of each gut punch passed straight through Ken's muscles to his spine. But he no longer felt pain; his soul was well on its way to leaving his body.

"Die, die, die, die," Ryu muttered, almost pleadingly.

"If you…"

Somehow, Ken found the strength to speak, and Ryu's fist stopped.

"If you want me dead that bad, just hurry up and kill me…"

Ken felt the numb corners of his mouth lift in a smile. He surprised himself with his relaxed tone. It almost sounded like he was inviting a friend to come out and play, which struck him as strange.

He was also shocked by his own lack of regrets. Oddly enough, he was ready to give up on the Masters empire, his own family, everything.

"I'll be satisfied, getting killed by you," said Ken, still smiling.

The strangest part was that he meant it.

Because more than being a father, a husband, or the head of a family, Ken was a man, and his life as a man was defined by his warrior nature.

Survival of the fittest is a fundamental rule in battle. If one fears being killed by the strong, then one has no right to enter the ring.

Ken had no regrets, for the man before him was stronger.

He would die, and that would be that. It was only fitting.

Not to mention, his executioner would be Ryu. Nothing could give Ken greater pleasure. No matter how far his friend's heart had fallen into darkness, Ryu was Ryu, and come whatever, Ryu was Ken's eternal rival and true friend.

With doom fast approaching, Ken understood that.

"Our last fight was fun, huh."

"Shut up…"

Ryu's fist stopped pounding Ken's stomach and rose slowly. It pulled back near the demon's head, poised to strike Ken in the face.

"Since this is the end, lemme say this much…"

Ken's voice was calm as he addressed his friend.

The raised fist quivered. Ken couldn't be sure if it was rage or distress that caused it, but the shaking was undeniable.

"Thank you. You made my life a fun one."

The fist flew as soon as Ken finished.

Darkness…

No pain. No sense of impact. Only darkness.

Even Ken's thoughts were cut off.

"M-ma'am! Y-your husband… He's awake."

A woman's high-pitched voice pierced Ken's ears. Why would the first voice one hears in heaven be so shrill and obnoxious? Ken sighed at the thought of it.

He sighed?

Could souls really sigh?

"Ken! Ken!"

A face appeared in his whited-out vision.

A familiar face…

"Eliza?" he said, calling out to his wife.

"Thank goodness… It's a miracle."

Tears began to spill from Eliza's eyes . They slid down her long eyelashes and dripped onto Ken's chest. The warm, fresh tears told Ken that he was indeed still alive.

"Where am I?"

"One of your hospitals."

"Right..."

Ken raised his right hand to remove the respirator from his mouth. He saw a doctor running over fretfully as he pushed himself into a sitting position.

A sharp pain ran down from head to spine. His muscles screamed in response.

"If you'd been found just one hour later, you might be dead right now. So don't overdo it," lectured the doctor. Someone must have found him lying in that alley somewhere in Eastern Europe.

"How long was I out?"

"Ten days," answered Eliza.

"What about Ryu? Where is he?"

Eliza shook her head from side to side, bringing her brilliant golden hair along with it.

"So I was just lying there, alone?"

"That's what the man who found you said."

"I see... *He* was gone, then..."

Ryu had vanished, leaving Ken by his lonesome.

Ken wondered why he was still alive when that last attack should have finished him off. Maybe Ryu hesitated at the critical moment?

It had been impossible to truly gauge the turmoil unfolding in Ryu's afflicted heart. Regardless, Ken was still alive. That was the truth.

In which case...

Ken wanted to believe his own theory.

No, he *did* believe.

He believed that Ryu hesitated to kill a friend.

He believed that Ryu hadn't really foresworn his dream to become a true fighter.

That's why he let Ken live.

"I guess our fight isn't really over, Ryu..."

Something splashed onto Ken's clenched fist. He realized it was his own tears just as Eliza wrapped her thin arms around his shoulders in an embrace.

His wife's love was a complicated thing .

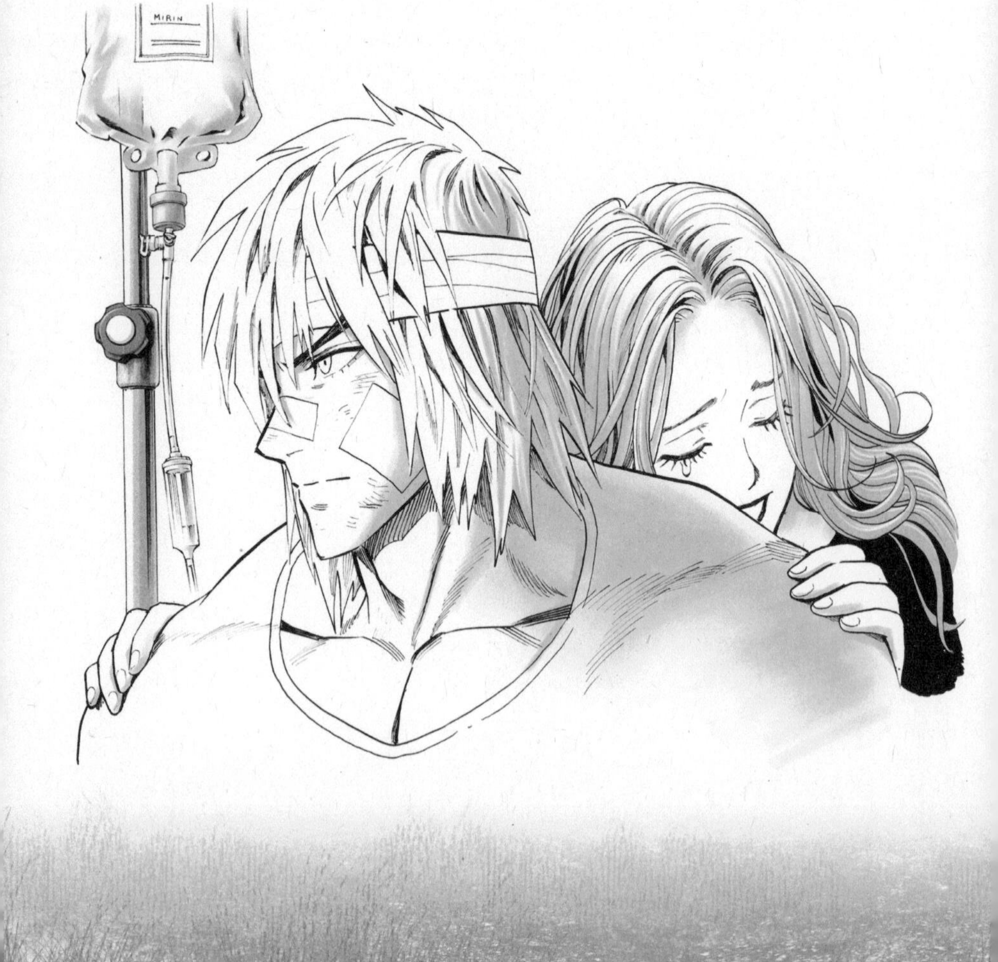
MIRIN

ROUND

5

焔と油

**FUEL TO
THE FIRE**

ROUND 5
FUEL TO THE FIRE

...Yep

It only took a moment of thought to come to a quick conclusion.

This man was bad news...

Hakan stared at the strange, slim, squirming figure before him and swallowed hard.

Some of the oil covering his body seeped into his mouth, where it mixed with saliva before ending in Hakan's stomach. The scent of olives wafted past his nose, calming his heart.

...No, no! This was no time for calmness!

As if to snap his heart out of its tranquil daze, he gave his cheeks a single slap. Droplets of oil flew where skin smacked against red skin.

...What to do, what to do, what to do.

Hakan had no answer, but he couldn't help but ask himself. Thinking was the first step to surviving.

It all came back to the man standing before him.

Hakan's eyes settled on the thin, dark-skinned man. "Thin" was an understatement; it was as if he had stripped himself of all non-essential flesh. The body was not so much well-tempered as retaining the barest minimum of muscle, mostly covering his chest. His ribcage bulged from the skin at his stomach. Every time he breathed, his stomach would inflate and deflate in that gap between the ribs on either side.

Hakan had no time for idle thoughts, but in more relaxed times, he might have likened the image to that of a frog puffing out its vocal sac.

For some reason, the man's chest shuddered with every breath.

One breath in.

One breath out.

"Yoga…"

As he muttered, a small jet of flame escaped his pursed lips before vanishing.

"Yoga."

Another jet.

"Yoga."

And another…

Over and over again.

What exactly was he practicing?

The flames kept coming, accompanied by an utterance of "yoga" every time.

This was Dhalsim.

One of India's preeminent street fighters.

Upon meeting the man, most would doubt his credentials. Even after witnessing him fight, part of that doubt would typically remain.

Breathing fire made him seem less street fighter, more street performer.

Still, what was about to occur on this street was most certainly a fight. A brawl entirely without rules. As such, it was obvious that his flames were meant for his opponent.

If that were really the case, then the drilling that Hakan now witnessed was not for nothing. The potential consequences sent a shudder down his spine.

For Hakan was an expert in *yağlı güreş*, or grease wrestling. His prowess was world-renowned, and he was widely considered a national hero in his homeland of Turkey.

Yağlı güreş fighters prepare for every match by first covering their bodies in olive oil. They wear special calfskin trousers called *kisbet* and aim to either pin the opponent–back to ground–or lift him in the air for several seconds, thereby winning the fight. The simple rules are similar to those of Olympic wrestling, but the presence of the oil demands considerable stamina.

Greased bodies easily slide off one another, so monstrous strength is needed to achieve a proper pin or lift. As a grappling style, yağlı güreş is far more exhausting than most.

Hakan believed there was no manlier fighting style in the world, and he took great pride in his role as a practitioner. Such was his pride that he would even lube up like this for a mere street fight. He kept supplementary bottles of oil in his back pockets should he start to dry out, and he had placed an entire barrel of the stuff on the roadside, just in case.

But now, it looked like Hakan's proclivity for oil might backfire in a big way.

What if…

What if Hakan was right, and Dhalsim preferred to fight by blowing fire at his opponent? He couldn't think of a worse matchup.

Even children know the dangers of mixing oil and flames. The smallest spark could ignite an inferno in an instant.

The wrestler was dripping with olive oil, and Dhalsim was blowing fire.

If that fire so much as brushed Hakan's skin, he would…

The end result was plain as day.

The street of the Indian village was packed, but the crowd gave Hakan and Dhalsim a wide berth. Onlookers formed a massive circle around the pair, eager to see how this confrontation might play out, and their eyes blazed impatiently as they waited for fists to fly. Once it looked like a fight would break out, no one would attempt to stop it or even dream of calling the police. They crowded with baited breath, as if they'd paid for tickets to the event.

What would happen if Hakan caught fire here?

He doubted anyone would help; they would only jeer at him as the crimson flames charred his skin black. The scenario played out in the back of the wrestler's mind.

Dhalsim stared at Hakan with pupil-less white eyes.

"Shall we begin?" asked Dhalsim, his jaw flapping independent of his otherwise motionless, shaved head.

The deep voice, at odds with the thin body, gave Hakan a sense of unease.

"Are you prepared?" questioned Dhalsim.

His right hand–raised as if in prayer–made him resemble a statue of the Buddha. Two metal bangles adorned the skin and bones of his right wrist, while another pair circled the lowered arm's wrist. Three small skulls hung from his large necklace. They had to have come from children under the age of ten, or possibly from small animals. Either way, the effect was unsettling.

Hakan had heard that Dhalsim was an ascetic of some sort, but did Buddhism or Hinduism really prescribe this sort of costuming? Being from Turkey, the wrestler was unsure.

"Are you okay, Turk?"

Hakan's shoulders leapt slightly at the sudden voice. Dhalsim had somehow appeared directly in front of him.

Three red stripes ran across the shaven head. Hakan was curious if they were tattoos or just painted on, but he didn't bother to ask.

"I-I'm fine," replied Hakan with a wide smile. His hardened moustache was soaked in oil, and it reflected the dazzling Indian sun right into his eyes.

"If you have a particular concern, we need not do this."

"I said I'm fine, didn't I?" shot back Hakan without hesitation.

He didn't like Dhalsim's tone.

Ever since spotting the jets of flame, Hakan's obvious worry had kept him from focusing properly. He considered himself a fairly grounded man, and as such, the sight of a fire-breathing ascetic was sure to shake him. That said, he wasn't one to back down from a fight.

He told himself not to take this particular opponent lightly.

"Let us begin, then…"

Dhalsim extended his right hand as he spoke.

This was supposed to be a street fight, and street fights needed no opening gong or other such formalities. It would begin with the first move, after which point all rules went out the window.

Dhalsim's offer of a handshake seemed a bit *too much* like fair play to Hakan, but he wasn't so boorish as to refuse the courtesy.

Acknowledging his misgivings about a potential trap, he reached for his opponent's palm with its unusually long fingers.

"Hmm?"

Hakan couldn't help but remark on the strange texture he felt.

Like a sponge? An inflated rubber glove? Mozzarella cheese? A woman's breast...?

None of the textures that came to mind were exactly the right fit. What he could say was that this hand was like none he had ever felt before. There were the bones and a decent amount of solid muscle. The dry, cracked skin gave off the usual amount of warmth. But it all came with a strange pliancy.

Hakan ran one of the world's top edible oil companies, so he was naturally forced to shake plenty of hands on the job. He was even prone to bragging about the number of hands he had shaken over the course of his life.

Upon feeling Dhalsim's hand, Hakan immediately thought to himself that the texture was like no other.

He pulled his arm back and released the strangely pliant hand. Dhalsim's mouth twitched for an instant before he turned and walked away.

The thin ascetic stopped after putting considerable distance between the two. He turned around slowly.

"Oh, honey," came a woman's voice out of the crowd. Dhalsim scanned to find its owner, and Hakan's eyes followed.

A beautiful woman in a bright, sky blue sari was staring at Dhalsim with a worried look on her face. The ascetic returned her gaze with a loving one before turning back to Hakan.

Dhalsim's wife...

Hakan knew it at a glance, and he was instantly reminded of his family back in Turkey.

He had a lovely wife and seven daughters of his own.

Real, tangible profits from his entrepreneurial success in the oil business.

Pitting his own yağlı güreş against other international fighting styles was just a hobby. Hakan drew a clear line between his private and public lives, which led him to roam the world in search of good fights, all while his family cheered him on from home. They had never once expressed discontent over his habits.

Such a wonderful family was wasted on him, which was all the more reason he couldn't afford to die here.

He had to defeat this man, and that meant doing something about those flames…

No solution came to mind.

"Well, I guess we'd better get this thing started," murmured Hakan as he carefully took his stance. He lowered both hands into a natural position and relaxed his shoulders. His hips dropped as low as they would comfortably go.

His right hand reached for the back pocket of his calfskin pants and produced a glass bottle, whose cap Hakan removed before he turned the bottle upside-down over his head. Slightly sticky, high-quality olive oil poured onto his crown and flowed down over his body. He tossed the empty bottle aside.

"Now! Let's do this!" said Hakan, taking a step towards Dhalsim.

A powerful attack struck his face.

"Wh-what the…?"

He had been hit…

But it wasn't possible.

The gap separating the fighters was, judging by the looks of it, at least five meters. No attack could possibly clear that distance.

"Of all the crazy…"

Hakan felt a dull pain in his nose. Warm blood trickled out and soaked his mustache.

Dhalsim wasn't moving. Both thighs were pinched together in a tight stance, and he held his right hand vertically in front of his face—the spitting image of an ascetic. There was no emotion to be read in his empty, white eyes, lending him a vaguely frightening appearance.

"So y'got me with some fancy magic spell, huh?"

Hakan kept his eyes focused on Dhalsim as he took another step forward, determined not to be hit by the same trick twice.

He couldn't believe what happened next.

As Hakan moved lifted his right foot, Dhalsim's raised hand changed into a fist. A punch from that same erect position shouldn't have gone far, but then the arm *stretched*.

Not the sort of stretching that might be achieved by dislocating one's shoulder and elbow joints.

Rather, the way a bungee cord would stretch when a fat man takes the plunge off a bridge in the hopes of just barely skimming the river below…

At this proximity, though, the reality of it was unmistakable to Hakan.

The fist easily bridged the five-meter gap to land another savage punch on the wrestler's nose.

He was dumbstruck at the idea of a stretching arm, and this second punch had been stronger than the first.

The blood that now flowed from Hakan's nose was no mere trickle. It sprayed audibly, like shaken soda upon removal of the bottle cap.

Hakan staggered back from the impact.

"Yoga…"

When he came to his senses, Dhalsim's elastic right arm was back in praying position. The dignified voice, which had no business emerging from such an emaciated-looking man, was followed by several bursts of flame.

"So are yeh even human, then?" asked Hakan instinctively.

The man before him certainly seemed like a monster. Ascetic or not, how could such a being be a real adherent of any religion that promoted goodness and truth? He more closely resembled that which faiths around the world have reviled since ancient times—a *demon*.

Stretching one's arms? Breathing fire?

Both acts were completely inhuman. If mastery of yoga granted such abilities, then was yoga actually some sort of dark art?

Dhalsim seemed far enough removed from humanity to conjure such thoughts.

"Have you had enough?"

"Sh-shut up," came Hakan's reply, full of false bravado.

A stiff smile emerged on Dhalsim's dark face.

"I'll be coming at you, then."

So come…

Hakan felt his whole body go rigid.

There are few things worse in a fight than allowing one's body to stiffen. The loss of speed renders one less able to cope with the opponent's attacks, and one's own attacks are blunted by the effects.

As Hakan desperately tried to loosen up, Dhalsim vanished from view.

With no exaggeration, he quite literally *vanished*.

"Yoga…"

A voice from behind.

Dhalsim's.

"How'n the hell…?" muttered Hakan as he spun around, his right arm extended and poised to strike. If Dhalsim had really snuck behind him somehow, that arm would mow him down.

He *was* there…

Close enough to touch.

But still, Hakan's sweeping arm missed its mark.

Dhalsim's thin upper body was bent back to an unbelievable extent. Bent back as if someone had snapped him in two where spine met hips, forming the shape of an uppercase "L."

So it was only natural that Hakan missed.

"What's this, now!?"

As he shouted, Hakan kept spinning to face Dhalsim. As if to confirm the wrestler's suspicions, the bent torso slowly rose back up.

The flesh between Dhalsim's ribs was sunken. His entire abdomen seemed as thin as a piece of cardboard, as if made of nothing but skin and bones. No sooner had Hakan thought as much than Dhalsim's stomach suddenly swelled, a deep breath transforming it into a balloon on the verge of bursting. Before Hakan's eyes, the stomach collapsed in on itself once again.

Dhalsim's eyes were suddenly filled with a strange bloodlust as his formerly sunken cheeks suddenly puffed up, as if he were a squirrel trying to store a bit too much food.

"Cr-crap!"

"Yoga Flame."

Just as Dhalsim's cheeks deflated, a jet of powerful fire shot from his mouth.

Pure hellfire.

But Hakan was already sliding.

He had sensed the unnatural bloodlust and thrown himself to the ground the instant Dhalsim's cheeks hollowed out. Being covered in oil meant that his momentum carried him into a slide across the ground when he landed. It was a trick that would shock most street performers, but by sliding on his back, Hakan put the necessary distance between Dhalsim and himself.

"O-o-one hit from that and I'd be a dead man…"

Hakan righted himself after getting far enough away, and upon standing, he felt something warm soaking his forehead. No telling if it was sweat, oil, or both. It was an unpleasant sensation either way, as it dripped down onto his face.

"Gahhh. Damn it all!"

Hakan reached for the opposite pocket as last time and pulled out another bottle of oil, the contents of which were soon covering his head and body.

Most people find that a splash of cold water is a good way to cool one's head, but Hakan was a different story. Olive oil to the head was all he needed to relax. Covering his body in it was just the thing to calm his muddled thoughts.

Now he could focus on how to win this fight.

Dhalsim's parlor trick ended with a final small puff of flame. His torso gave a single undulating shudder before he took his fighting stance. With hands neither open nor quite in fists, he spread his arms wide and began to spin them, every revolution causing his bangles to clatter. His spine was bolt straight, but his head and neck jutted out awkwardly. This was like no other fighting stance that Hakan had ever seen, but the peculiar posture was clearly helping Dhalsim control his breathing.

"Wh-wh-what the hell's all that about…?"

The monster wore a faint smile, which threw Hakan off his game all the more.

No amount of oil would be enough to get him through this ordeal, because none of it made any sense.

What on earth *was* Dhalsim?

A fire-breather with rubber arms who could disappear and reappear behind his opponent?

That last point, especially.

The word "teleportation" floated through Hakan's mind, but he still couldn't believe that such an absurd thing was possible.

That was no normal element of yoga.

It was magic.

"Yogaaaaa."

Dhalsim began shifting his head from side to side. When his body moved right, his head went left, and vice versa. All of this while still facing Hakan. The wrestler finally realized that the dance was meant to provoke him.

An invitation.

But not one Hakan felt like honoring.

His opponent here was a genuine, full-fledged monster, and Hakan, despite his natural-born stature and demonic visage, was only human.

He and Dhalsim lived in different worlds.

This was not an opponent he could beat; Dhalsim's fire would char him to the bone, and that would be the end of it.

Not a good matchup by any stretch of the imagination.

"Shall we stop?" asked Dhalsim, still smiling, head still bobbing.

Yes!

The word reached as far as Hakan's throat before he forced it back down. He looked as if he was about to scratch his head, but his fingers only slid across the oily surface.

"Continue, and you will only receive more of the same, as you have seen. We ought to stop."

Dhalsim's reasoning was sound, but the comical head movements made him all the less persuasive. And it was that same lack of persuasiveness that made him even more unapproachable.

Hakan shuddered at the thought of having to deal with Dhalsim as a business partner.

In the end, business is all about two cunning parties trying to outfox each other. An expert businessperson is able to read a dozen steps ahead of his or her negotiating partner in order to engineer the best possible deal.

Trying to read Dhalsim, however, would be a lost cause. He would probably take Hakan for his last red cent, and it was for that reason that the wrestler felt he shouldn't enter Dhalsim's range at the moment.

Business and fighting are much the same. Read one's opponent, make a move, and reap the profits. Both are battles in the truest sense.

Hakan could only come up with a single significant difference–the nature of what was at stake.

So much could be lost from a business deal gone wrong. Should his company collapse, his former employees would be out on the street, and his extended family would be forced to wonder where the next meal was coming from. Needless to say, his wife and daughters would suffer as well.

Compared to all that, the potential loss from a fight was far more straightforward.

His own life–plain and simple.

Should he prove too weak, he would die. Such was the unforgiving nature of battle, and Hakan accepted that.

If he were to die, his company's VP and directors would take over; there were plenty of able individuals lined up to keep the enterprise going. His immediate family would grieve, but Hakan's considerable savings would ensure their survival, so losing him would not leave them destitute.

When it came to betting his own life, Hakan didn't hesitate one bit.

"No answer? Then I will once more make my move."

Dhalsim's head stopped bobbing.

"Sure are one annoying bugger, I tell yeh."

Hakan gave his cheeks a slap.

"Enough talking just to hear yerself. If yeh wanna win, come at me."

The wrestler thrust an open right hand towards Dhalsim, showing the back of his hand, and flicked his four fingers towards himself exaggeratedly.

He repeated the motion—an obvious provocation.

The limp corners of Dhalsim's mouth lifted in a smile, and his thin legs kicked off the ground. He flew into the air as if he weighed nothing and crossed his legs mid-flight. Then, yet another unbelievable act.

He froze in place.

The ascetic's head was bowed slightly, and he thrust his arms to his sides as he floated.

"What the hell planet did yeh come from, y'damn alien!"

The still-smiling Dhalsim gave no indication that he heard Hakan's jab. Instead, he simply vanished.

"T-teleported, did yeh?"

Hakan felt stupid even saying the word. He spun around madly, the oil helping his feet glide across the ground. He spun like a brutish ballerina, desperately searching for the spot where Dhalsim might pop up.

His opponent performed a vanishing act, and he was a twirling ballerina.

How did it come this?

Then Dhalsim reappeared, still in mid-air, still cross-legged.

"Found yeh."

Hakan braced himself to stop spinning, but the oil served to supplement his momentum. When he finally planted his feet and faced Dhalsim, the ascetic had already touched down.

It was time for a grab.

The main moves of yağlı güreş involve grabbing the opponent and performing either a throw or an extended hold.

Once the wrestler took hold, the match would be his. Dhalsim's slender spine would crack and crumble when subjected to the grip strength that made Hakan a national hero back in Turkey. He wouldn't have another chance to blow so much as an ember.

Grab him, break him, and win the fight.

After all, this opponent might look the part of a holy man, but hadn't he breathed those flames with the intent to kill? Hakan couldn't afford to respond to that with any degree of mercy.

His mind made up, he took a step towards Dhalsim and raised both arms high. The arms would snap closed like the pincers of a stag beetle, and it would all be over.

"Say yer prayers."

"Yoga," shouted Dhalsim, just as Hakan shot his arms forward with a burst of power.

"Gotchaaa!"

The wrestler's momentum sent him to the ground, face first, and he immediately felt something warm on his back.

From the prostrate position, Hakan whipped his head up and found Dhalsim staring down at him, cheeks fully inflated.

"Thought yeh might try that," said Hakan with a smile.

He wasn't enjoying this, but neither was he hating it.

No visceral sense of battle. No grim reflection on the fact that he might lose his life here.

Nothing.

Hakan was empty.

Not even the man himself knew why he was smiling.

"Yoga Flame."

The fireball descended from Dhalsim's mouth and hurtled towards the grounded Hakan.

He gave a dexterous twitch of his legs, from thighs to knees to toes, which sent him sliding across the ground with a kick, aided by his trusty oil. He slid straight for the gap between Dhalsim's legs.

Hakan's plan was a cunning one.

Just as he passed into reach, he grabbed for both of Dhalsim's bangle-adorned ankles and kept sliding.

Dhalsim fell forward as if the rug had quite literally been yanked out from under him.

"Here we go."

After confirming that Dhalsim had really fallen, Hakan flipped over, dove onto Dhalsim's back, and wrapped both arms around his trunk. With left hand gripping his own right wrist, Hakan had the thin man in a foolproof hold.

"Finally gotcha."

Blood pumped to Hakan's pecs, delts, biceps, and abs, strengthening every muscle he needed to maintain the vicegrip.

Both men lay on the ground.

Hakan twisted his torso at the hips and began to spin into an Oil Dive, the oil reducing friction against the earth. He pumped his legs in bursts, steadily gaining speed.

Dhalsim and Hakan became a spinning blur of brown and red.

"The fun starts here," shouted Hakan, kicking off the ground abruptly.

They hurtled towards a wall, and it would soon be Dhalsim's head taking the brunt of the collision.

"Move aside!"

The crowd parted at Hakan's urgent request, and the wall of a mud-based dwelling came into view. That was the target.

Slap…

A sudden sound from near the wrestler's chest. He immediately understood, because his arms were woefully empty. Dhalsim had vanished against, leaving Hakan to grip his own pecs in an awkward embrace.

"Not this crap again!"

He smashed against the wall but managed to avoid hitting his head by curling into a ball first. Still, a sharp pain shot through his back at the point of impact.

As Hakan lifted himself on one knee, a fist came flying.

He dodged Dhalsim's punch with a quick flick of the head.

The ascetic's hand went snapping back to him like a rubber band.

The wrestler's respite was brief, as a rubbery kick soon followed.

"Yer legs too…"

The comment was cut off by the dry, cracked sole that collided with Hakan's face.

He struggled to stand while seeing stars.

Dhalsim was flying now. Not floating, not posing cross-legged, but truly soaring.

Hakan idly thought to himself about Dhalsim's impressive jumping abilities, which had propelled the ascetic over two meters into the air. At the peak of the jump, Dhalsim stopped for a moment before going flat as a board. That's when he started to rotate. It was his slow descent that made the move almost comical. Hakan watched agape as Dhalsim spun towards him.

So slowly, though…

"Think y'can hit me with *that*?" mumbled Hakan.

He leapt high, hoping to jump straight over Dhalsim, but just as he neared the thin legs- now aiming down, diagonally- something hit Hakan's body.

The unexpected blow cut off his momentum and sent him falling to the ground in a clumsy heap.

A leg? A fist? Maybe a head?

All Hakan knew was that something had smacked him out of the air.

Dhalsim was still airborne, spinning like a screwdriver on his way to the ground.

The wrestler lashed out with one arm but felt another blow to his head.

This time, the culprit was clearly one of Dhalsim's legs. The kick wasn't all that damaging, but it succeeded in stopping Hakan's attack.

Before he knew it, Dhalsim had landed.

"Crap!"

Fire was incoming.

Hakan attempted to bend over backwards in a dodge, but a hand from nowhere gripped his head, locking him in place.

The wrestler's hairstyle was reminiscent of the kind exhibited by so many statues of the Buddha, with a series of spiraling protuberances. In Hakan's case, the bumps were more geometric looking, and although they appeared as solid as stone, they were still just hair, hardened in place by oil.

Dhalsim's fingers tore into the carefully sculpted hairstyle. He had astounding grip strength for a man so slender. Hakan attempted to wrest himself away to no avail.

"Yoga."

The utterance came with a quick punch to Hakan's face from Dhalsim's free hand.

The punch didn't have much oomph to it, but it was heavy enough to shake Hakan's core.

"Yoga."

Another cry of "yoga," another punch.

"Yoga, yoga, yoga…"

Dhalsim went on, sounding almost disinterested. The punches kept flying.

No single punch was all that threatening, but Hakan ground his teeth in fear as the flurry continued. Repeated blows to the same spot could cause fractures in his skull. If he wasn't careful, a splinter of bone could break off and pierce his brain.

Then it'd be too late to react.

It was the plainest of attacks, but even ants can be threatening in a large enough swarm.

"Yoga, yoga, yoga…"

"Really gettin' mad, here."

Hakan's grumbling never reached Dhalsim's ears.

The ascetic's dogged devotion to the punches and the steady repetition of "yoga" stirred anger within Hakan.

"What's with all the yoga, yoga, yoga while yeh punch?"

Hakan grabbed the hand holding him in place and glared up at Dhalsim.

"Why the chant, huh? Is 'yoga' what yeh call punching here in India?"

As he spoke, he slid his hands up Dhalsim's arm.

"Don't tell me the 'yoga' yeh monks do is actually all about punching? How can yer training be named after the art of hittin' folks!"

The wrestler's grip slid up past the ascetic's shoulder to clasp around his neck.

"Ack," grunted Dhalsim.

"Yeh don't happen to know any words besides that 'yoga,' do yeh?"

Hands still gripping the thin neck, Hakan lifted Dhalsim as he stood and bent over backwards, aiming for the ground. In pro wrestling terms, the move would be called a suplex.

As Dhalsim's head met the earth, it gave off a dry, dull sound, like a wooden bucket hitting the tile floor of a bathhouse.

His skull wasn't broken. If it had been, his sloshing brain matter would have given the sound a wet quality, and Hakan knew that.

Despite the impressive-sounding crack, Dhalsim took little damage.

This was no death match. It was Hakan's pride that kept him from strangling his opponent outright, so he released his hands from Dhalsim's throat and stood.

The ascetic's body remained erect for a second, head planted in ground, before falling over with all the lightness of a dried-out tree branch.

"Now it's my turn."

Hakan licked his lips and extended his hands towards Dhalsim's motionless body, hoping to grab him around the waist.

Something suddenly snapped, like a glancing blow.

Dhalsim—still facedown—had hit the ground with his own stomach. The degree to which he could inflate and deflate it was almost revolting. Still, given the remarkable control he had over those muscles, it was no wonder that he could force himself up off the ground with such a trick.

It wasn't the sound that shocked Hakan. It was the way Dhalsim's body rose into the air, almost floating.

"How light *are* you?" muttered the wrestler in disbelief. Dhalsim transferred into a backwards somersault and turned his gaze on the wrestler. He formed a bridge position with his body, as if resting atop an invisible board in the air.

The suspended Dhalsim stared at Hakan with those white eyes.

"Yeh really gross me out, man…"

Hakan began to charge, head first.

"Yoga Fire."

Dhalsim's cheeks collapsed and the flames flew, charting a course straight for Hakan.

"Not this old trick. S'getting boring."

He moved his massive, red body with surprising agility to dodge the fire.

"Yoga."

More flames.

Dhalsim, still floating, had transitioned to the cross-legged position.

"Persistent, huh."

The first dodge had been to the right, but now Hakan went left.

"Yoga."

A third burst.

"Enough of that already!"

The wrestler leapt into the air, and as his toes left the ground, the fire grazed the spot where he had only just stood.

He wouldn't let the fourth attack happen. Hakan landed right in front of Dhalsim.

"Have yeh now!"

Both arms shot out to grab his opponent in another hold.

That was the plan, anyway…

Once again, Hakan was left embracing his own shoulders. Muscles smacked against muscles violently, sending splashes of oil into his face.

"Pbbfft."

Hakan spat oil and kept on the move while trying to assess the situation.

His opponent had vanished again, and there was only one answer.

Teleportation.

An explanation Hakan couldn't believe in spite of himself.

There was no denying it anymore, though; this man was capable of teleporting. He had warped away in order to dodge the grab, and he would soon reappear elsewhere.

Hakan tried to imagine where he would go if he were Dhalsim.

"Over *here*," he shouted as he whipped his body around.

In battle, the most advantageous position is always at the opponent's back, and Dhalsim was floating just where Hakan expected him to be, confirming his suspicions.

The ascetic's cheeks bulged.

"How inhuman d'yeh have to get before yer satisfied…?"

Hakan had put all his energy into spinning around, so once again, he wasn't able to stop on command. It didn't matter though, because he never could've defended against the incoming attack or evaded in time. Only a god could cope that quickly, and Hakan was no god.

"Yoga Flame!"

There it was.

The fire connected, and Hakan lit up.

"Ohhhhh."

The crowd roared at the sight of the blazing wrestler. It was no cry of horror, but rather a resounding cheer.

Fire spread instantly across the surface of Hakan's oily body.

If he couldn't extinguish the flames in short order, he was dead.

His body moved to roll on the ground faster than he could think, covering itself with the dry, baked sand. Every rotation added more sand to the mix of fire and oil.

The flames began to lose their ferocity.

He didn't stop rolling, because he'd already decided on his destination.

Burning black smoke infiltrated his nose and throat. Hakan had long since stopped feeling the heat; his body was going numb.

Oddly enough, his mind was clearer than ever, and it told him to keep rolling.

The gallery stepped aside as Hakan rolled towards his goal.

A massive barrel…

It was uncovered and filled to the brim with olive oil.

"Rahhhh."

Body still ablaze, Hakan jumped into the barrel up to his neck.

Fire will naturally die out when deprived of oxygen, and the risky move would also serve to cool down the hot oil coating Hakan's body.

It was all a big gamble, but one he was confident he could win.

There was a dull hissing from all over his body.

He hadn't just doused the fire in oil; he had drowned it.

Hakan leapt from the barrel.

"Whaddyeh think about that?"

He spread both arms wide, dropped his hips, and turned to face Dhalsim.

"Extinguishing fire with oil…? You are one very foolish…yet amusing man."

"Me n' oil are friends through thick and thin. If I tell it to put out a fire, the oil obeys."

"Turning the impossible into reality… You remind me of *him*."

Dhalsim spoke fondly of this old friend from his cross-legged position in mid-air.

"A warrior who hailed from the farthest eastern reaches. A man named Ryu."

Hakan was no stranger to that name. Ryu was an infamous street fighter who used a style resembling karate. Hakan never saw the man fight, but if the rumors were true, then he was strong beyond strong.

Dhalsim himself was a renowned fighter in India, so it came as no surprise that he had actually met Ryu.

"In order to overcome your natural limits, you found the resolution and determination to achieve the impossible. I commend you for that."

"Can't say I'm all too thrilled to get praise from a *monster*," replied Hakan, attempting to hide his embarrassment.

Every person is glad to earn respect. All the more so when it's given face-to-face.

"Now, warrior who has traveled from the crossroads of east and west. Shall we clash fists once more?"

As Dhalsim spoke, he thrust out both rubbery arms and began to shake them slowly. The swaying arm movements betrayed his obvious joy.

"Weird thing for a holy man to say…"

Hakan's grumbling was too quiet to hear, and he was on the move again in no time. He had no plan of attack, but that was fine. He believed that straightforward moves without guile were the best sort.

This wasn't about winning or losing, or even about some gaudy display of power. Rather, by immersing himself in the purity of battle, Hakan was able to forget everything else. The essence of "fighting" could be found only when both fighters left the material world behind and ascended to a higher plane.

His simple way of thinking resembled the concept of freeing one's mind through meditation. Scheming and plotting in order to win a fight would be evidence of unnecessary attachments. Once one accepted the righteousness of battle, any planning would seem a foolish act.

Victory depended on the luck of the draw.

That's how it was for all things in life.

It would be enough to "win" at the moment of death.

Having no plan or even an inane one was fine.

He would laugh in death's face.

That was the sort of victory Hakan could appreciate, so it only made sense to fight without regrets.

"Rahhhhhh."

He charged.

The already airborne Dhalsim somehow lifted himself even higher before stretching out both arms.

"Come with me, my friend."

Hakan heard the words as he felt Dhalsim's hands grip his head.

The ascetic was far overhead, but the two fighters were linked by the pair of rubbery arms.

"Yoga."

Dhalsim's shout was accompanied by what felt like a thunderclap to Hakan's head.

A headbutt.

By the time he realized, a second headbutt was already incoming.

"Yoga."

A shockwave of pain.

The elasticity of Dhalsim's arms allowed him to perform this novel series of headbutts, and there was no way to deal with an attack so off the beaten path. Hakan was already stunned stiff as the third headbutt drove into his crown.

The wrestler felt Dhalsim rise up again. He was completely out of view, but the long airtime suggested that this leap was higher than any of the previous ones.

A sudden force started wrenching Hakan's head to one side. Dhalsim's arms were twisting around each other on the way up, until the built-up tension caused him to spin in the other direction as he fell and smashed into Hakan's head.

Another direct hit.

The fourth headbutt didn't end there, though. The spin transferred to Dhalsim's head, effectively turning it into a drill that violently rattled Hakan's brain itself.

He was losing consciousness, and with all his power was drained, Hakan's legs collapsed, sending him to the ground, splayed.

"Gah!"

An irritated cry.

His hazy view was obscured by Dhalsim's dark skin.

The ascetic had fallen on top of him…

Hakan somehow knew it instinctively. Dhalsim had attempted to land on the wrestler's stomach, but he had forgotten about the oil and ended up slipping.

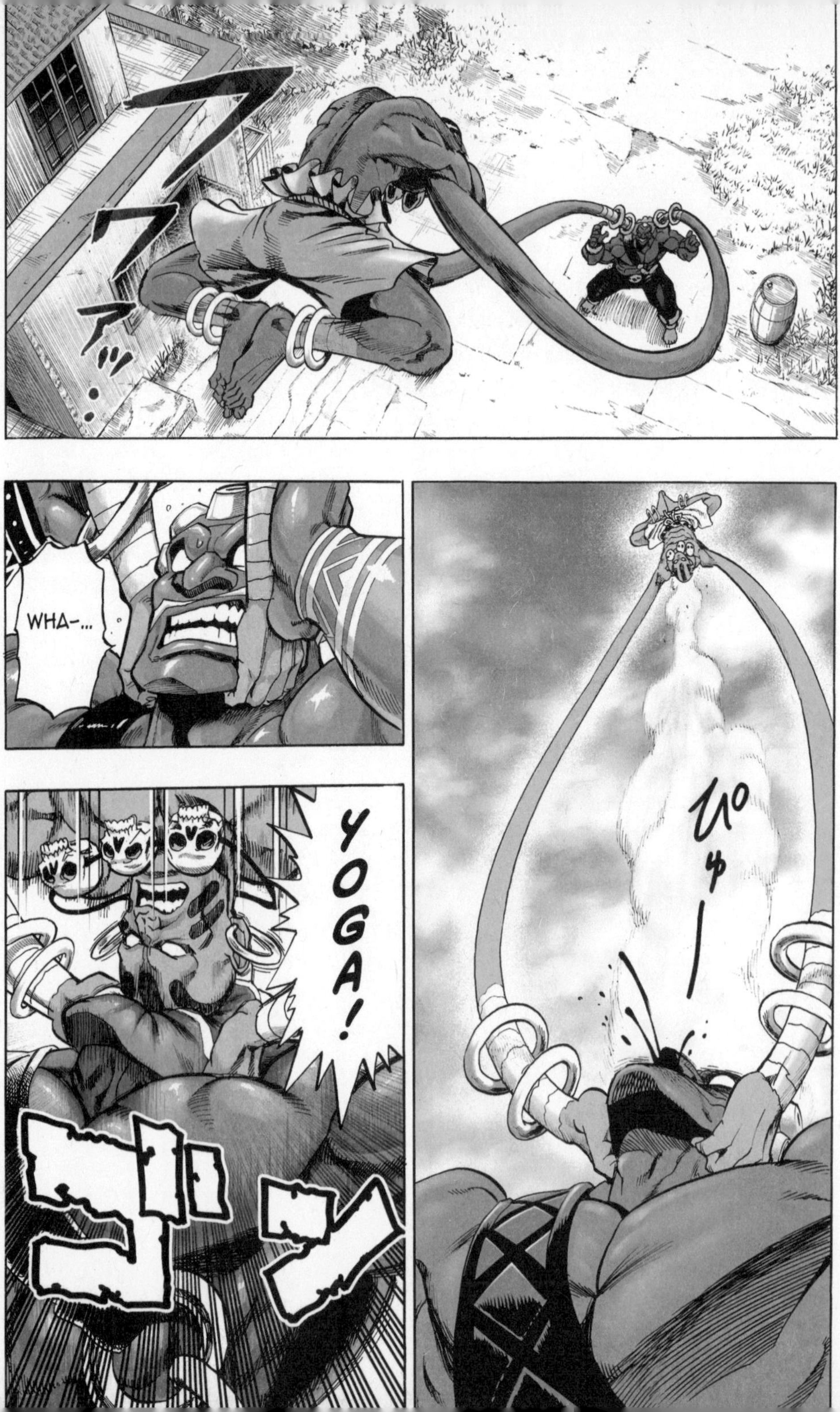
ぴゅー
WHA-...
YOGA!

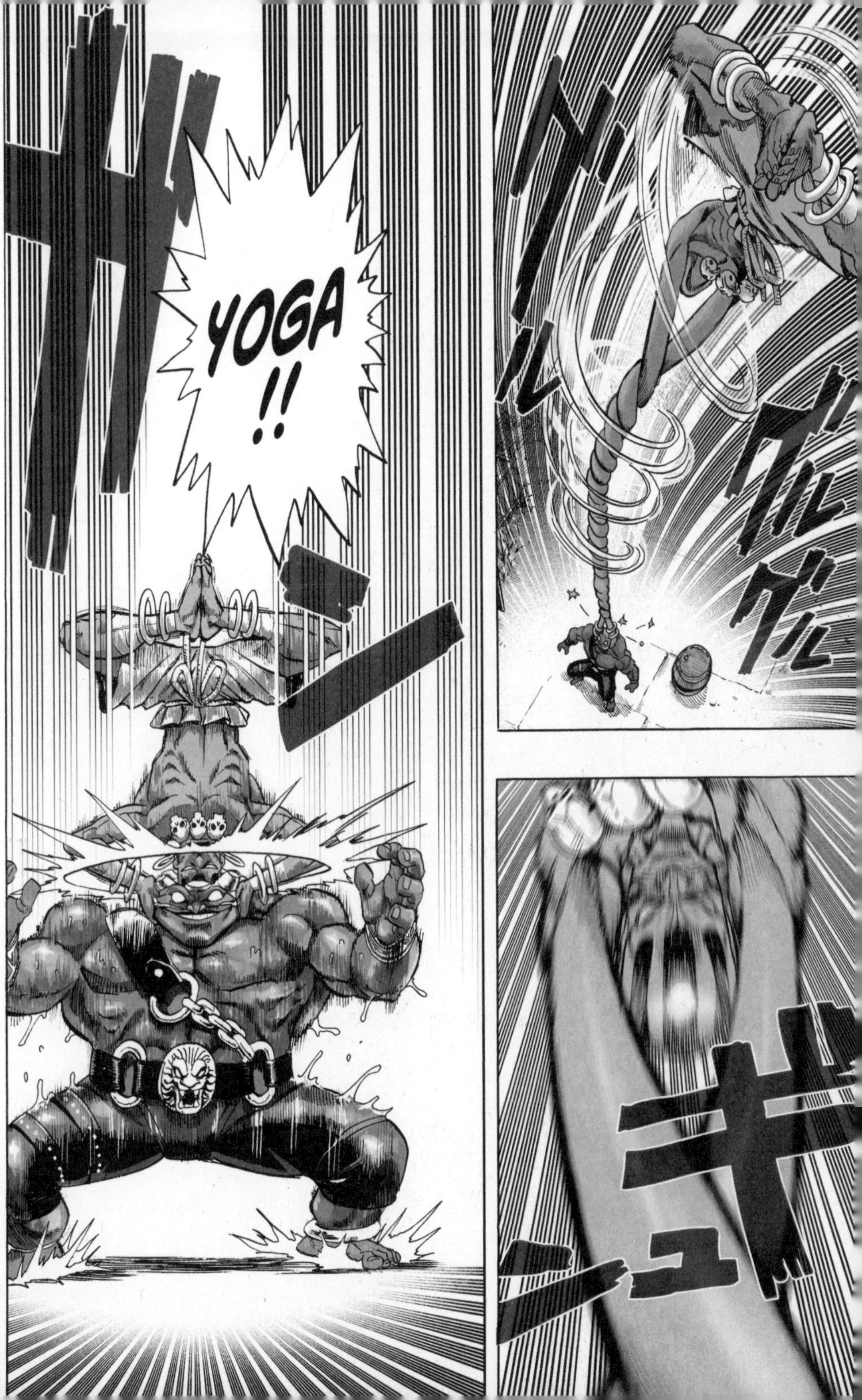
YOGA !!

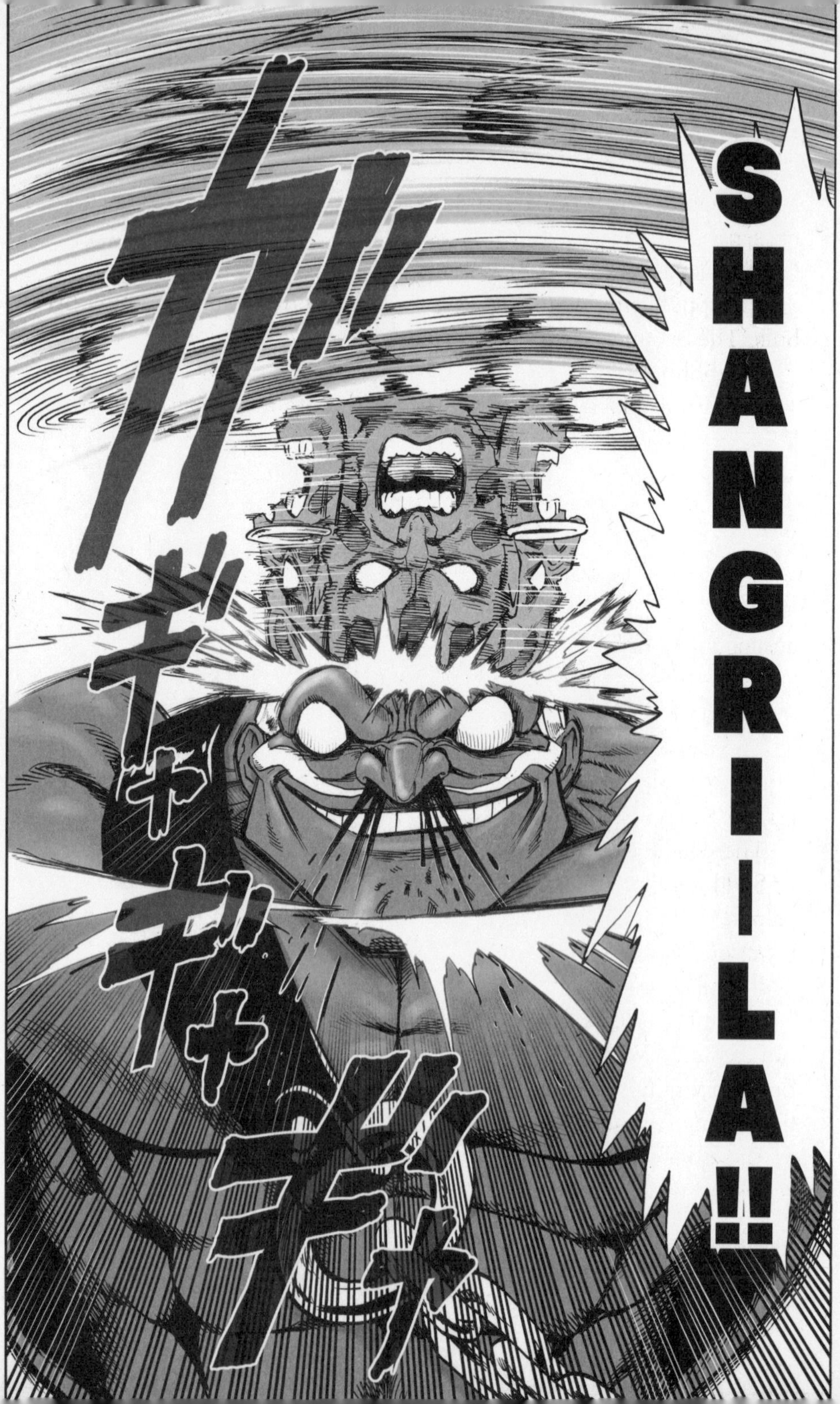
SHANGRI-LA!!

The last bit of rotational energy from Dhalsim's twisted arms was now causing his body to spin atop Hakan's slick body.

Though on the verge of losing consciousness, Hakan came back to his senses with a shake of his head.

"S'my chance!"

He flipped, pinning the defenseless, still spinning Dhalsim under his bulk. The two men were aligned head-to-foot.

"Urahhhh."

Now it was Hakan who started spinning, with both arms and both legs extended. A diversion meant to distract from the impending attack. Unable to react, Dhalsim could only go rigid in an attempt at defense.

He was good and confused.

It was time for the next move.

Hakan stopped spinning and grabbed Dhalsim with all four limbs, curling into a ball.

The ascetic's head stuck out just past Hakan's rear end.

"Here we go!"

The wrestler poured all his strength into squeezing the space that Dhalsim occupied. Under that pressure, the small, dry body gave off a series of cracks and groans.

There was nowhere to run.

Suddenly, a loud "pop," as if someone were slapping his or her palm against open, rounded lips. The sound came from near Hakan's lower quarters.

Dhalsim was gone.

The crowd clearly realized that *something* had flown past them, but none could be sure what it was. The people in the object's path had been knocked over by the force, their legs swept out from under them. Something soft had collided with a wall behind that particular part of the mob. Those who heard the "splat" it made might have been reminded of their childhoods, when the crueler among them had thrown frogs at walls for fun.

A series of cracks began spreading across the wall. The parted crowd was soon aware of what had caused the cracks, and the stunned Hakan eventually brought his gaze to the site of impact as well. Laying on the ground in a heap, bent nearly in two and unconscious, was Dhalsim.

His oddly limp and rubbery looking tongue lolled from his mouth, and though his eyes–white as ever–gave no clue to his state of consciousness, his utter motionlessness was more than enough evidence.

"Honey!"

The worried woman from earlier rushed over, screaming.

Hakan realized she must have been his wife after all, but the idle thought soon vanished from his mind.

"Nothing to it."

Victory depended on the luck of the draw…

No doubt about it.

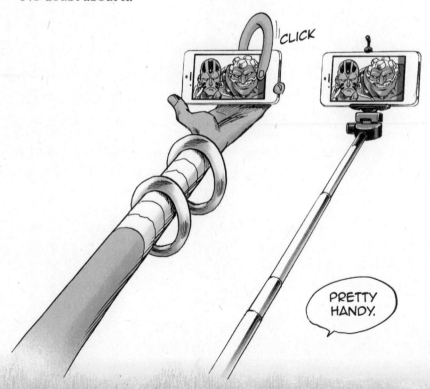

ROUND

6

暴力と品格

VIOLENCE
AND DIGNITY

ROUND 6
VIOLENCE AND DIGNITY

"**I** daresay there is nothing quite like second flush Darjeeling tea."

Dudley spoke with his usual air of satisfaction and composure as he breathed in the tea's aroma.

A smattering of early afternoon sunbeams lit up his gazebo, which was surrounded by bushes of multicolored roses in full bloom. Here he was–drinking quality tea and feeling a refreshing spring breeze brush by his face. The roses were just the icing on top of what Dudley knew was the very pinnacle of luxury.

"Another cup, sir?"

Dudley nodded in silence to his head butler, a man with meticulously styled gray hair and a silver tea pot in one hand that he wielded with practiced deftness. A loyal man who was a fixture in the family since Dudley's father's time. Even when times were hard and Dudley had been forced to deal with the massive loans meant to cover a loss in his father's business, the butler had believed in Dudley and agreed to continue working for next to nothing. No one had rejoiced more when Dudley's heavyweight boxing career took off, allowing him to pay back every loan and amass even greater fortune. "Devotion" might as well have been the butler's middle name.

"Thank you, Mr. Gotch."

The loyal butler was getting on in his years, and he now wore a pair of round spectacles–a gift purchased with Dudley's first ever boxing winnings.

Ten-odd years had passed since that day.

Dudley was now an unstoppable force in the boxing world, and he had even made a name for himself in street fighting circles thanks to his participation in a number of no-holds-barred fighting tournaments.

Even in fights without rules, Dudley refused to remove his boxing gloves. His gloved fists were weapons enough.

His opponents would come at him with their fists, too. And kicks, and throws, and strangleholds. His fists would always win the day, though.

Boxing was almost a religion to Dudley.

He believed that no other fighting style in history had done more to explore the art of striking, and that its flexibility was perfect for coping with any given scenario using nothing but one's fists. He knew he could triumph in any bout without resorting to the myriad strikes favored by other fighters, and it was that confidence that led Dudley to leave the world of professional boxing and dedicate himself to street fighting.

Before the momentary financial setback, Dudley was born into a British family of high pedigree, so it was his belief that dignity was at all times essential.

No matter how destitute one's upbringing, one could always fall back on dignity. Dudley constantly sought to be dignified in his own actions, and he thought it was a quality worth pursuing for every man and woman alive. It had nothing to do with his station. He happened to be born into a noble family, so Dudley was taught the concept from an early age, but he had met plenty of people from lesser backgrounds who made a point of maintaining their dignity.

This train of thought brought to mind a certain man.

Ryu…

Anyone remotely involved in the world of street fighting knew the Japanese fighter's name. He was a stoic man who sought out the strong, earning him the respect and admiration of many a young fighter.

Dudley knew nothing about Ryu's upbringing, but through the latter's worldwide quest for strong fighters and his resulting lifestyle, it was clear that he embodied the concept of "honorable poverty." There was an unshakable dignity about Ryu in spite of his humble way of life, and the powerful will that drove him granted him a dignity that shined brighter than that of most nobles.

Dudley had felt nothing but fondness and affinity for Ryu when they had crossed fists.

The boxer had lost that fight. The first black stain on his record as a street fighter. On his record as a boxer, even. Indeed, Ryu was the only person Dudley had ever lost to.

Yet...

He felt no anger or regret over that loss.

It was no wonder, given Ryu's overwhelming ability. Ryu was on a completely diferent level, and Dudley realized he had lost their match before it even began.

"Hmph..."

With a self-derisive snort, the boxer picked up a porcelain teacup with a single, tasteful pink rose painted on its surface.

The tea's sweetness and roses' fragrance mixed within his body to create an overwhelming sense of euphoria. He could die right here, and all would be well.

Mr. Gotch's large ears twitched, and Dudley took note from over the rim of his teacup. The twitching ears led to a furrowed brow and a glance to the right. Dudley was already searching for whatever had disturbed his loyal butler.

Near the edge of the estate's sprawling garden, a group of men seemed to be making some noise. There were four or five voices in total, and Dudley knew them all.

It was the head gardener and the mansion's security team, all shouting.

"Allow me to investigate, sir."

The butler dropped his head at precisely a 45-degree angle as he took up the teapot. He then hurried away to the source of the commotion, all the while maintaining perfect posture.

For a moment Dudley thought Mr. Gotch might carry the teapot with him to the scene, but no- he would never do anything so boorish. He was probably going to bring it into the house first.

Mr. Gotch disappeared behind a hedge of rose bushes.

Dudley's teacup remained mostly full, so he continued to sip in silence.

The shouting grew louder.

One voice was conspicuously more boisterous than the rest. It was grating on the ears and without a hint of dignity as it hurled abuse at the others. The owner of this voice must have been at the center of the conflict, and whoever it happened to be was a stranger to Dudley.

When the tea was halfway drained, the vulgar voice started to draw closer to the gazebo. Dudley couldn't make out Mr. Gotch's voice, always the embodiment of reserved dignity, though the butler had surely reached the source of the discord by this point.

One-third of the tea remained…

The voice drew even nearer. From beyond the ring of rose bushes that circled the gazebo, Dudley heard a ferocious roar followed by the screams of his employees.

This unknown intruder was beating down the mansion staff as he approached.

One sip of tea left…

A hedge wall of white roses exploded in from the outside, producing a black hole amidst the exquisite white and green. A giant of a man stood on the other side.

"Finally found you," said the man while sporting a smile vulgar beyond words. The mansion staff cowered at his feet.

"Where is my Mr. Gotch?"

"Huhh?"

Dudley remained seated in his white chair as he asked his question, to which the intruder replied with a bulging right eye.

The man's kinky hair was cropped short, shaven into a series of sharply angled points that framed his face . A pair of blazing yellow eyes and a complete lack of eyebrows were evocative of the wicked-looking gargoyles that adorned the roof of Notre Dame cathedral.

"I refer to my esteemed butler. He ran off to see about the noise you were raising."

"That old four-eyes?" muttered the man as he bent forward, the muscles bulging from his back seeming to envelop his head in that position. He wore a light blue tanktop over a white running shirt whose sleeves were ripped off at the shoulder. Each shoulder was the size of a basketball, and from them hung a pair of grotesquely muscled arms.

What drew Dudley's eye more than anything, though, were the man's fists.

He wore boxing gloves.

Six-ouncers, by the look of them.

The lightweight kind no longer in use. Punches from six-ounce gloves are all the more damaging due to their relative lack of stuffing and reduced load, so they were banned in all formal bouts starting in the early 1990s.

The six-ounce gloves looked even smaller when compared to the man's unnecessarily thick arms.

"All it took was one little push to put that geezer down for a nap," said the man with a pleased look on his face. He brought his fists together, and the thin gloves produced a dry slapping noise.

"Do you mean to say you *punched* an elderly gentleman clearly unaccustomed to fighting?"

"I'm saying I did."

The man spat, and Dudley looked down on him, still seated in the gazebo.

"Anyone who tries to stop me is gonna get what's coming to them. Doesn't matter how many you send."

"You have no mercy, even for those unable to fight back?"

"How many times you gonna ask? I've got no patience for a man who can't get the message."

"Then I will readily ask once more. Did you truly punch out my elderly butler?"

"Shut up, already. Like I told you, I did."

The cruder the man, the lower his boiling point and the sooner he bellows. Dudley knew this man was just that type.

"Balrog…" said Dudley, picking up his cup.

"Glad to hear you know my name."

The right corner of Balrog's mouth raised in a sneer, his every action showcasing his undignified nature.

"Yes, I recall an American heavyweight competitor by that name."

Dudley drained his teacup and placed it down on the saucer in a single elegant movement. He stared down at Balrog coldly.

"People had high hopes for this Balrog, but in the end he could never quite leave the street-fighting behind. He would employ headbutts, bites, kicks… Those dirty moves left his opponents marred beyond recovery, so he eventually left the world of boxing. You are the spitting image of that foolish man."

"Yup, that's me."

Balrog punched his own fists together once more and tilted his head side to side. Pops and cracks rang out from his neck.

"Fight me," he said, staring at Dudley.

"Why should I?"

"Don'cha wanna know which of us two is stronger?"

"Is that why you've made a mess of my garden, knocked out my staff, and disrespected one of my oldest friends?"

"That's right."

Balrog gave a series of quick nods, excessive enough to get on Dudley's nerves.

He had never met such a galling individual.

"So, we gonna do this or not? I need an answer. Hell, even if you turn me down, I'm still gonna beat the tar outta you."

"And then I suppose you'll spread word of your victory?"

"You catch on quick. Good."

Balrog's laugh was jarring, and thin blood vessels began to pop out across Dudley's forehead. The man himself didn't realize this, though; he refused to acknowledge the rage building inside.

"Very well…"

He rose gently, but his piercing glare never shifted from Balrog.

"I'll need a moment or two to prepare, if you'll permit me."

"Long as you're not thinking of running."

Another grating laugh. As Dudley walked down the gazebo stairs, he fought hard to suppress the urge to smash the man in the nose right there and then.

"Would you care to follow me?" spoke Dudley as he passed Balrog, neglecting to turn towards the man.

"So you really are a boxer through and through, huh?"

Dudley could tell Balrog was following, but he didn't stop walking towards the mansion.

"If this was a street fight, you'd already be a dead man."

"I'll ask you not to underestimate me," came Dudley's indifferent answer. He kept his eyes locked on his destination.

"I'm fully prepared for you to attack from the rear, even now. Do not think such base tactics will be enough to defeat me."

"I'm praying that's more than just a bluff."

The sound of Balrog licking his lips from behind. Dudley kept walking.

Dudley faced his opponent in the practice ring he had built in one corner of the mansion. He wore blue boxing gloves and a button-down shirt with a starched frill and rolled-up sleeves, topped off with a bowtie. His green slacks with yellow stripes were held up by suspenders, which ran under a cummerbund a similar color as the pants. A pair of Church's Consuls were his choice of footwear.

This was Dudley's street-fighting style.

Even while fighting, he preferred to maintain his dignity as an English gentleman.

Though he stood in a ring, and though his opponent was a fellow boxer, this was sure to be a street fight, as it were, so he had opted for his back alley garb as opposed to the usual trunks.

Dudley's gloves were ten-ouncers—the same weight used by professionals in the ring. He would never stoop so low as to match his opponent's thin, lightweight gloves. Whatever fighting style he might come up against, he would respond as a boxer with those ten ounce gloves. It was a matter of pride, which itself was an element of his all-important dignity.

"No one here to ring the bell. How do we do this?"

Balrog's dark red gloves–worn down from excess use–slapped together as he spoke.

They had no audience, either.

Dudley had given his staff strict orders to keep away. No one was to step foot on this floor until their employer gave the go-ahead.

Balrog's boxing shoes squeaked in the otherwise silent ring. Eager to begin, he was bouncing around on his toes, causing the thin soles of his worn shoes to cry out in protest.

Dudley's gloves were blue, and Balrog's were red. The poles behind each of them, cattycorner to each other, matched each fighter's gloves.

A red corner and a blue corner.

In title matches, it's customary for the reigning champion to occupy the red corner, while the challenger takes the blue. Going by that reasoning, Balrog was the champ here and Dudley the challenger.

But there was no reason to fuss over the particulars in this case. This was no title match, so there was no implicit, preexisting hierarchy to acknowledge.

Still…

The man in the blue gloves was pumped, all the more so when his opponent happened to be wearing red in the red corner.

Despite his current affluence and success, Dudley always saw himself as the challenger.

After his father had nearly ruined the family name by losing everything in a bad business deal, it had been Dudley who rebuilt it all with his own two fists.

Never one to succumb to adversity, he was no stranger to fierce battles where life and death hung in the balance. Whenever fate reared its ugly head to block his way, he had fought back with desperation.

A man who challenged fate itself.

That was how Dudley saw himself.

Even after transforming his father's liabilities into assets and earning back the family fortune and then some, his disposition never changed.

A person can only know true defeat once he or she stops struggling against fate.

It was a lesson taught to Dudley by his father. What defeated his father, in the end, wasn't the business blunder or the loans. When business turned bad and former partners turned their backs on him, the man fell into despair. He drowned his sorrows in alcohol, shirking reality and deceiving himself by saying, "It wasn't supposed to be like this." He shifted the blame for everything wrong onto someone or something else. He ran from fate.

Fate was the opponent that had defeated Dudley's father.

He had cowered in the face of that greatest of foes- one very much worth overcoming.

Dudley would not follow in his father's footsteps.

He had decided a long time ago to struggle against fate, and he had ever since.

He saw fate as a beast, and if one was to succeed, one had to bring the beast to heel. "Life" was merely the battleground, and in that sense, every person was an eternal challenger.

True dignity could only be found in that struggle.

Dudley believed that with all his heart, which was why standing in the blue corner with those blue gloves was just the thing to get him fired up.

"Did you really come seeking a fight with a gong, referee, and other such trappings?"

The blue boxer clenched his right fist to test the glove's resistance, all while staring at Balrog. The latter responded with a hateful smile, veins like writhing serpents rising on his forehead.

"As long as you're good without, I'm down."

Balrog's grating voice had barely stopped before he kicked off the cerulean blue mat, his shoes giving off a high-pitched squeak.

The red boxer moved forward with head brought low and fists on either side of his face.

He wasn't favoring either side, and as far as Dudley could tell, both shoulders were equidistant from his opponent.

It was the head-on style of the peek-a-boo stance.

A specialized stance meant for the exchange of blows at nearly point-blank range, and one preferred by in-fighters.

"Hmph…"

Balrog began to charge at Dudley, as if a mad bull at a matador. The latter watched lucidly and slowly spread his hands apart. He crouched to half-height and thrust his left shoulder forward, forcing his right to pull back with a natural kink in the arm. Both fists sat slightly below his chin, unclenched, in the orthodox boxing stance.

When Balrog passed the ring's center mark, Dudley began to bounce up and down with a certain looseness of motion. His feet tapped lightly against the mat as he stepped forward. His shoulders bounced too, in time with Balrog's movement.

One.

Two.

Three.

He counted the opponent's steps.

There.

Dudley's left fist shot out from his shoulder. The light thrust warped, like whip being cracked.

A left jab.

The most basic of basic moves in boxing.

Having synced his own rhythm with Balrog's, Dudley landed an explosive, direct hit to the red boxer's forehead. A dry "whap" rang out, and Dudley felt the satisfying recoil in his own glove-covered fist.

The mad bull stopped charging.

Just as planned.

A second, and then a third.

An entire series of jabs in quick succession.

But if Dudley's fists could reach, then so could his opponent's.

Still facing forward with fists protecting his face from the nose down, Balrog wasn't merely enduring the flurry of jabs. He was *waiting*.

"Guheh!"

An ugly bellow. The red boxer thrust his own fist between a gap in the jabs, but Dudley didn't miss a beat.

"Fsshh."

With a short, quick breath from pursed lips, Dudley bent backwards ever so slightly.

The corner post being directly behind him, there wasn't exactly anywhere to run.

So he swayed, instead.

Swaying is another fundamental boxing technique where the boxer shifts only his or her torso up and down or side to side in order to dodge a punch.

From the swaying position, Dudley responded to the ferocious hook with his own right fist.

A power-packed straight.

It sounded as if a paper bag had exploded in the small space separating the fighters.

Feedback to his fist.

Meanwhile, Balrog's fist sailed past Dudley's eyes.

The mad bull staggered back a few steps, and Dudley, still bent backwards, was suddenly aware of the corner post digging into his back.

A gap had opened between them.

After retreating to the center of the ring, Balrog eyed Dudley, motionless, with both fists raised to his chin. His eyes brimmed with a hungry light, as if he were a beast watching his prey.

"You got some power there, but…doesn't look like you're too good at reading my moves," muttered Balrog.

Dudley wondered to himself what his opponent could possibly mean by that. Their first, brief exchange had shown Dudley to be the superior fighter. Unable to endure the storm of ferocious jabs, Balrog had only lashed out with a single hook, which Dudley had adeptly dodged and countered with a straight to the forehead. The sheer force of it had pushed the red boxer back.

The only hits so far came from Dudley's fists…

"Hmm?"

Something warm in the corner of his left eye.

Blood.

The realization came with sudden pain that gradually spread across his entire eyelid.

But the punch hadn't hit? Dudley clearly saw Balrog's fist fly past. No mistaking it.

So how…?

There was only one explanation. His thumb.

The traditional boxing glove separates the thumb from the other four fingers, meaning that the thumb alone is able to act independently.

Balrog's gloves were only six ouncers, and the thinner the material, the easier it is to thrust out one's thumb.

So he had thrown an exaggerated hook. One he knew full well that Dudley could dodge. In the process, though, he stuck out his thumb and grazed Dudley's eye.

Nothing else could explain the injury.

The rules of boxing naturally forbid attacking with single fingers, but this was a street fight. One without rules.

There was nothing *wrong*, per se, about Balrog's attack.

Still…

It was unforgivable.

Especially during street fights, and especially when there are no rules, boxers must always be a boxers. Once they put aside the gloves and resorts to kicks and grabs, they are boxers no longer.

The man standing before Dudley wore those gloves and stepped into the ring, so he too was a boxer. Any violation of the basic principles of boxing could not stand.

It was a matter of dignity.

This man was entirely unprincipled. He abused the techniques of boxing for his own pleasure, harmed the innocent, and stormed onto another's property like a common criminal without second thought. Dudley could never forgive him for wearing those gloves.

"Will you promise me one thing?" asked Dudley, blood still dripping from his eye.

Balrog took a single step but continued to listen.

"If by chance I win this bout, you will never again don a pair of boxing gloves."

"Sure thing. But there's no way I'm losing this."

"By 'sure thing,' you mean to say you agree to my request?"

"Take it however you wanna take it."

"I see…" replied Dudley, sinking into his stance.

"Then what I shall take is my win, and without reservation."

Step.

He advanced, closing the gap in an instant.

Still in the orthodox stance, Dudley's left shoulder was nearly close enough to graze Balrog's solar plexus.

Shocked by Dudley's speed, Balrog launched a panicked right hook.

Step.

The blue boxer spread his legs wide to drop even lower and tilted his torso diagonally into a shoulder roll. The red boxing glove skimmed past his face.

A paper-thin margin.

This time, Dudley was fully aware to watch for a stray thumb, so it was a perfect dodge.

He straightened back up immediately after swaying and used the momentum to launch a right uppercut.

A body blow.

The wild swing had left Balrog unable to defend, so the blue glove exploded against his flank.

"Guhh."

An unmistakable grunt of anguish. Dudley's fist was already on its way back.

In pulling back his right, his left was driven forward all the faster.

The blow to the side had left Balrog breathless, and now Dudley's left fist smashed into the opposite flank.

When one's body is hit from both left and right, one will inevitably curl forward. It has nothing to do with logic or reason—only reflex.

And Balrog was only human. With the second body blow completed,

Dudley's left was pulling back in preparation for a third hit, and it was all his opponent could do to remain standing with a stunned expression that seemed to say, "Hit me!"

"Short Swing Blow!"

The rotational energy that went into the straight had been transferred from toes, to knees, to hips, to shoulder, to arm, to wrist, giving the punch more than enough power.

The fist drove into Balrog's gargoyle-like face, sending the force straight through to the back of his head. Had it been a bullet, it would have opened a hole in the middle of his face. Dudley's fist could only produce a piercing shockwave, however, and once finished, he swiftly brought the hand back to his jaw.

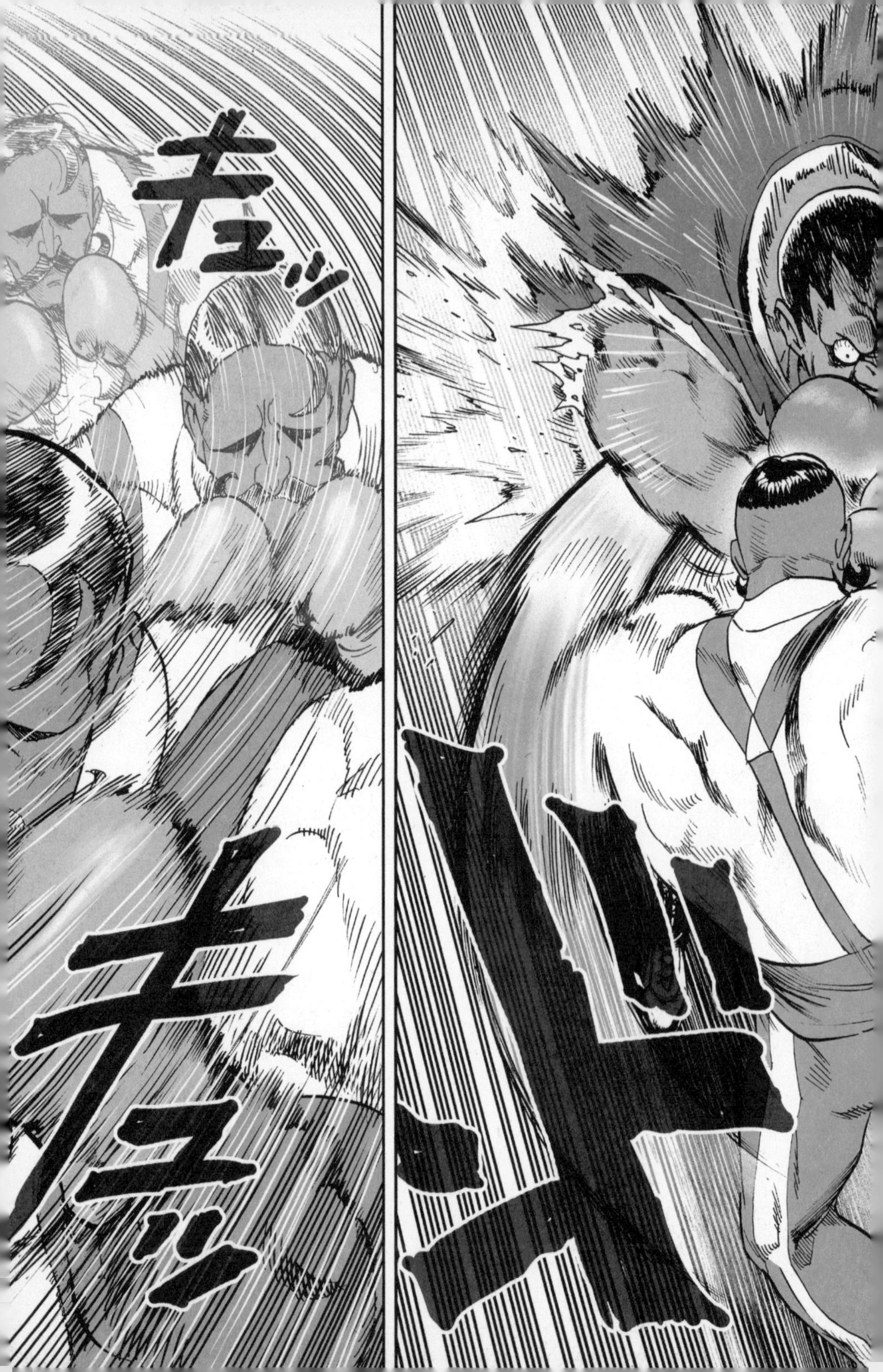
ドン
ギュッ
キュッ

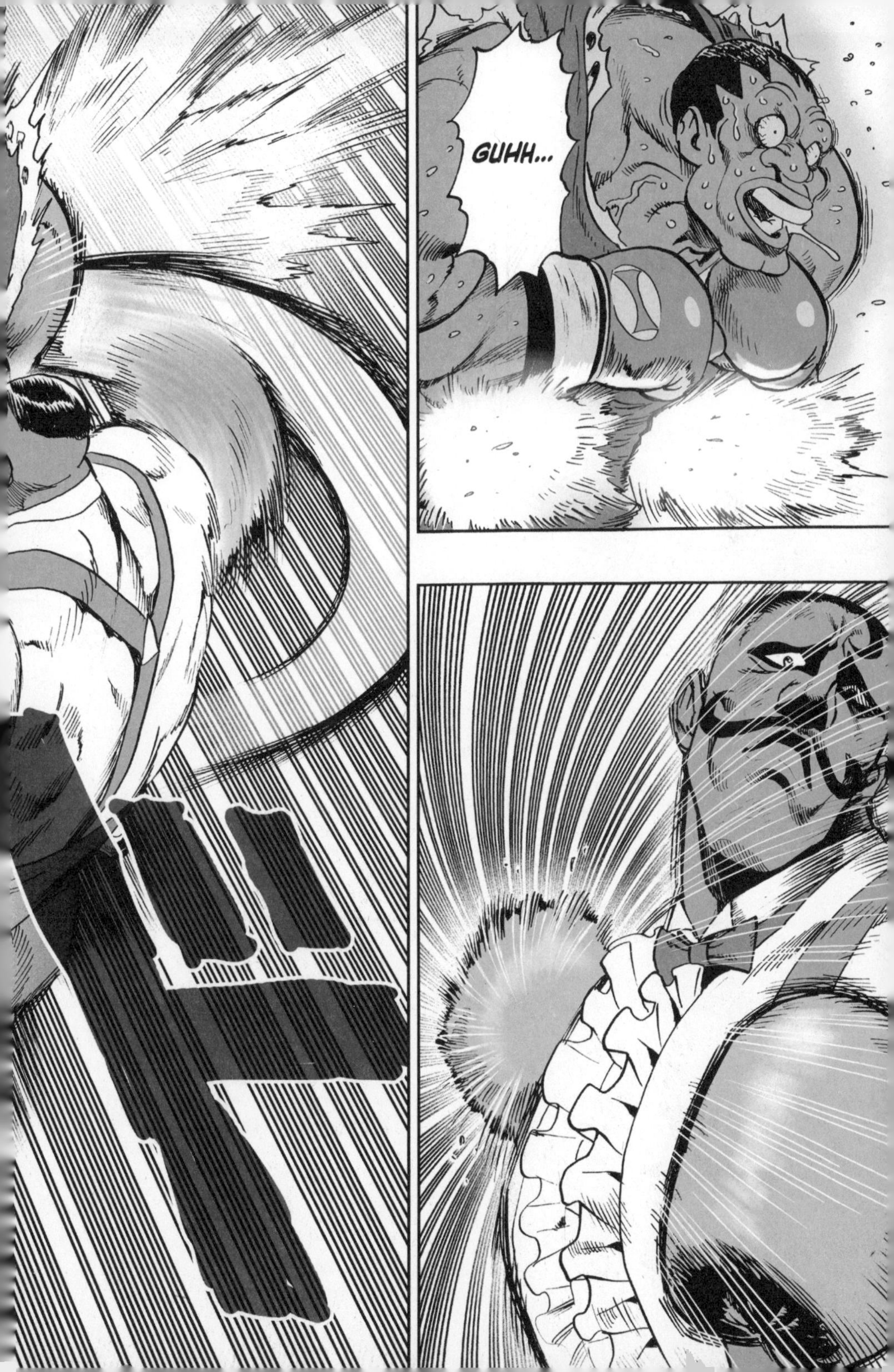
GUHH...

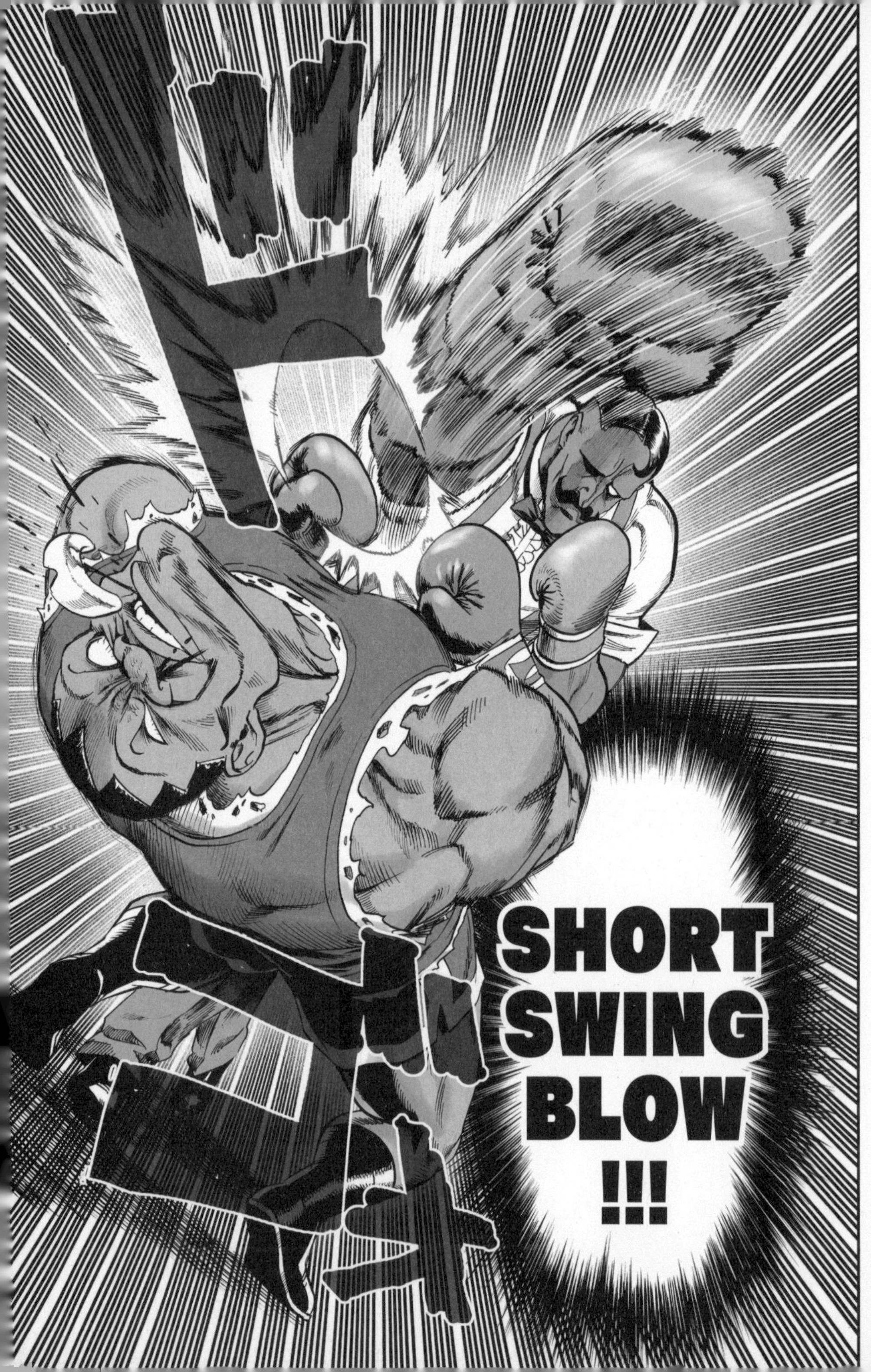
SHORT SWING BLOW !!!

Balrog's torso flew back, and when he could no longer brace his legs against the shock, he fell backwards to the mat. The force of the hit was such that he flipped lengthwise upon falling–heels over head–landing face down and sliding another meter across the surface of the ring.

A perfect knockdown.

In a real bout, the referee would have started the count, but the two fighters were the only witnesses in this case.

Well over ten seconds had passed, and still Balrog didn't stir. Even accounting for his own strength and skill, Dudley couldn't believe he had caused enough damage to KO his opponent. Surely Balrog was lucid by now, so why did he refuse to move?

This was a street fight, so some might take the red boxer's reluctance to stand as him throwing in the towel, but he didn't seem like the type to do that.

"Are you planning to stand anytime soon, by chance?" asked Dudley, leaning against the blue corner. Balrog still lay face down, limbs splayed.

"Kehkehkeh …"

It sounded like he was sobbing.

The guttural noise grew louder, and as the coarseness came back into Balrog's voice, Dudley realized that his opponent wasn't crying. He was snickering.

"And just what is so funny?"

Balrog's shoulders began to shift, but his expression still wasn't visible. He gave no reply but continued laughing.

"Enough of all this nonsense…"

"Bahhahahahahahah!"

As if to cut off the approaching Dudley, Balrog slapped the mat, lifting his torso. His ruined face stared up at the ceiling as flecks of saliva flew from his gaping mouth. He rose slowly, swaying left to right. With his right hand at his nape, he wrenched his head back and forth, producing a bone-cracking series of pops.

"If you are able to stand, then why do you not do so?"

"Hmph."

The laughing finally stopped, and Balrog's face broke into a wide, vulgar smile.

"I demand to know what's so funny!" screamed Dudley, unable to stand the jeering any longer.

"Nothing could be funnier, my man," answered Balrog with tears in his eyes. Ever the embodiment of crassness, he went on with a feverish madness in his voice.

"This is a *brawl*. Not some weak little match that's gonna be decided by a bullshit count to ten."

That was clear enough without Balrog's clarification. Deep in their hearts, both fighters knew it.

Balrog finally stood, and that was enough. Forget a ten count; two or three whole minutes had passed, but that didn't mean he was done. If Balrog could still fight, then the bout would go on.

"What's so *funny* is you knocking me down and heading back to your corner."

The red boxer kicked off the mat as soon as he finished, threatening to close the gap.

Dudley's stance was set.

In the end, this opponent was nothing more than a mad bull. A tactless in-fighter whose direct attacks displayed no breadth of technique.

Dudley's own techniques would be more than enough to overwhelm and defeat him.

He could run his mouth all he liked, but once he was laid flat on the mat, he would know how very *small* a man he was.

Some fools need their lessons taught by a pair of fists.

"Come, then…"

Dudley casually lowered his left arm to dangle in front.

A dropped guard. An invitation.

From Balrog's perspective, this meant that the blue boxer's face was completely undefended.

All the techniques and polish in the world can't strip a person of basic instincts. When an opponent presents unguarded vitals, the impulse to strike at them is almost overwhelming. Even when the move is an obvious ploy, the urge remains.

"Let him come…" spoke the voice inside Dudley as he watched the charging Balrog.

Even in the peek-a-boo stance, a boxer tends to one side or the other when walking and striking. By observing which foot takes on more weight and taking note of minute changes in center of gravity, one can tell which hand is dominant before a single punch is thrown.

Balrog was right-handed without a doubt, so he would be aiming a straight right at Dudley's undefended face. No question about it.

Dudley would invite the straight, sway to dodge, and follow up with a counter.

Balrog was charging.

The driving force from his body alone would be enough to floor an amateur, so the power behind one of his straight punches was likely beyond belief.

However, a counter punch makes use of the opponent's very momentum.

In all martial arts, one is most open to retaliation when attacking. One rarely has the wherewithal to focus on defense when victory seems close at hand, and lashing out with a fist that should be guarding also leaves another body part exposed.

There is no better ambush than a strike that takes advantage of both fighters' forward drive.

The plan was already set in Dudley's mind.

With his face as the bait, he would coax out a straight right from Balrog. He would then sneak a left hook of his own past his opponent's extended elbow, driving it into his jaw from below at a 45-degree angle. That would be more than enough to rattle Balrog's brain, cutting of all thoughts and bloodflow for a quick KO.

The match would be Dudley's, and upon waking, Balrog would know his limits.

Dudley waited calmly.

"Now die!"

The charging bull yanked his right arm as far back as his head and took another step.

It was the most overblown, obvious telegraphing of a straight right that Dudley had ever seen. Balrog must have gone soft in the head to be foreshadowing his attack to this extent, because in the professional world, such a punch would never hit its mark.

Balrog's right foot stomped down onto the mat.

The straight came flying.

Pull back and dodge…

That *was* the plan.

"Hmm?"

When Dudley attempted to curve his back, he found his foot immobilized.

A dull pain, coming from his toes.

For a brief instant, he glanced downward.

A worn boxing shoe was sitting atop his own foot. Balrog was pinning him down.

"That's a violation!" shouted Dudley's mind, but he didn't voice the complaint because, of course, this was no boxing match.

He couldn't move, and the fearsome straight punch was coming.

Guard…

Dudley brought both fists to his chin in a flash.

He braced himself for the hit.

Suddenly, something exploded deep inside his right ear. Then the left.

His head was clamped by a pair of red gloves, and Balrog was saying something with a smile. With his ears covered, though, Dudley couldn't hear a word.

He struggled to break free, but everything suddenly went black. Dudley saw stars.

A splitting pain across his forehead followed by a shockwave that roared through his entire body.

A headbutt.

Another violation he had no business protesting.

The gloves came off Dudley's ears, but the holes still felt covered, almost like the air itself was pressing against them.

Balrog spread his arms and shrugged his shoulders exaggeratedly.

With a twisted smile plastered across his hateful face, the red boxer kept shaking his shoulders in a series of shrugs.

Stars were still dancing across Dudley's vision, and he felt as though his ears were covered in plastic wrap.

It took all he had to find his stance.

Clearly reveling in Dudley's crippled state, Balrog stopped shrugging, struck his own stance, and fire off a straight right.

Direct hit.

The shock of it pierced through Dudley's nose out the back of his head.

Funnily enough, he found himself thinking, "Not a bad punch," as if it were someone else's problem.

There was no telling how many times he spun end over end. When he came to, his back was resting against the pole in the blue corner, having landed in a sitting position by happenstance.

"Even funnier that you ended up *there*, after that dumb shit you pulled earlier."

Balrog's shouting sounded muffled, and it was then that Dudley realized that one of his eardrums must have burst. He wouldn't hear anything at all if it were both, so a muffled sound implied that he had lost his hearing on just one side.

The semicircular canals of the ear are thrown off when an eardrum bursts, causing a loss of balance as well as hearing. Sitting in the blue corner, Dudley still felt as though the world were spinning around him. His very vision jerked about, making it seem like the charging Balrog was flipping and twirling like a circus performer.

He had to stand…

His shaking body needed some encouragement before it dared to lift itself, back pressed against the pole for support. One knee was bent at a right angle. Dudley was nearly half-standing.

Suddenly, his spinning vision was wrenched towards the ceiling.

A hit had knocked his head back.

By the time he had time to reflect, Dudley felt a blow to the left side of his face.

Then the right.

It had been an uppercut followed by a pair of hooks—one, two.

After struggling so hard to find strength, his legs once again failed him.

Knees hit the mat, and he began to crumple.

But Dudley's body didn't complete the fall.

Eyes cast downward, he saw Balrog's left fist driving deep into his stomach, effectively holding his body up and keeping it from collapsing.

"I hate your type the most," came the muffled voice.

Balrog's nose brushed against Dudley's right cheek. His right ear was still working, so that meant it was the left whose eardrum had burst.

Another impact to his stomach sent Dudley's vision spinning anew.

"You rich and powerful guys hold your damn heads so high, thinking you're the chosen ones while looking down on the rest of us. Just looking at you makes me wanna beat you black and blue."

Yet another blow to the gut.

There was no pain; Dudley was well beyond such an earthly sensation. He would die…

Some part of him suddenly realized that.

"I hated you since the first time I saw one of your matches on TV. Whaddya say to that…?"

Dudley felt his head being pulled back, bringing his face to meet Balrog's head-on.

The red boxer was lifting him by the hair.

"But boxing wasn't enough for you. No. You had to go and mess around with street fighting, too."

The right hand grabbing Dudley continued to lift him into the air, while Balrog's left slowly drew back.

"Little rich boy thinks the world is all puppies and rainbows, so he needs a good whupping… Nah, even a whupping's not enough for *you*."

Bloodlust shone in the sickly yellow eyes.

"Die."

Balrog had pulled his left fist as far back as possible, and it now sliced through the air, charting a direct course for Dudley's undefended face.

Natural instinct...

An unconscious reaction...

Tenacity towards life...

Fruits of all that training...

Even Dudley himself wasn't sure of the source of the sudden burst of power.

The right uppercut he threw came from a place beyond logic and thought. Given his suspended state, the punch was powered only from the shoulder down , without any torque from the hips.

Still...

The most dangerous point of any bout is when one believes that victory is at hand.

Dudley's earlier blunder, even, had come just after the moment when he saw his win playing out in his mind.

Now it was Balrog who was convinced. Dudley was on his last legs, and one more punch to his face would end it all.

So the red boxer never saw the reactionary uppercut coming.

Like a bird on the wing, the blue-gloved fist rose through the air almost gently before burying itself into Balrog's solid jaw.

Dudley never heard the dull crunch through his damaged left ear.

His body shook, and the hand supporting his head was gone, sending him crashing to the mat.

He attempted to rise on limp arms.

Only able to bring himself to his knees, Dudley looked up and saw Balrog unceremoniously floored with limbs splayed, once again.

He was unconscious.

Even a light hit to the jaw can be tremendously effective, because jarring the opponent's head like that does far more than any damage from the actual impact. In that sense, the uppercut that Dudley managed to fire off subconsciously had gotten the job done. It didn't have much power behind it, but the simple, natural motion had rocked Balrog's brain.

He likely fell unconscious before he knew what hit him, quite literally.

Dudley was now upright, though the joints throughout his legs shook like they had fallen out of place. It was a wonder he could stand at all.

Had he won?

The blue boxer couldn't be sure.

It was apparent, though, that Balrog couldn't continue the fight.

That *would* imply that it was Dudley's win, but it still didn't feel that way to him.

He took a quivering step towards Balrog.

"Just what did you hope to achieve in coming here?"

From the ankle down, Dudley's foot was suddenly gone.

Concealed under a red glove.

"Y-you bastard…"

Balrog's brain still hadn't recovered from the blow, so his convulsing body couldn't find the strength to lift itself.

Dudley knew that a good stomp to the head from his free foot would knock Balrog unconscious again, giving him no choice but to admit total defeat once he came to.

His right foot was still pinned, so Dudley gave his free left foot enough power to rise slowly. With knee bent, Dudley hovered the leather shoe- still marked with grime where Balrog had tread on it- over the opponent's twitching face.

One swift stomp. That was all it would take.

"Tch…"

A bitter grunt.

He couldn't do it.

Kicking a fallen opponent's head was something Dudley could never forgive himself for. Even if such an act won him the match, it would simultaneously destroy everything he had worked so hard to build.

Hadn't he sworn never to be like his father?

To possess dignity is to wield a will sublime enough to combat the might of reality itself.

A quasi-victory like this would strip Dudley of all dignity. He would be choosing to live as his father did.

That was the one thing he could never do.

Dudley placed his left foot back on the mat just as Balrog summoned the strength to stand.

Both fighters had seen better days at this point.

A bit of white froth emerged from the corner of the red boxer's mouth, and he brought his shaking fists up to guard his jaw.

The peek-a-boo stance.

Dudley struck his own stance.

Balrog was red, and he was ever the blue challenger.

Those blue gloves lit a fire in him like nothing else.

"Let's make this fight fair and aboveboard, shall we?"

"Guess you and me are never gonna see eye-to-eye, huh," replied Balrog with a smile.

But it wasn't the frenzied, bloodthirsty smile of earlier; this one radiated sympathy. Acceptance, even. Whatever it was, the hatred for Dudley was gone from Balrog's face.

"Shall we let our fists do the talking?"

"Just what I wanted to hear."

They two men smiled.

Suddenly, the gong...

Both turned to look outside the ring and spotted a gray-haired old man.

The incomparable Mr. Gotch was smiling.

The fighters faced each other once more.

"Here I come."

"Very well."

Without a hint of cunning, each threw an honest straight right at the other's face.

Their fight had only just begun.

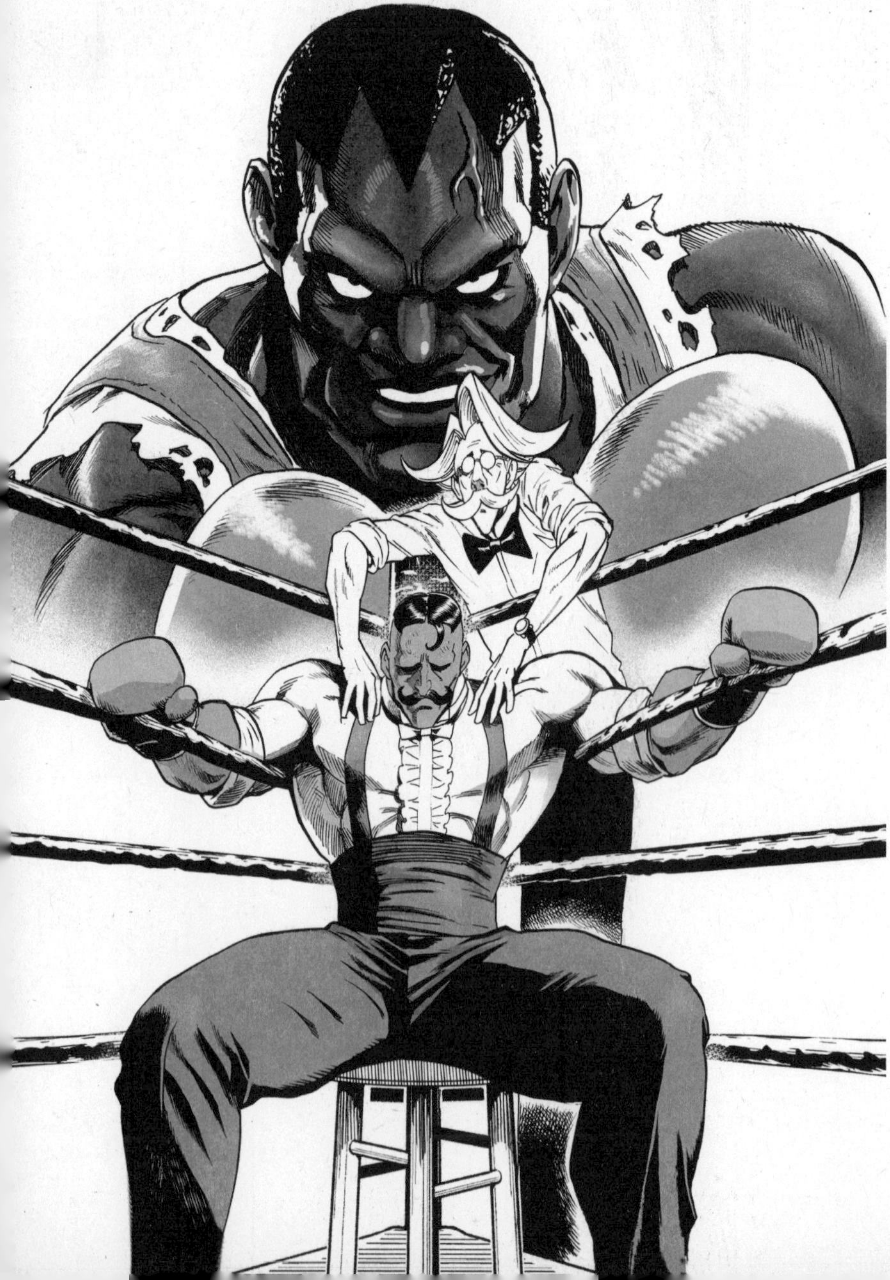

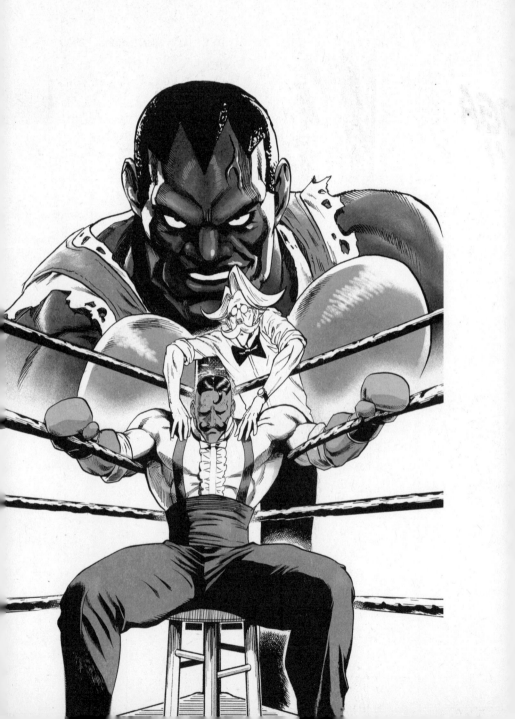

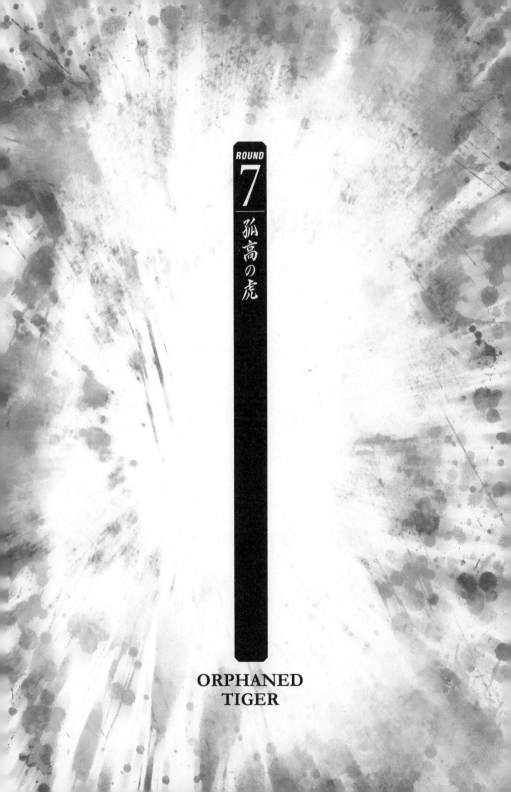

ROUND

7

孤高の虎

ORPHANED
TIGER

ROUND 7

ORPHANED TIGER

The man sat on the opposite side of a polished, jet-black desk. His elbows rested on the surface, and his square jaw sat atop his folded hands. A row of clenched white teeth were just barely visible inside his large mouth, which was curved into a sickle of a smile.

"It's been too long, Sagat."

Every hair on Sagat's body stood on end at the sound of the man's unearthly voice. It rippled with an overwhelming aura of darkness.

In the face of this embodiment of wickedness, Sagat took a deep breath in an attempt to maintain his composure.

"What have you come for this time?"

An enormous pane of glass loomed behind the man, constituting one entire wall of the spacious room. Beyond the window, skyscrapers filled the nightscape. The flickering reds and yellows of the city illuminated the shadowy man from behind.

His crimson military uniform with silver epaulets gave the impression of an imposing commander. The eyes that peered from below the military cap were white and without pupils, though ringed with black and almost blurred by the violet miasma he gave off.

Sagat raised one hand to his own chest, laying it over a darkened scar. A massive one that ran straight from his right collarbone to left flank. In times of intense emotion, it always prickled painfully.

His overall appearance was not one that people typically forgot.

Only his left eye bulged from his face; the right was covered by a black eyepatch.

Sagat opened his mouth–locked into a permanent scowl–and spoke the name his heart was itching to say.

"Ryu…"

The military man's eyes twitched.

"You're after him, right?" asked Sagat.

"So that rumor's found its way to you, then?"

The man removed his chin from his hands and leaned back in his chair. He went on, completely unflustered.

"Yes, a man believed to be Ryu has been slaughtering other fighters across the globe."

"But none of them have actually died, right?"

"That part doesn't concern me. The problem is how he's doing it."

The man looked delighted as he spoke.

"Ryu was always so damn upright. Sincere. Honest. Irreproachable, even. But now he fights like a bloodthirsty beast? He's fallen to some dark magic, no doubt."

Sagat's old wound throbbed at the man's words.

Ryu and magic…?

It was a hard thought to reconcile.

Still, it fit with the unbelievable rumors Sagat had heard.

Someone was roaming the earth, bloodying fighters within an inch of their lives. Someone who resembled Ryu and used Ryu's techniques.

It seemed absurd, but Sagat couldn't help but think there might be some truth to the stories.

"I'm thinking it *wasn't* you who transformed Ryu, right Bison?"

Sagat spoke the man's name, bringing an ominous smile to Bison's face.

This was a man he once considered a kindred soul, but now they walked opposite paths.

"I'm under no obligation to answer you."

Sagat stepped forward with his right foot at Bison's provocation. White bandages wrapped his bare feet and thick calves, and his feet clung to the polished marble floor. The coolness of the stone traveled up his feet and legs, chilling his heart and causing Sagat to grunt in protest.

"No obligation, sure, but I'll still have my answer."

"What's it worth to you?"

Bison pulled away from the chair once more and leaned across the desk.

"What can you offer me for information about Ryu? Will you agree to join my organization and work for me again?"

"That, I refuse."

Shadaloo. That was Bison's organization.

With deep ties to the underworld, it wielded tremendous wealth and authority, which it used to foster all manner of illicit activities worldwide. A terrifying organization powerful enough that its goal of "world conquest" didn't actually seem like a pipe dream. In fact, it was already well within reach.

Sagat used to be an agent of Shadaloo; one prominent enough to be called Bison's right-hand.

It had all started with Ryu...

Sagat was once known as the Emperor of Muay Thai , and he used to boast an unblemished record. His first ever loss had come at the hands of a humble fighter from the Far East , back when Ryu was only just starting out.

The young up-and-comer's head had been filled with big dreams, so Sagat had seen it as his duty to crush the boy, teaching him about the cruelty of life via a painful defeat.

But in the end, Sagat's arrogance had been unable to stand up to Ryu's earnest fist.

Shoryuken...

The name of the technique that had changed Sagat's life. After a mighty blow from Ryu carved the scar across his chest, he had joined Shadaloo in the hopes of strengthening his resolve.

It was his own naïvety that had defeated him...

Sagat had been determined to raise himself to greater heights by steeping himself in darkness, but then it was Ryu, again, who had broken that determination.

Sagat's second loss to Ryu had come during a fighting tournament hosted by Shadaloo itself. The Japanese fighter had gone on to best Bison as well before setting out on his journey once more.

Pride had led to Sagat's first fall; doubt, the second.

He had resolved to reform himself once again. After parting ways with Shadaloo, Sagat had returned the world of Muay Thai, starting from square one.

He had pledged to hone his skills in preparation for his eventual third match against Ryu.

But what now…?

Ryu himself had fallen to darkness, apparently. It was still too hard to believe, so Sagat's doubt had led him to this place.

"Stubborn a bastard as ever, I see," said Bison from a leisurely stance. Sagat remained silent and motionless as the dictator addressed him.

"You demand information about Ryu, yet you refuse to join me. We seem to be at an impasse."

With an air of composure, Bison walked around the large desk, keeping his eyes trained on Sagat.

"Though, judging from your appearance, it doesn't seem you *expected* this to end peacefully."

The keen words slipped from the ever-smiling mouth. It was true; the Sagat that Bison saw through those white eyes was not a peaceful-looking man.

His chest was bare, and his hands and feet were wrapped in layers of white cloth. His only clothing was a pair of blue trunks with red lines running down the sides.

The garb of a Muay Thai fighter.

"A fighter is obstinate by nature. His desires are everything to him, and he seeks them with his fists. That is how he must live. In that sense, I applaud your determination."

Bison bounced his shoulders up and down and stuck a finger under the seam of his collar to loosen it a bit. Now in front of the desk, he crouched down to half-height, right fist to chin and left extended out, looking less soldier, more grappler.

The dictator himself was quite a capable fighter.

A purple aura rose from the red-clad Bison, a sign that he was ready to begin.

Sagat took his stance, too. With most of his weight placed on his right foot, his left heel hovered above the ground in front of him. He placed his fists equidistant from his face in order to protect it. In this low stance, he faced Bison.

"So, was it you who changed Ryu, Bison?"

"Who can say?"

The corners of Bison's already wide smile curled even higher.

"I'll get you to talk, whatever it takes."

"Try me."

Both fighters shot into action.

Bison opened with a full body leap, propelled off the floor by both feet.

Sagat, on the other hand, pulled both arms behind his back.

"Psycho Crusher!"

With right palm extended straight ahead, Bison began spinning through the air. Wreathed in his own fighting aura, he shot towards Sagat like an arrow of light.

"Tiger!"

Sagat's cry came just as he swung both hands around. They formed vacuums where they tore through the air, and when both arms were stretched to the limit in front, their energies combined into a single blade.

The blade left Sagat's hands and hurtled towards the incoming Bison.

Tiger Shot.

Sagat's signature projectile attack.

Just before the moment of impact, Bison stopped spinning and landed.

He almost seemed to smile at the looming Tiger Shot.

Bison leapt straight up, a blur of red.

The Tiger Shot missed its mark, smashing into the black desk before vanishing, but Sagat was already taking aim at the airborne Bison.

The dictator flew straight for Sagat's head, with legs clenched together and arms crossed.

"Hahhhh…"

Sagat exhaled and brought his right fist to his hips.

He dropped low and, like a compressed spring, launched skywards, fist first.

"Tiger Uppercut!"

The attack stretched Sagat's body to its limit.

His bandaged fist flew past the dictator's military boots and red-clad legs as it rose, eventually landing a solid blow to Bison's jaw.

Sagat kept rising.

Bison's descent coupled with Sagat's upwards momentum to make the impact that much fiercer.

Sagat felt it in his fist.

The sensation of the cool marble under his feet returned as he watched Bison curl backwards and fly across the room.

But this opponent wasn't one to be defeated by a single attack.

He kicked off towards the spot where Bison would meet the floor, head first.

Just as the red cap brushed the marble, the dictator shot out both hands and performed a flip to right himself.

Sagat was already in striking distance, though.

He crouched, focusing all his energy in the knee he planned to attack with.

The knee exploded up at an angle.

"Tiger Knee!"

A knee strike aimed at Bison's jaw.

Sagat's agility propelled him through the air, but by the time he realized his attack had missed, Bison had vanished entirely.

Teleportation.

Strictly speaking, Bison wasn't a fighter. Nor a soldier. Nor even human, exactly. Not anymore.

With the considerable finances and influence of Shadaloo at

his command, Bison had made a point of researching all manner of supernatural phenomena. He hadn't shied away from human experimentation and other abuses of science in his quest for power.

One of the fruits of his labor was the so-called "Psycho Power."

It allowed him to transform his own force of will into tangible energy, forming the basis for a system of spirit-based techniques.

That was the extent of Sagat's knowledge of Psycho Power, at any rate. He wasn't sure of the actual science behind any of it, but he suspected it was similar to whatever powered Ryu's Hadoken and other such techniques.

Given that Psycho Power grew stronger based on the user's will, it was unrivaled in the hands of a man as charged and driven as Bison.

Teleportation was just one of the techniques it granted.

The technique, which Bison himself called "warping," allowed him to vanish before reappearing in another location. Sagat had seen the dictator use the move against countless opponents, so it didn't take him by surprise.

Surprised or not, though, he still found himself exposed.

The strength he had poured into the Tiger Knee meant Sagat was still airborne. Even at his quickest, it would still take a second or two before he could react.

There was only one place Bison would choose to reappear.

From behind.

The enemy's presence...

He was coming.

Sagat landed and swung around, but it was too late.

An overly saccharine smile came spinning into view just as something hard struck his nape. The shock traveled down his spine and out through his limbs.

Sagat was thrown to the ground in a heap.

A brown-soled boot stomped down onto his head, and his vision went black.

"Your first defeat by Ryu lost you your title of 'emperor' and drove you to my doorstep. Your second defeat drove you away again. You're hardly destined for greatness, yet still you struggle."

The foot twisted, grinding Sagat's head into the floor.

"You're even weaker than when you first came to me, seeking power in darkness."

The words cut at Sagat with the force of a great axe.

He tried to push himself up, but Bison's foot was unyielding.

Waves of Psycho Power oozed from the sole, permeating Sagat. The evil aura ate away at his skin and stripped him of the energy to push back.

"You've been reduced to such a pitiful state, so I might as well tell you what you want to know. It *wasn't* my Psycho Power that corrupted Ryu."

Sagat breathed a momentary sigh of relief before a new concern struck him.

Bison was a living mass of will. In a sense, Psycho Power itself constituted his very being. As long as he had a new body to transfer his soul to, he could revive himself time and time again.

The stronger the vessel, the better, so Bison had had his eye on Ryu for a while. That was the reason for his current search.

But if Ryu hadn't fallen to Psycho Power, then what had changed him?

Sagat prayed it wasn't a force from within Ryu himself.

"His school has long concerned itself with a wicked power that they call the 'Dark Hado.'"

"The Dark Hado…"

"Indeed."

Despite Sagat's efforts to stand, Bison's foot wouldn't budge. He continued to struggle as he focused on the dictator's explanation.

"The one who slaughtered Ryu's master is well-versed in the Dark Hado. That same man led Ryu down this terrible path."

"Akuma?"

"Oh? So you know the name."

The would-be Ryu's recent heinous acts reminded Sagat of another series of incidents, years ago.

Akuma.

All anyone knew was that the man was Japanese and that he would show no remorse when it came to the opponents he beat bloody.

"Ryu gained the Dark Hado himself through his battle with Akuma, elevating him to new heights as a fighter."

Pain ran across Sagat's chest.

Not the pain from Bison's attack, which had long since faded, but a deeper pain within his scar.

Pulsing blood rushed to his chest. The wound closed up long ago, but sometimes it felt to Sagat as if the jagged scar would burst open in a torrent of blood.

It was anger that caused it.

When Bison explained how the awakened bloodlust in Ryu made him a stronger fighter, Sagat became enraged. He had clung to a certain, precious notion ever since Ryu beat him, but even that was sullied, now, and it fanned the flames of anger within him.

"After all is said and done, the art of fighting is all about harming the opponent. Once that first punch flies, all your platitudes and high-mindedness become so much hot air. Now that he's realized that inevitable truth, Ryu is that much closer to true strength. Indeed, he's been the one spilling the blood of so many fighters across the globe. The Dark Hado compels him."

"But he still hasn't killed anyone."

"So what?"

Bison's foot rose for a moment before stomping down on Sagat's head again.

"Whether he kills or not is inconsequential. Far more important is the sheer power he's exhibiting."

The heat building in Sagat's old scar began spreading to the rest of his body. Unwilling to be contained, the rage began to vibrate through his very skin.

Vision still clouded in darkness, a hazy figure came into view and steadily grew more distinct.

An East Asian man with a red headband...

Beneath thick, raven-black eyebrows lay a pair of eyes burning with wisdom. His clenched mouth radiated integrity and firmness.

Ryu.

The one fighter Sagat respected.

"I thought our fight actually meant something."

Sagat shouted at the phantom floating in darkness. He recalled the time they had squared off, all in the pursuit of strength.

His own arrogance had caused him to lose his first fight against Ryu, and it was doubt that led to his second defeat.

Both of those losses he could accept.

Sagat had lost to Ryu as a man. As a human being.

That was why, all the more…

Ryu *had* to keep walking the path of strength ahead of Sagat, so that when the day of their third bout finally arrived, Sagat could claim true victory. All of his life had been leading to that eventual day.

"Unforgivable."

His thoughts emerged as a single word, and his body was suddenly rising of its own accord.

The Psycho Power might have stripped Sagat's strength away, but it couldn't overcome the sudden burst of life-force that exploded from deep within. Slowly but surely, his body began fighting back against Bison's foot.

"Give up. Surrender to my might, Sagat."

"No way in hell."

Bison replied with a swift kick to the face, the force of which lifted Sagat off the ground. He found himself kneeling before Bison.

"Then you will die."

The dictator thrust out an open palm that seemed to grasp the air itself and aimed it at Sagat's face. His arm began to glow faintly from the silver gauntlet down.

A ball of purple light flickered to life in the open palm and shot towards Sagat.

He crossed his own bandaged arms in front of his face just in time for the ball to strike them with a low-pitched crackle.

His arms went numb, but there was no time to worry about that.

Sagat rose immediately and used his upward momentum to lash out with his right leg.

The kick connected with the left half of Bison's face, distorting it. His expression remained frozen in a grin, adding to the eeriness of the sudden warping.

Face separated from foot as the red-clad dictator's body went tumbling to the polished marble. Near the end of his slide across the floor, Bison slapped his hands down and popped up, looking completely undamaged.

But Sagat was close behind, having rushed to close the gap. He had the now standing Bison in his sights.

Sagat was about a head taller than his opponent, which allowed him to aim a right elbow strike at Bison's crown.

In Muay Thai, elbows become blades. A direct hit from one will quite literally slice through flesh.

In a forward lean, Bison twisted his torso to dodge.

Quick reflexes.

Sagat had to give the man credit for that.

But the next round was already loaded in the chamber.

With his right elbow still extended, Sagat wrenched around, driving his left fist into an uppercut aimed at Bison's flank.

Direct hit.

The dictator stopped moving, but only for a moment.

Sagat's wealth of experience translated to instincts, and those instincts told him to keep going.

This was no time to let up.

He drove a right hook into the opponent's stiffened face. The blow rocked Bison's entire body to the left.

Next, a left elbow strike.

Not even Bison was able to maintain that grin anymore. Not with blood pouring from a fresh laceration on his right cheek. This hit forced his head to whip back to the right.

Sagat flew into a Tiger Knee that buried itself in Bison's undefended jaw.

Not even the mighty Bison could stay standing after such a barrage. Yet...

He didn't fall.

Even with the knee driving into his jaw and threatening to topple him, Bison braced his legs. Still close enough to reach out and touch the opponent, Sagat was ensuring his own safe landing when he noticed the crooked smile return.

"You underestimate me, Sagat."

Purple flames blazed in those white eyes.

As Bison whipped his torso back up, his hand shot out to grab Sagat's head. The dictator dipped low and transitioned into a fastball pitch, with Sagat as the ball.

The thrown Sagat smashed into the desk and chair, but his momentum didn't let him stop there.

The piercing sound of shattering glass echoed through the room.

He was falling...

Sagat threw his right hand out to save himself, but it landed on the windowsill, which still retained pieces of the broken window. Sharp pain as the shards drove into his open palm.

"How unsightly."

Bison looked down from the window at the dangling Sagat.

"It's almost as if this predicament represents your sorry state in life."

A boot came down on Sagat's wounded hand. He pushed past the incredible pain and grabbed the sill with his left. The boot's heel ground his right deeper into the glass, each press sending waves of agony to his brain.

"You've lost the fight, but still you refuse to die. Even when reduced to a pitiful mess, you insist on living. The simple act of letting go would bring you peace, so why endure the pain? What meaning does your life hold should you live to see tomorrow? You're nothing but a whipped dog. A pitiful fool, neither righteous nor wicked. Death is all that remains for a dethroned emperor, so this pathetic determination to live shames you. The day you lost to Ryu was the day you should've died."

Maybe Bison was right.

During his days as the Emperor of Muay Thai, Sagat had known neither doubt nor hesitation.

He would defeat all challengers, ever victorious.

His faith in himself had been unshakable.

Opponents would fall precisely as he had willed them to. Not even the gods could experience what that had felt like. Sagat had truly believed that he was born to become an emperor.

But then…

It had all crumbled away when Ryu showed up.

"It was just a single loss," people would say, but Sagat knew that his fight with Ryu couldn't be summed up in such trivial terms.

The loss hadn't crippled him physically or merely broken his will. He had lost *as a person*.

It was a matter of Sagat's essence. His very being.

What had he even been, before that point?

He had suddenly felt ashamed of lording his "emperor" title over others for so long. Ryu led a simple life, seeking strength for strength's sake, unconcerned with recognition, status, or glory. It had all left a deep impression on Sagat; an impression that turned to self-directed fury.

His admiration of what Ryu stood for had been an implicit rejection of his own lifestyle until that point. A rejection of Sagat the emperor, who had reigned.

Maybe he really should have died back then.

What was the value in the life he had led since then?

Nothing.

Sagat had existed in the darkness since that day.

When he had become Bison's confidante as an agent of Shadaloo, and even when his rematch with Ryu had spurred him to return to Muay Thai, Sagat had lived behind a shadowy veil, ever lost.

Was he truly strong?

What constitutes strength?

What could he do to reach the plane that Ryu existed on?

The more he had trained over the passing years, the darker and more unclear his path had grown.

What even kept him going?

Sagat hadn't come up with any definite answers, but Ryu had always been at the center of whatever it was he pursued.

And now that same Ryu was consumed by bloodlust.

"Nonsense," thought Sagat to himself.

How could something so hackneyed as "bloodlust" be part of his ultimate goal?

Did this mean that even the great Ryu couldn't run from the darkness forever?

Did seeking the strong necessarily mean walking a path of shadows?

"No, wrong…"

The words escaped Sagat's mouth before he realized it. With his foot still on Sagat's hand, Bison opened his right eye a little wider.

"Wrong? What's 'wrong'? No. Death is indeed all that awaits you."

"I have to live."

As he spoke, Sagat filled his arms with the strength to lift himself.

A raindrop hit his face, turned up towards Bison.

Then another, and another, falling from the heavens. The rain began to pound as Sagat slowly pushed himself up.

"Enough of this pathetic charade, Sagat!"

Sagat's head emerged over the windowsill, but Bison leaned forward with a swift kick to the face.

The wounded right hand was finally free. With splinters of glass still embedded in the palm, Sagat reached out for the ankle of Bison's offending foot. The move clearly rocked the dictator's footing, but he was far too well-trained to let himself go tumbling out the window. He pulled the leg back into the safety of the room, ignoring the grasping hand. Now it was the other foot that kicked Sagat in the face.

He could do nothing to defend.

A fountain of blood burst from Sagat's nose, but still he focused on raising himself.

"There can be no comebacks for a fallen emperor! Death is the only path for the feeble tiger who's lost his fangs! So allow me to send you to your grave, Sagat!"

"I'm not about to be killed by the likes of you…"

Sagat crawled into the room, ignoring Bison's kicks. It took all his strength to drag himself onto the marble floor and pull his legs past the threshold.

"Tch!" clucked Bison's tongue.

Sagat was finally back on solid ground, now in a low crouch.

The dictator wore an expression of pure resentment, and he swung out with a mid-kick in the hopes of lopping his opponent's head clean off his shoulders.

Sagat raised his right arm to defend.

The kick sunk into his upper arm, and the force of it dislodged several shards of glass from his hand. They scratched his cheek, causing minor pain, and the accompanying flecks of blood dyed his eyepatch red.

"A mere dog who doesn't know when he's beat."

Bison's insult came as Sagat started to rise.

The dictator's boot somehow clung to Sagat's right arm, so the entire leg rose along with him.

"I have to live…"

At hearing the determination in Sagat's voice, Bison's smile gave a small spasm.

"Maybe I really should've died the day I lost to Ryu. But I'm still alive. Why?"

"How should I know?"

"So I could lose my way."

Sagat shoved the kicking leg away from his right and swung out with the kinked elbow of his left.

Bison dodged backwards just as the elbow swept through the air where his face had just been.

"No matter how dark my path is, it's all about what lies *beyond* that doubt…"

A straight right. The dictator crossed his arms in front to defend.

"I know I'll find my answer. But…"

The force of the punch pushed Bison back ever so slightly, and Sagat claimed the territory for himself.

He stepped forward into a crouch and drew his left fist down to his hip.

"Mark my words—it won't be the answer you and Akuma found!"

He flew.

Bison's guard dropped for an instant, but when he realized what was coming, he scrambled to defend again.

It was too late, and Sagat knew it.

The fist threaded the needle between the formerly crossed arms.

Like a tiger with wings, Sagat's body and heart soared.

The thrusting fist met Bison's jaw, but there was no recoil.

So perfect was the hit that the apparent lack of feedback made Sagat wonder if he had connected at all.

The sight of Bison now reminded him of the first time he had taken a Shoryuken from Ryu. The attack that had given Sagat the scar across his chest.

Perhaps he had been reborn that day. Blinded and controlled by pride, he had lost sight of the quest for greatness, so it was no wonder that Ryu's honest attack had broken him.

But what had he become?

A troubled man.

And maybe that was just fine…

Maybe there was no such thing as "true strength"…

It could all just be a fantasy.

But Sagat would continue his journey, even if the destination were unattainable.

It didn't have to end in darkness. Not necessarily.

No one can say what the future holds, so it's human nature to be troubled by such things.

Searching for some formless answer that might not exist could very well amount to a life worth living.

Doubt and confusion were inseparable from the search for true strength.

None of it was to be feared.

Sagat believed his answer lay ahead in the darkness, so he would keep walking that path as long as he lived.

His body—with left fist piercing the heavens—seemed to hang in the air unnaturally. Meanwhile, Bison flew slowly with limbs dangling. Sagat felt a strange sensation, as though time itself were dilating.

The stretched moment began to return to the normal flow.

Sagat's seemingly weightless body suddenly felt burdened by heavy flesh and bone until the moment gravity took over and sent him plummeting to the floor at an astounding speed.

He landed.

Across the room, Bison fell head first, smacking to the ground face up like a broomstick knocked over.

Sagat didn't let down his guard.

This particular opponent was a demon whose abilities surpassed those of ordinary humans. One tenacious enough to get back up even after such a fierce attack.

One step forward with a braced right leg sent a stabbing pain racing through the sole of Sagat's foot, up his body, as if from hundreds of needles.

"Urghh."

He ignored his own grunt of anguish and stepped with his left foot. More sharp pain.

Every step he took was agony.

His body begged for relief, but that wasn't in the cards.

He began to run, shutting out the cries of agony from his wounded flesh.

Sagat had to keep walking; like the eternal doubt, this fresh pain was just another bitter pill to swallow.

A weak, selfish part of him wanted to stop, but he knew that beyond the torment lay a new self waiting to be discovered.

The Sagat of today would overcome the Sagat of the past, and the man he woke up as the next day would go even farther.

Each painful step was a guidepost for that future self.

Sagat himself wasn't the enemy.

No, the enemy was right before his eyes!

He locked onto Bison, who was now moving to stand.

The dictator was smiling...

"*Still* you continue this pointless struggle."

Daring words from that crescent grin. Sagat cleared his mind to drown out the taunt and kept running.

"Ahhhh!"

His right foot fell in the gap between him and Bison, and his left was already off the ground.

A middle kick ...

Bison rushed in to meet the attack by guarding leisurely with his right knee, as if to show how unthreatened he was.

Just as planned.

The feigned middle kick was strategic groundwork in order to close the gap. The left leg Bison was guarding against didn't kick at all, but instead stomped down, bringing Sagat within point-blank range.

"Fsshh!"

A clipped puff of breath escaped Sagat's downturned mouth.

With a pair of bent elbows, he began to strike the dictator.

One hit wasn't enough.

In the style of boxing's one two punch, he delivered a barrage of elbow strikes from either side, with each blow coming as soon as the last finished.

Bison was quick to sense the incoming attacks, but the arms he raised high to guard didn't last long. The violent assault beat the dictator's defense down until the path to his head was clear.

"Grahh, arghh, oof ..."

Each hit elicited a gasp from Bison.

Not enough. Still not enough...

Sagat would beat the air out of Bison until his lungs were empty.

"Lowly insect... Make light of me, will you?"

Bison's tone was unlike any Sagat had ever heard. Full of overwhelming doom. Suddenly, his elbow struck air.

More warping.

He whipped around, but the dictator was nowhere to be seen.

Where had he gone?

Something heavy crashed down on Sagat's crown.

A military boot…

Bison stood over the fallen Sagat.

"Kneel before the might of Psycho Power!" roared the dictator as he shot out his left arm at Sagat's head.

That terrifying grip and brutish strength.

In the blink of an eye, Sagat's massive body was dangling in the air. Bison laid into his stomach with a solid punch.

The purple haze of the Psycho Power radiated out across Sagat's entire body, draining him of his very will to fight. After ravaging him, the violet flames returned to coil around Bison's right arm.

The arm–still buried in Sagat's gut–kept shining. Bison's smiling face also glowed eerily beneath the brim of his cap.

"Weak… So very weak!" bellowed the dictator.

Psycho Power continued to swirl about Sagat's stomach before penetrating his body and emerging out his back. The purple torrent exploded like a spray of blood but soon dissipated in the air.

Bison's hand released Sagat, and he fell. First to his knees, then face to floor.

"Try as you might, you have no hope," came the voice from above.

"Can't let it end like this…"

Both of Sagat's arms hit the floor to lift him.

"Still, you refuse to see how hopeless you are!"

Bison swung a sweeping kick at Sagat's head, as if it were a soccer ball.

It only hit air.

Sagat stood as he dodged. He brought both fists equidistant from his face and pushed his left foot forward, heel barely off the ground. Sensing his opponent's breathing, he found his own internal rhythm and aligned his own labored breathing with the bobbing of his shoulders. This was a stance he had been performing since before he could remember. It came as naturally as breathing to Sagat.

Yes…

Now he remembered.

He remembered who he had been before the days of "Emperor" Sagat. Back when his only, pure desire had been to grow stronger. The days when money, glory, and status had meant nothing compared to the pursuit of strength. *That* was Sagat's true essence.

The notion of Emperor Sagat was the warped illusion…

He wasn't "lost" now; the only time he had been lost was when he had lorded his achievements over others. In his younger days, Sagat had known that strength could be found through constant questioning. He had lost his way with age.

But his true self was no different than Ryu.

He had found himself again…

All was suddenly clear, and Sagat had never felt so pure.

What was strength?

It was continuing to doubt.

Those who march ever forward without fear of regret are the strong.

"Come on, then!"

Sagat's voice was finally free of hesitation, and the sound of it gave Bison pause for a moment.

"It will always end the same way."

With that, the dictator thrust an arm out, sending an orb of purple light at Sagat.

"Tiger!"

Both of Sagat's arms shot forward.

Blade of air met ball of light midway between the fighters, producing a dazzling explosion.

Sagat moved in.

So did Bison.

They clashed right where their projectiles had collided just a moment ago.

Bison blocked Sagat's high kick with his right arm, while Sagat caught the dictator's spearlike thrust in his own right hand.

They glared at each other, locked in place.

"I feel hesitation in your kick."

"I'm not lost anymore. What you're feeling is your own fear, Bison."

"Silence suits you better. Such bizarre reasoning will only get you hurt."

The spear hand grew heavy with power, threatening to break free of the hand holding it back.

Sagat responded by pressing harder with his kicking leg. Bison's right arm began to quiver as the extended shin inched towards his face.

Both attacks had already been blocked, so neither would amount to much even if pushed through by sheer force at this point. Still, whoever retreated now would be late to the next exchange, so pulling back wasn't an option.

A perfect stalemate.

"It seems that nothing but fools fill the ranks of you so-called fighters…"

Bison's fingertips brushed Sagat's forehead.

"Maybe we just believe that anything's possible as long as we keep moving forward."

Sagat's shin drove into the dictator's grim face just as the spear hand tore through flesh. Blood oozed from his forehead and dripped down his nose. Another stream flowed over his left eyelid, clouding his only good eye with a layer of red.

A single blink and shake of the head.

Over in an instant, but…

Not missing a beat, Bison took action.

The hand that had blocked the kick burst towards Sagat's neck.

Setup for a throw.

Predictable.

Blinking to clear his eye of the blood hadn't been mere reflex but a calculated invitation.

One performed with the knowledge that Bison couldn't help but take the bait.

The dictator was looking down on Sagat and other true fighters like him, believing them to be nothing but charging brutes incapable of strategy. Bison's eyes could see through any move so long as he was calm and collected, but in the heat of a death match, things would start to unwind.

He couldn't imagine that Sagat would feint.

This particular battle had long since made Bison lose his cool, so the prejudices deep in his heart took over, skewing his judgment.

Having fallen for the tactic, he moved into position for a throw, but the hand that shot out to grab Sagat's neck found only air. Sagat was, of course, crouching.

"Tiger..."

The word was tinged with the ki emerging from the pit of his stomach.

Sagat flew, knee first.

A direct hit to Bison's face, but it wasn't over yet.

No sooner had Sagat landed than he unleashed a full-body uppercut.

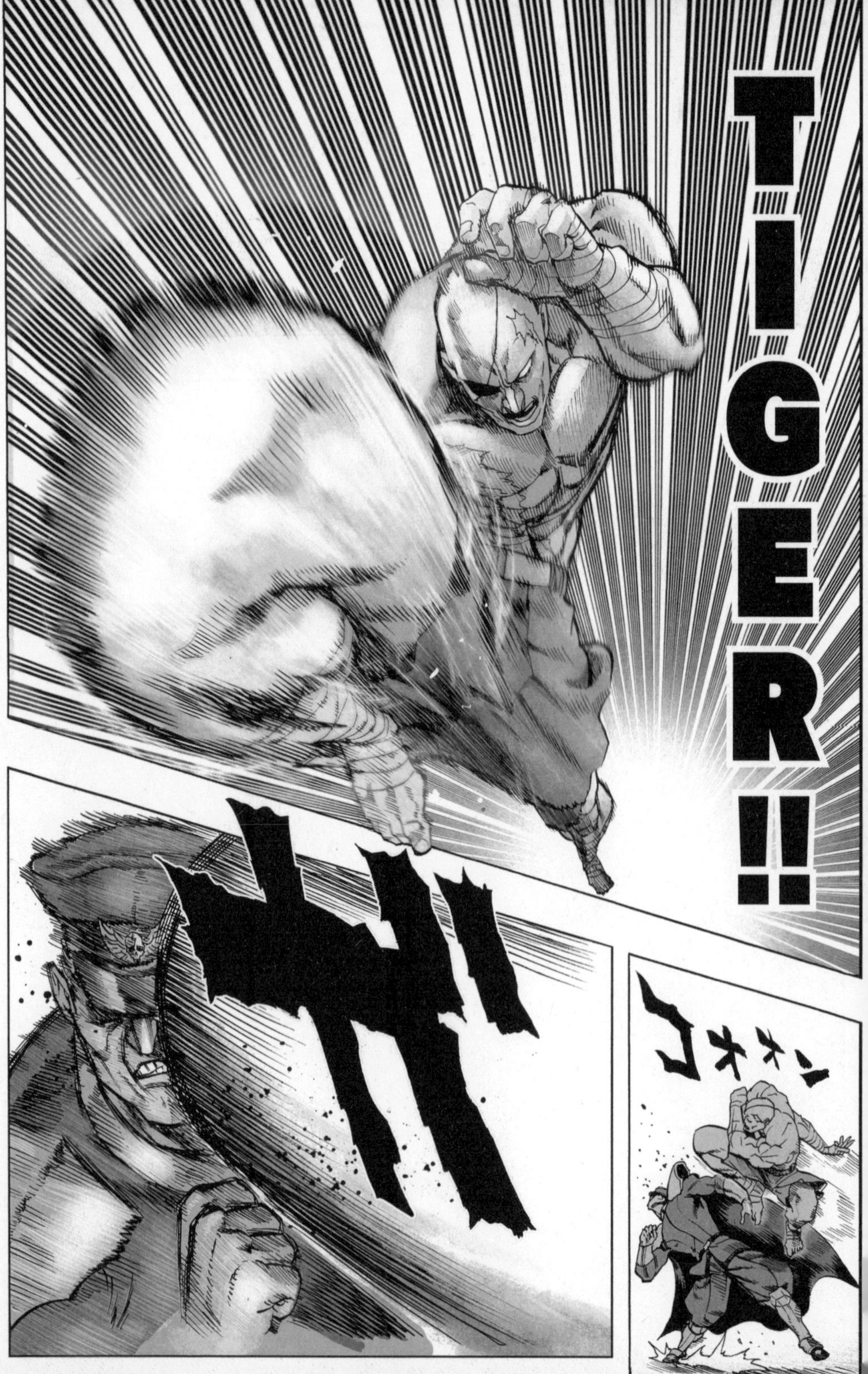
TIGER!!
ガッ
コオオン

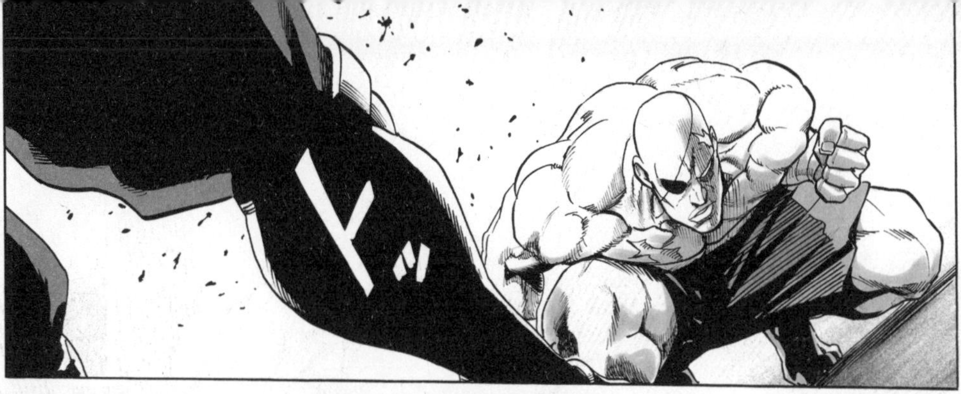
ドッ
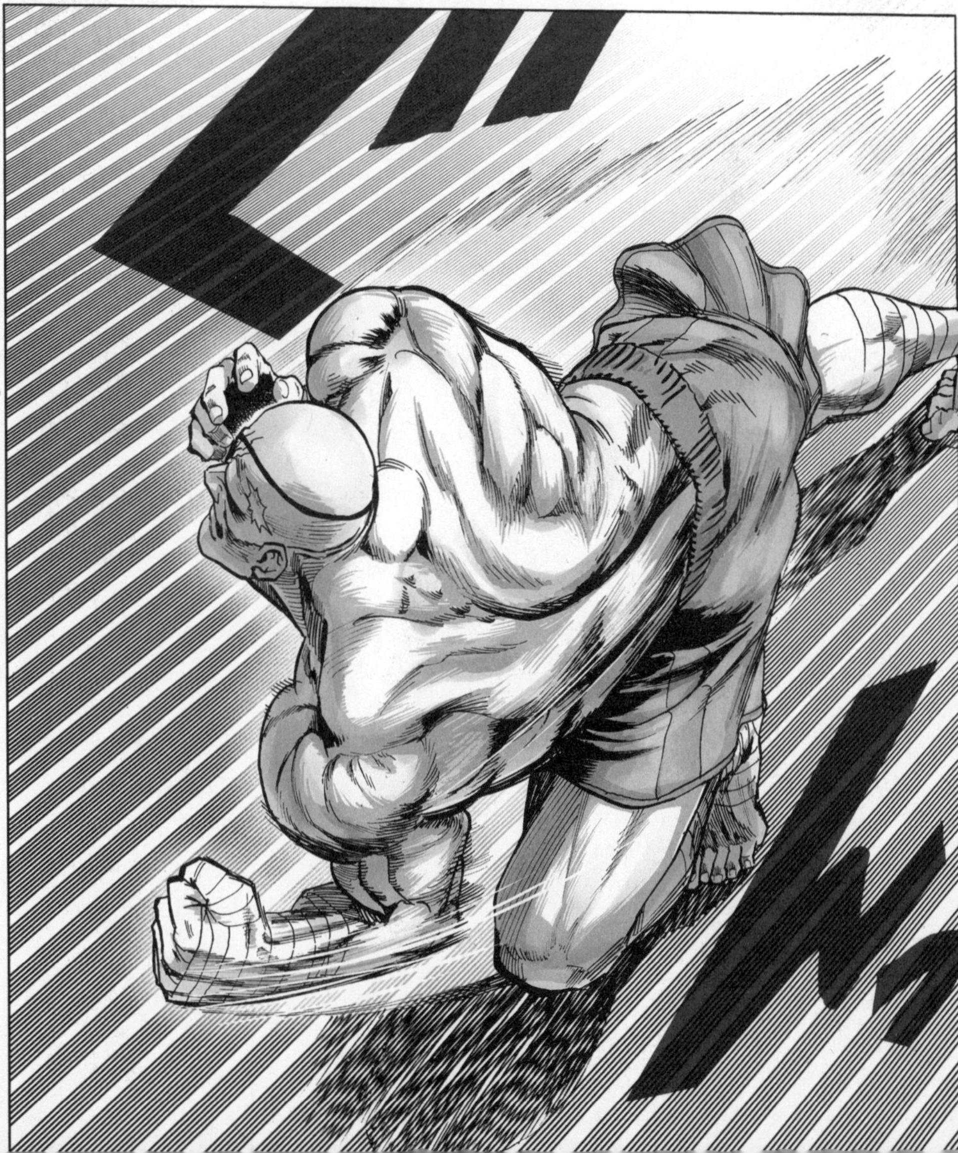

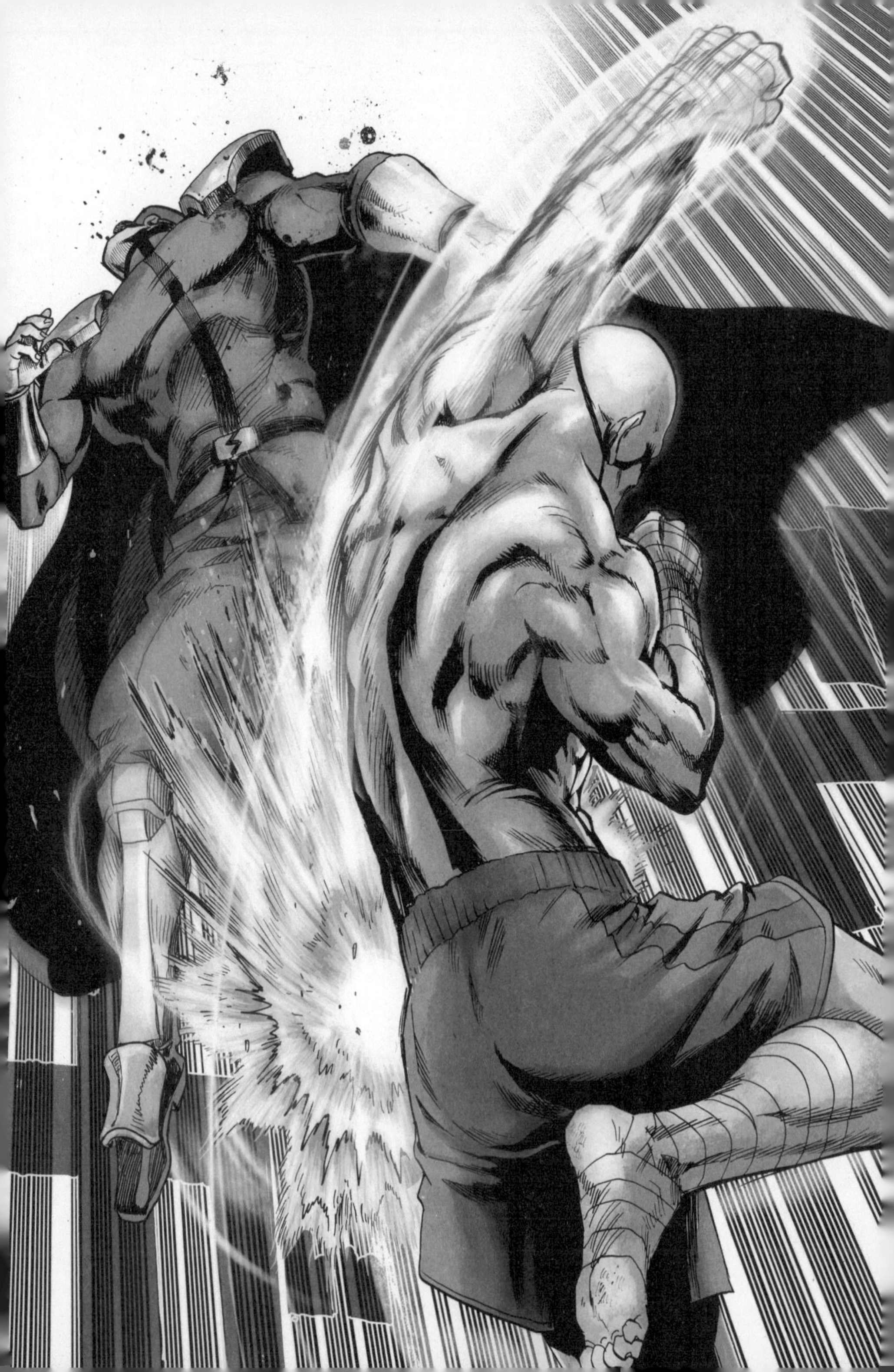

Bison sailed through the air, and Sagat followed.

Another uppercut–this one to the splayed Bison's spine.

A gust blew in from the shattered window.

Wind coiled around Sagat's soaring fist and roared like a ferocious tiger.

The attack pierced Bison's back, threatening to snap him in two at the waist.

Sagat kept rising.

Purple haze seeped from the military outfit. It didn't wrap around Bison like earlier but was rather swept away by the violent wind before vanishing.

"Gahhhhhh…"

Sagat's fist separated from the howling Bison, and he began to descend.

Once safely standing on the marble, he raised his gaze to the opponent, who was now floating in the air.

The demonic cry of anguish continued.

Bison's limbs writhed and shook, and he seemed to be muttering something in his delirium. This went on for a good while until his anguish appeared to abate and he found his composure. Still hovering in mid-air, Bison crossed his arms, brought his legs together, and stared down at Sagat with a pale gaze drained of all blood. His very musculature seemed to have withered away.

Sagat wondered if the dictator was finally drained of all Psycho Power.

"Hard to believe it would be *you* who pushed me this far."

Still floating, Bison drifted towards the broken window.

Sagat remained silent, staring, but didn't pursue.

"You seemed to come unbound partway through our bout. What changed?"

"I found the way I had lost."

"What a very Zen answer…"

Bison smiled before hovering out the window, past the edge of the building.

"I find myself wanting you once more."

"I'll never kneel to you again."

"Join me at Shadaloo, Sagat."

"No way."

No hesitation.

The corners of Bison's mouth rose eerily into a wry smile. Rain pelted his shriveled body, and the red of his outfit grew faint. His pallid face seemed to melt into the array of skyscrapers.

"What about Ryu!?"

"Like I said, my organization had no hand in that. He fell to evil all on his own."

"Bison!"

"Should you ever hear the call of darkness again, come to me. I'll be waiting, as long as it takes."

The wicked smile faded into the dark, and Bison's very presence vanished.

A rush of footsteps from behind.

The heavy double doors slammed open as a squad of armed men flooded the room to surround Sagat.

"You won't be leaving this place alive, Sagat!"

The men raised their weapons.

Glaring at the enemy, Sagat kept his calm and spoke.

"I can't be stopped here, of all places. Sorry, but I won't be holding back."

"Fire!" screamed the man in command.

"Tiger!"

The vacuum blade flew from Sagat's fists, and he dashed into the hail of bullets.

Oblivion…

Leaping towards his moment of death, Sagat kept the image of Ryu in his heart.

ROUND

8

邂逅と覚醒

ENCOUNTER
AND AWAKENING

ROUND 8

ENCOUNTER
AND AWAKENING

T he presence grew stronger.
  With each passing moment, it became harder to breath.
The Dark Hado….
How long had it been since he last felt it? Back during the battle
against his younger brother, he supposed.
  That brother probably assumed he was dead. It had certainly seemed
that way.
  He felt ashamed that he now lived; what right did he have to survive?
The presence was almost upon him.
A familiar aura.
His old disciple.

"Ryu…"
Gouken spoke the name with eyes shut. The moonlight streaming in
from the torn roof fell on his eyelids, clouding his darkened vision with
a haze of white.
  A full moon. The perfect sort of night for a bout.
"Hohh…"
With a great exhale, he slowly opened his eyes. The pair of Deva
king statues towering over him on either side glared down, their forms
brimming with apparent power.
  Not a single priest remained in the ruined Buddhist temple where
Gouken now sat. His legs were crossed, and his hands formed the

meditation ring of Mahavairocana. Both palms faced upward, right atop left, with the tips of each thumb just barely touching the other.

A *zazen* pose.

But Gouken was no student of Buddhism. Though he wore a black robe draped over one shoulder in the style of a monk's *kasaya*, it was no holy garb.

That said, he was of the opinion that Buddhism had plenty to teach. Why do we live?

Humans are inherently born with 108 polluting *klesha*, and they experience myriad sufferings according to their *karma*. It could be said that one central focus of Buddhism is concerned with severing those klesha and overcoming one's karma.

Gouken had developed his own fighting style out of ancient assassination techniques. He had transformed the art of murder into a means of respecting others through combat.

Still, the fundamental goal of any fight is to harm another.

If one were to err, a fight could end in death.

Assassination techniques meant to kill were more than effective enough in battle and, if used in their original form, would render the average opponent utterly helpless.

Unsurprisingly, the opponent would most likely die.

That did not sit well with Gouken, as he believed that crossing fists with another could lead to mutual understanding.

Could those killing techniques somehow leave the opponent alive? In Gouken's mind, this question mirrored the one posited by Buddhism, about whether or not a person could overcome their inherent karma and klesha.

Hence his fondness for Buddhism.

Life and death.

Salvation and sin.

Enlightenment and earthly desires.

Yin and Yang.

All of creation is balanced around two extremes, so humans, who exist in the interstice, must endure all manner of troubles and anguish.

Both light and dark exist within the heart of every man and woman. Should one attribute grow stronger, the other will follow suit.

Gouken's school of fighting and the killing techniques that inspired it represented yet another reflection of the two poles governing creation.

"So you've come…"

The wooden door at Gouken's back—already rotting off its hinges—burst open, never to close again. Though the master felt a sinister aura approaching from behind, he didn't turn but only waited for the presence to reveal itself.

"Who's there?" came a muffled voice.

No reply from Gouken as he continued to focus on the aura.

It was the Dark Hado, without a doubt. A fearsome bloodlust at least as intense as Akuma's own.

"Answer me. Who are you?"

The source of the voice and aura stepped foot into the temple. The already-cracking floorboards of the ruined structure groaned under the heavy stomp.

"Have you already forgotten your own master?"

Gouken lifted his bulk off the floor but still didn't turn.

"My 'master'…?" the voice queried.

The Dark Hado shot from the man's body with a hiss.

"It has been too long, Ryu," said Gouken as he spun, settling his gaze on his disciple.

Ryu's dougi hung in tatters, exposing a crater in his chest that pulsed in time with his heartbeat. His gloves were stained dusky red by the blood of his foes, and loose threads emerged from a series of rips and tears. Black hair stood on end, held up by a headband beneath which a pair of eyes glowed red. From his clenched mouth poked a pair of sharp, beastly fangs.

"What a terrible form you've taken," said Gouken, pained by his disciple's shocking transformation.

Ryu wasn't listening.

He stood near the center of the main hall, leaning forward slightly with right hand raised to the caldera of a wound on his chest.

"Who did that to you?"

Gouken already knew the answer.

Akuma.

In order to awaken the bloodlust within Ryu, the demon had pierced his chest and imbued Ryu with a taste of his own Dark Hado.

"A-are you Gouken?"

Without answering Gouken's, Ryu replied with a question of his own. The master couldn't help but sigh at his disciple's lack of manners.

"You're supposed to be dead."

Ryu was right.

When Akuma had awakened to the Dark Hado and perfected his killing techniques, Gouken had put his life on the line to stop his brother. Their fierce battle had nearly broken Akuma, but in the end it had been the elder brother's loss.

Strictly speaking, Gouken *had* died. His heart had stopped.

Several months had passed before he regained consciousness, and he had found himself in an unfamiliar land, being cared for by strangers.

Gouken couldn't say whether he had been carried by the flow of the river or perhaps by a pack of animals, but he had found himself far away from the battle site.

That was when he had vanished from Ryu's life, having taught both his disciples everything he thought they needed to know. Going forward, it would be on them to polish their skills.

Ryu and Ken.

Akuma had ripped Gouken away, leaving them unsure of their master's fate.

And Gouken had believed that to be just as well, until recently.

Until the rumors about Ryu had reached him…

"If either of you were to lose his way, I imagined it would be you."

Ken had a natural brightness to him. Never the type to brood or become obsessive, he would seek broad knowledge with an open heart and mind.

Ryu was different.

What is strength? The question consumed him.

In constant pursuit of strength, he would forever seek out other strong fighters. As the answer seeped deeper and deeper into his core, Ryu would start to internalize that ultimate truth. Gouken was proud to call this truth seeker his disciple.

Still, the loftier the path, the greater the danger of a catastrophic fall.

Strong light begets even deeper darkness, as no person can be ruled by just one pole of the dichotomy.

In seeking to perfect himself, Ryu's perception had become skewed and he had begun to cultivate the evil within. In that precarious state, it would take only a small push to flip him to the other side.

So it made perfect sense that the Dark Hado now corrupted him.

Ever since hearing that Ryu was committing atrocities around the world, Gouken had resolved to wait for his disciple in this place.

Surely, he would come to the temple where the three of them had once trained together…

Finally, he appeared.

"You've found your destination."

In a half-crouch with legs spread, Gouken raised both arms in the manner of the Deva kings who guarded the room.

It was his own, personal stance, different than the one he taught Ryu and Ken.

They had learned every technique he had to offer, but not every one he *knew*. Gouken reserved some moves only for himself out of his pride as a fighter and his love for his disciples.

For the teachings of a master should not represent the sum of the pupil's abilities. Ryu and Ken were destined to depart Gouken's school and form their own techniques. They would leave with knowledge of the basic stances, but no more than that.

"You hope to find your own style looking like that?"

Gouken's voice was filled with affection for Ryu, but the words never reached his beloved disciple.

"A-are you *really* Gouken?" asked Ryu with brows furrowed. Gouken nodded wordlessly, still in his stance.

"U-urghhhh…"

Clutching his own chest, Ryu began to writhe in agony.

Smoke rose from the cavernous wound, which glowed red beneath the heavily muscled arms. It pulsed violently, as if a torrent of blood might burst forth at any moment.

"There is only one thing I can do to ease your suffering."

A deep breath from Gouken caused the straw rope around to waist to creak in protest.

He channeled ki to his open left palm, and a sparking sound began to ring out from where the hand hovered, raised to the side of his face.

"Wh-why…? Why now…have you come, before me…?" muttered Ryu, still clutching his throbbing chest. Something wet spilled from his red eyes. Either sweat or tears.

"You were the one searching, Ryu. Not I."

"Sh-shut your mouth…"

"I only sat waiting in this temple. In the place where you and Ken spent your days training. *You* are the one who has come."

The sparking stopped.

It was ready.

"Hadoken!"

A ball of blue lightning flew at Ryu.

Though Gouken's was fired off with just a single hand, it was at least as powerful as Ryu and Ken's two-handed version.

This "Gohadoken" was a league above their ordinary Hadoken technique.

The wild orb of light hurtled towards Ryu.

"We shall let our fists do the talking. Come at me, Ryu," said Gouken to his disciple. Ryu still touched his own chest, unflinching.

The Gohadoken loomed.

"Guohhhh!"

A roar to the heavens, with head bent back, before vanishing from Gouken's sight.

The master raised his eyes to track Ryu.

In his effort to dodge the Gohadoken, Ryu had leapt nearly high enough to smash through the already crumbling roof. His bloodshot eyes flashed at Gouken with deadly intent.

With right leg poised to kick, Ryu plummeted to the ground faster than gravity alone would propel him.

Tenmakujinkyaku…

A technique reserved for those awakened to the Dark Hado. The force of the kick would be more than enough to pierce any half-hearted guard or counterattack, leaving the opponent defenseless against the blade of the foot.

Gouken analyzed Ryu's path calmly and shifted just enough to dodge. Such was his incredible judgment. Two steps backward was all it took. The master's eyebrows didn't even twitch as he watched his disciple come down.

A cloud of dust rose before his eyes.

Ryu had fallen just where Gouken predicted, and not an inch closer.

Moonlight illuminated the ashen cloud just before the demon burst through the veil.

Threads of saliva hung from Ryu's clenched teeth as he glared at Gouken in anger. He was barely recognizable as human anymore.

Just a beast.

The man who began as Gouken's disciple had lost all sense of self in his dogged pursuit of strength.

"Pitiful…"

Right hook into a left straight. Then an advancing front kick with the right leg into a spinning back kick with the left.

Ryu's four-hit combo.

Gouken dodged every strike by a hair's breadth.

The bloodthirsty demon his disciple had become didn't stop there.

"Urghh! Grahhh!"

One blow after another, each accompanied by a bloodcurdling grunt.

Not a single one connected, because Ryu's bloodlust was laid a little *too* bare. His intense focus on each subsequent target made his moves all too easy to read. Gouken might have appeared precognizant as each elegant dodge flowed into the next.

"Dieeee!"

Now well within range, Ryu prepared to launch a Shoryuken.

"Hmph."

Gouken filled his tanden with ki as the crouching Ryu's knee began to straighten.

But the leap never came.

The master's hands—each like a massive crag—came down from above to grip the fist aimed at his chin. All of Gouken's considerable weight pressed down, preventing Ryu from soaring.

"You fool… Who do you think taught you that move?"

"Urrrgh."

Gouken controlled Ryu's center of gravity now, leaving his disciple immobilized in a half-extended stance.

Ryu's shame only fueled the Dark Hado, though, forcing waves of it from his body. In an effort to clear the air of the suffocating miasma, Gouken flared his nostrils and took a deep breath.

"What is it you truly seek, Ryu?"

"Get off me."

Gouken ignored the pained request and continued.

"I asked you what you seek! Can you hear me, Ryu? If even the smallest shred of light remains in your heart, then I know you can! So answer me! What is it you seek?"

No one is completely dominated by darkness. There had to be light in Ryu, still. Even the dread Akuma couldn't purge himself of all conscience.

For all of creation is governed by dual forces, and eradicating one or the other is impossible.

So his words *had* to be reaching Ryu.

Gouken was sure of it.

As if to confirm that suspicion, Ryu's rage-filled eyes trembled ever so slightly.

The briefest shudder across his eyelids, and a deep sigh that escaped his twisted grimace.

"Think back to when you first appeared before me! What was it you said to me? What did you want for yourself?"

The memory was clear in Gouken's mind. Though still an adolescent, Ryu's eyes had revealed age beyond his years.

"I want to be stronger than anyone."
A cry straight from his heart.
Back then, Gouken had had no idea what drove the young man to such a desire. Strength of that sort was hardly essential in peaceful, modern times. An ordinary life in Japan was attainable to anyone who put in minimal effort, so why did the boy want so much more?
To be strong...
The thought had consumed Ryu.
Despite all else, Gouken imagined that that, at least, hadn't changed.
"I-I want..."
Ryu struggled to squeeze the words out of his throat.
"That's right! Remember what you told me."
"I want to be strong..."
"Now look at yourself. Is this what you sought? Are you satisfied now?"
Ryu trembled, but not out of doubt or hesitation.
The only emotion controlling him at present was *rage*.
He couldn't help but feel vexed by Gouken, admonishing from on high with a tone of superiority. Ryu wanted to shout about how little his master understood, but the force keeping his body in check also kept him from vocalizing. Still, the Dark Hado was not so simple a thing as to be cleansed by mere criticism.
"Sh-shut up..." came Ryu's voice, tinged with rage.
"Worry not, Ryu. I will wake you from this nightmare."
Gouken released his grip.
"Gwahhh."
Finally free, Ryu flew straight up, thrust out his right leg, and began to spin.
"Tatsumaki Senpukyaku!"
Attacks from those possessed by the Dark Hado are leagues more powerful than those of any ordinary person, and Gouken's body was

now assaulted by a hurricane of such kicks. Even the master's solid defense couldn't stave off all damage.

"Urgh."

He felt his right shoulder go numb after the heaviest hit yet. His right arm would be rendered useless if it kept up.

Gouken knew full well that retreating backwards would do little to evade the onslaught.

The spin behind the Tatsumaki Senpukyaku sent the user hurtling forward at the foe, so attempting to move away would only play into the attacker's hands. The one on the receiving end would eventually be left with nowhere to run.

Gouken could only wait until the storm abated, so he endured, prepared to sacrifice his right arm if necessary.

He knew a chance to counterattack was coming.

The kicks stopped, and Ryu touched down.

This was it…

Gouken lunged but hit only air, as Ryu had vanished.

Asura Senku.

A technique that allowed the user to conceal both spiritual and physical presence while shifting across the battlefield.

Following by sight was impossible, so Gouken tried to read Ryu's ki.

It felt far away, despite how close the two had just been. Ryu would be sure to close that gap again before reappearing.

The air blurred where a hazy outline came into view, well within the master's range.

Gouken's left hand took hold of the dougi, solid and visible once again. His disciple's face twisted in shock.

He braced his legs and threw Ryu in a single, sweeping motion. The latter's head hit the ground first, and he fell in a splayed tangle of limbs.

"Allow me to show you that I am like no other opponent you have faced."

Ryu attempted to rise but could only muster a spray of blood from between his lips.

"For this is not my first fight against a Dark Hado user."

The disciple uttered a deep groan as he stood, but Gouken was already in range again after seeming to slide across the floor.

"Hah."

A palm strike from a low stance, aimed at the solar plexus. Ryu had only just regained his footing, but the palm dug into his stomach, sending Gouken's ki shooting through his body and out his back. Ryu began to fly backwards, and his master kicked off in pursuit.

Gouken's body began to spin about his hips.

"Tatsumaki Gorasen."

A technique he had never taught his disciples. In fact, he hadn't perfected it until after they had parted ways. Unlike the Tatsumaki Senpukyaku, which was notable for its forward momentum, the Gorasen variation would drive the opponent upward at an angle with an even stronger spin behind it. There was truly nowhere to run from such a move.

The first strong blow smashed Ryu's face and forced his feet off the ground. His master's kicking leg became an unstoppable force that landed hit after hit.

"Rahhh."

The final kick connected with strength to smash the heavens, and Ryu soared, released from the combo at last.

"I'm not done just yet."

Gouken landed and began to focus ki in his tanden.

Lightning surged about his fist before the orb flew at and collided with Ryu.

The undulating waves of Dark Hado blended with the Gohadoken's light to form a mottled blend of black and blue.

Ryu convulsed silently as he plummeted to the floor, where he lay motionless after landing.

His master released his stance as he put some distance between the two.

The Dark Hado continued to seep from Ryu's body, undeterred. The raging storm was not something to be quelled by even a fierce beat-down.

What really mattered was Ryu's *heart*.

No sound thrashing would awaken him so long as he couldn't bring himself to reject the Dark Hado with all of his being- not even if he were killed. It was Ryu himself who invited the Dark Hado in, so he had to be the one to drive it out.

"Still not finished, then?"

The disciple didn't respond to his master's kind voice. His body only gave a sharp spasm before his face turned up at a queer angle. His crimson eyes locked onto Gouken in a frozen glare, and his teeth gnashed with a dull crunch.

"You are weak."

Within Gouken's provocation was love for his disciple. The sentiment was lost on Ryu, however, and he took the insult at face value. More grinding of teeth. Controlled by bloodlust and lacking a shred of humanity, Ryu hardly looked like one to be pitied.

Still, Gouken couldn't abandon him.

He *would* awaken, and he would open his eyes to the nature of true strength. Gouken still had faith in the man.

To that end, it was just a matter of figuring out how to do it.

The master was determined.

"It seems as though the strength you found cannot faze me. Note that I haven't accepted the heresy of the Dark Hado myself, but still you cannot manage to beat me, a mere human. So ask yourself…what good does the Dark Hado do you?"

Gouken stroked his long beard.

He could tell that Ryu was still seething, because every wave of anger sent another pulse of black miasma shooting from his body.

"Now stand. I am prepared to crush you as many times as it takes. Until you realize how useless the Dark Hado is, I will not fall."

"Grrr."

The guttural noise coming from Ryu could have been mistaken for that of a wild animal. He continued to glare at Gouken as he stood.

"Ready to try me again?" asked Gouken with a single raised eyebrow and a tilted head. Ryu's answer came in the form of his stance.

"Very well."

As Gouken took his own stance, an easy smile rose to his face.

He wasn't enjoying the fight, per se, but it reminded him of better times.

Squaring off against Ryu brought back memories of the boy who had turned up on his doorstep years ago. Within the black-garbed demon now before his eyes, Gouken saw the determined young man who would always stand back up after a defeat.

"Let us fight to your heart's content, then."

Both men kicked off towards each other and were in range in an instant.

Gouken made the first move.

His uncalculating and honest straight right made a beeline for Ryu's nose.

"Nuohhhh!" screamed Ryu, firing back with a punch of his own. A right hook, just like a boxer's.

The two hits landed simultaneously, meaning that the disciple had been slightly faster than the master.

"Hmph."

Gouken nodded with satisfaction. His left fist was already whipping towards Ryu.

Unfazed, Ryu launched another attack, and both fists met their marks for a second time.

And a third.

And a fourth.

Right, then left, then right again, fists flying faster than either fighter could process.

But neither fell. Each could only see his opponent before him.

The space they occupied seem to transcend time itself, and the only sounds ringing out were those of fists on flesh.

"This isn't the strength I remember! Hit me like you mean it, Ryu!" roared Gouken, his face quickly swelling. Ryu's own face twitched, as if in response to the taunt.

His next punch flew with slightly more force behind it.

"Yes! I knew you had it in you! Hold back, and you will never triumph over me!"

"Silence."

Ryu's voice wavered, his emotions in a frenzy.

"Are you even hearing me? It is I, Gouken! Your master! You now fight against the master you thought dead!"

"…"

His disciple sunk into silence once more, though their fists continued to fly.

Gouken was determined to reach Ryu, so he continued speaking even when his pummeled cheeks were torn on the inside by his teeth, causing his mouth to fill with blood.

He would entreat Ryu as they exchanged blows and glares.

The essence of Gouken's words might never reach a man possessed by the Dark Hado, but their fistfight might just do the trick, because Ryu was a natural-born fighter.

Even when lost to darkness, the part of him that lived to fight could never die. Ryu was as true to himself as he could be while engaged in combat.

As a fighter himself, Gouken understood that much. The master knew that his words had the best chance of touching Ryu's heart when he was at his purest and most genuine. Hence the pleas between blows.

Even Gouken was reaching his limit, though. Strong as he was, repeated blows to the head couldn't simply be shrugged off.

His vision suddenly grew hazy.

It might have been a cut on his face, leaking blood into his eyes, but he couldn't be sure. Whatever the cause, bloodstains bloomed across Gouken's vision.

Ryu, on the other hand, was nowhere near as fatigued or damaged as his master.

Yes, his face was twisted, swollen beyond recognition , and dripping with blood, but despite the extensive physical injuries, there were no signs that he felt pain. Nor was he on the verge of passing out.

Had the Dark Hado dulled his senses to this extent? Having never been seduced by the sinister power himself, Gouken wasn't sure. What was clear from looking at Ryu, though, was that his already impressive tenacity had been magnified tenfold, which had to be the Dark Hado's handiwork.

It also eradicated any reluctance about killing. Each strike was stripped of all hesitation, meaning that the victim would receive far more damage than he or she might otherwise. On the flipside, such attacks would also take a toll on the bones and muscles within the attacker's fists.

Ryu's gloves were evidence enough. The fraying seams showed that the material couldn't keep up with his sheer power output.

Such abuse of his own body should have resulted in considerable pain and fatigue, so it had to be the case that the Dark Hado was somehow invigorating him and numbing his nerve endings.

"This is no time for such idle thoughts…"

Just as Gouken chided himself under his breath, the fiercest blow yet struck his right cheek. The force of it sliced open his skin, producing a dry snap and a spray of blood.

The master staggered back several steps unwittingly, but his disciple wasn't one to let prey get away.

The Hadoken stance…

"Nuohhhhhhhh."

Ryu pulled both hands back to grasp the familiar ball of air. This time, however, the orb of light that appeared was purple. As it grew, it seemed to absorb the misty waves of Dark Hado emanating from Ryu, which lent it a wicked aura.

Gouken was at a loss for words at the sight of this ominous Hadoken, which barely resembled the technique he knew so well.

A hit from this one could be serious.

Deadly, even.

A voice inside him screamed at him to act, so Gouken immediately mimicked Ryu's Hadoken stance. Although he was more than capable of executing the move with a single hand, this time he used two.

Almost instantly, the ki within the air around the fighters formed into a massive blue orb between Gouken's hands. Tiny bolts of lightning flashed about the orb before dissipating.

Ryu's red eyes glinted in response.

"Metsu Hadoken!"

Both hands shot out, and the purple ball of dark energy flew.

Gouken wasted no time.

"Denjin Hadoken!"

His own orb of blue lightning left his hands.

A thunderous boom, as if a bomb had gone off inside the hall.

In the immediate aftermath, Gouken could only see white.

He knew that the two balls of ki had exploded against each other, but even Gouken wasn't prepared for a shockwave of this magnitude.

The white faded, and the master's vision slowly returned.

Night sky…

The moonlight seemed that much brighter, now, because the ruined temple's roof had been blown apart by the clashing Hadoken attacks.

"Urgh!"

In the center of Gouken's returning vision stood Ryu, already back in his battle stance.

Too late to react.

"Messatsu…"

Suddenly, Ryu's hand gripped Gouken's nape.

A flash…

This time, the master's vision went dark.

A seemingly unending barrage of agonizing blows assaulted his body. He understood that he was being hit, but he couldn't tell where, or how.

The combo attack left him without a moment to breathe as it ravaged him from head to toe.

A distant memory surfaced.

The death match against his brother…

Akuma was curled at Gouken's feet.

"This final blow will end you."

The younger brother responded to the older's words with a piercing stare.

"Farewell, brother of mine."

Gouken's fist flew with those parting words, but Akuma had already vanished.

The demon's hand was at Gouken's neck.

Darkness…

And a full-body barrage.

"One instant, one thousand strikes."

His brother's voice, as if from some far off place.

The memory of their match ended there, and the sensation Gouken felt now was nearly identical.

Suddenly, the stream of strikes ceased. No longer pinned in place by the merciless attack, Gouken fell forward.

"Ultimate technique of the Dark Hado, Shun Goku Satsu…" whispered Ryu from near Gouken's head.

He was still conscious.

Already an improvement over last time.

He had somehow endured.

Yet…

Gouken's numb body refused to obey him.

"What a shame, Gouken," came Ryu's voice from above.

Unable to move a muscle, the master could only listen.

"This might be your second fight against a user of the Dark Hado, but unfortunately for you, I'm different than Akuma."

Different, indeed…

Ryu might have been claiming superiority over Akuma, but Gouken found different meaning within his words.

When his brother had hit him with Shun Goku Satsu, Gouken was knocked unconscious. Not so, this time around.

But it had nothing to do with relative strength.

It was Ryu's naiveté.

He hadn't yet fully accepted the Dark Hado within his system, so he couldn't properly end a fight with an ultimate technique like Shun Goku Satsu.

That Gouken was still conscious represented a glimmer of hope for

Ryu.

"U-ughh…"

He attempted to rouse his failing body.

Arms…

His right arm dragged itself across the floor far slower than he willed it to.

Legs…

Gouken tried to stand in vain. He could only manage to scrape one knee onto the floorboards.

"After all that self-righteous prattle, is this the best you can do?"

Ryu's hand stretched towards Gouken's neck and clamped around the space between his chin and Adam's apple. The master felt himself suffocating as he rose off the ground.

"The Dark Hado reigns supreme… I alone am destined for the heavens."

Gouken's feet now dangled above the floor, and Ryu looked up at him with a triumphant smile.

"Do you really mean that?"

Uttering those words in his cracking voice took all the master had.

"What was that?" asked Ryu, right eye bulging in a glare.

"Do you truly believe that, from the bottom of your heart?"

"Of course I do. Just take a look at what the Dark Hado has allowed me to do to y-…"

"Mankind is meant to walk the *earth*," interrupted Gouken.

"We may yearn for the heavens, but we are born without wings. We may pursue godhood, but we cannot even perceive the truth in our own hearts. Because we, as people, are foolish and weak. Our humanity leads us to seek strength, even if the search leads us into the darkness. A true god would never lose his way. He would have no need to harm others. You cause pain and suffering to assert your own dominance, but it will not lead you to true strength. This rampage shows you, instead, to be a pitiful weakling."

Gouken could barely breathe, but he managed to choke the words out, pushing his body beyond all natural limits in order to convey his will to his disciple.

"The only weakling is you. And your words are no more than the howling of a whipped dog."

"Howling or not, my words ring true."

"I've run out of patience for your pathetic speeches."

Ryu released Gouken's throat, and the master succumbed to gravity.

But his disciple wouldn't let him fall that easily. A swift spinning back kick to the solar plexus sent Gouken tumbling across the floor until his back smacked against the wall.

"No... We're not done just yet."

Their earlier exchange had bought him a bit of time. Feeling was returning to Gouken's limbs, so he used the wall to support himself as he stood.

Waist still propped against the wall, he leaned forward in a crouch with arms spread in the Deva king pose.

Again, his fighting stance.

"You still want to go on?" asked Ryu without breaking his own stance, walking calmly towards his master.

Gouken smiled and nodded.

"Then this time, you will truly die."

"You don't have it in you!"

"Nonsense."

As Ryu broke into a run, Gouken sunk low and gathered ki in the pit of his stomach.

He knew he only had a few counterattacks left.

Just one or two good blows...

Then his body would fail him.

Gouken brought the entirety of his focus on Ryu. With more than a mere stare, he *perceived* every bit of his beloved apprentice, down to the last strand of hair.

A bloodcurdling visage.

But there was a glimmer of *something* between the wrinkles of that furrowed brow. Not quite a sign of kindness, but evidence of some feeling, deep in Ryu, the man, etched onto the demonic face.

ACKNOW-
LEDGE
YOUR
WEAKNESS
AS A MAN,
RYU!

GAHHH!!

ACKNOW-
LEDGE
YOUR
INHERENT
WEAK-
NESS...

...BUT
CONTINUE
TO MOVE
FORWARD,
EVER
FORWARD!

THAT
IS TRUE
STRENGTH!

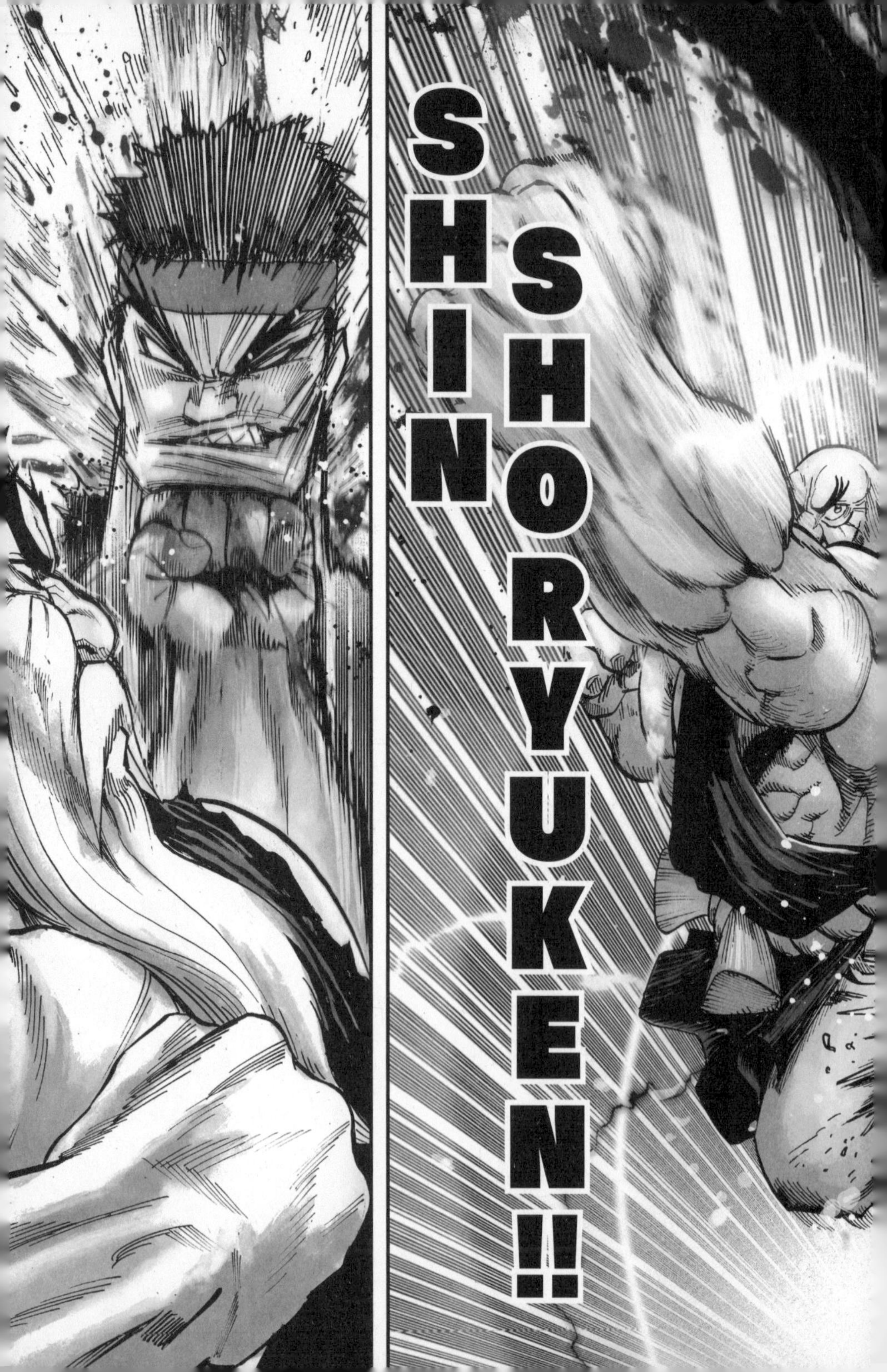
SHIN SHORYUKEN!!

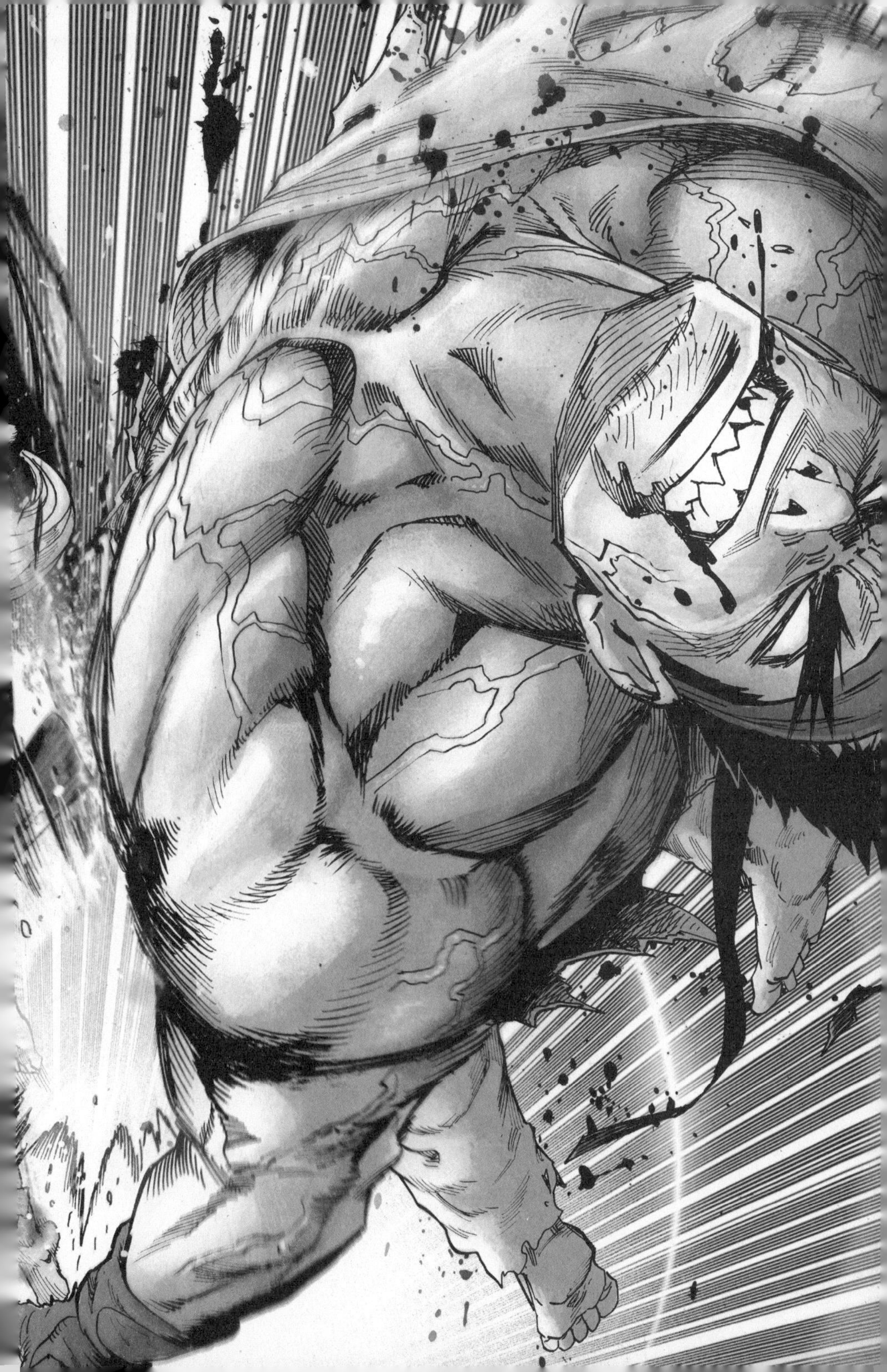

"Do not fear your own humanity."

Gouken's whisper went unheard.

His disciple took a great step forward.

"Hahhh..."

Ryu exhaled from deep in his tanden as he amassed ki within.

The two were now within striking range of each other.

A low stance.

A fist pulled down past the waist.

Preparation for a Shoryuken.

"Hmph."

Gouken steeled himself and moved in just as Ryu began to rise.

However, his disciple's attack fell short by a hair.

A battle was raging inside Ryu, between good and evil.

The two sides jostled for control, throwing him off by the barest amount in the final instant.

"Acknowledge your weakness as a man, Ryu!"

The fist grazed Gouken's nose, and he retaliated with his own right fist, driving it into the rising Ryu's stomach.

The impact cut off Ryu's upward momentum, bringing his feet back to the ground.

"Acknowledge your inherent weakness, but continue to move forward, ever forward! *That* is true strength!"

Gouken's fist flew once more, this time into Ryu's exposed jaw.

The disciple went stiff from the shock.

Shoryuken was a technique full of openings to exploit, so Gouken would only ever unleash it when his victory was assured.

Facing the shell-shocked Ryu, Gouken thrust upwards with his lowered fist.

Shin Shoryuken.

The solid hit connected, and the master felt himself soaring like a dragon bound for the heavens.

The moon shone bright high above.

Under the pale, gentle light, Ryu's energy finally gave out, and he found himself helplessly aloft.

Gravity stopped Gouken's ascent and began to pull him back to earth. His feet touched down, but he was too drained to hold himself up anymore. The master slid across the floor clumsily and only stopped upon hitting the wall. With back to the wall, he raised a single knee and slumped.

Across the room, Ryu had reached the peak of his arc before plummeting to the floor, head first. He now lay motionless.

Silence settled over the ruined temple. All Gouken could hear was his own ragged breathing.

Splayed and face down, Ryu was still enough to be mistaken for dead, but the waves of ki enveloping his body told a different story.

To accept one's weakness while continuing to move forward…

That described Ryu in his younger days to a T. His single-minded quest for strength had spurred him to spend day after day training with his friend, Ken. His unbending will had propelled him ever forward.

But time passed, and he had matured. One cannot remain a child forever.

Ryu had lived through all manner of experiences duringhis tedious years of adulthood, so little by little, that pure will of his had begun to change. The distortion had been subtle enough to go undetected.

People change, and people forget.

As they should, for they are inherently weak.

That is why they doubt and why they lose their way.

Strength is the capacity to accept those truths while still striving to be a better person than the day before.

The road to true strength has no real end, and rushing to find elusive answers will only result in straying from the path.

If anyone could understand that, it would be Ryu.

"Guohhhh!"

A sudden howl.

Though he hadn't so much as twitched until a moment ago, Ryu now stood in the Deva king stance and glared in Gouken's direction.

The master, however, was spent.

He could only wait for death's embrace.

The Dark Hado cloaked Ryu's body just as it had earlier.

"Lose your way, Ryu. That is how you are meant to be."

A final, bitter plea.

"G-Gouken…"

Ryu tottered forward while clutching at the wound on his chest.

Gouken–utterly stripped of the energy to resist–watched in silence as his disciple approached.

Then Ryu stopped, just a few paces away.

"Urgrahhhh…"

He crouched, hand still at his breast.

The ki surrounding his body began to swirl, and at the eye of the storm was the crater in Ryu's chest, which seemed to be sucking up the Dark Hado itself.

Ryu's internal struggle was raging; his human weakness struggled violently to suppress the monstrous strength.

With nothing left to say, Gouken watched wordlessly while his disciple writhed.

"I-I am Ryu…" he said, seemingly to no one in particular.

"Silence…"

The struggle continued.

Already, the black mist had retreated to a small radius around the wound.

"Just a bit more, Ryu…" murmured Gouken to himself.

"*I* choose my own path!"

With these words, Ryu spread his arms wide and tossed his head back.

The sunken cavity on his chest suddenly swelled like a balloon before flattening once more. The bulging blood vessels vanished and his skin was clear, as if it had always been that way.

Gouken could feel that Ryu's body was free of the Dark Hado.

Tears poured from the master's eyes. He was shocked to discover he still had it in him to cry like that at his age, but he did nothing to hold back the warmth that flowed down over his cheeks.

Finally released from his dark imprisonment, Ryu wobbled side to side like a marionette with cut strings before finding his footing and righting himself, the world still a blur.

He stared forward with vacant eyes at the seated Gouken.

"You've gotten strong, Ryu."

"M-Master…"

Gouken watched the tears well up and fall to his beloved disciple's cheeks.

CONTINUE?

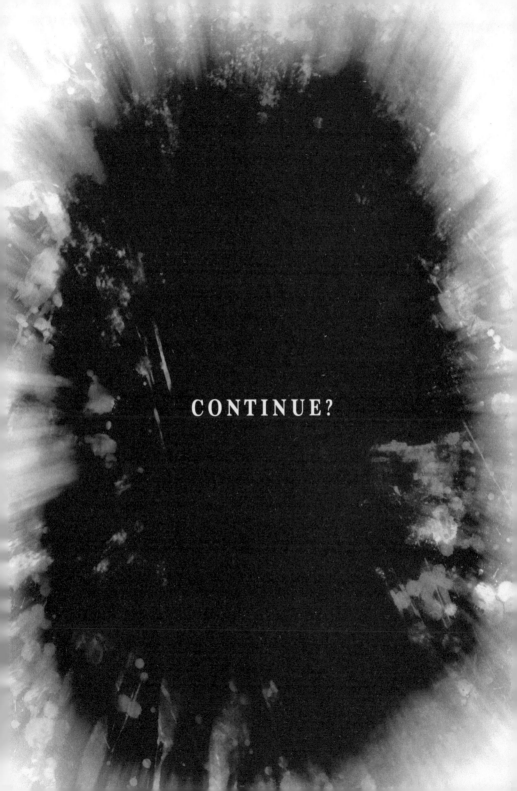

The resonant energy was extinguished…

Akuma could feel it clearly. Whatever had just happened, worlds away, sent a shudder across his skin.

"Dead, then? Or perhaps…" he whispered to himself, alone in the darkness of the cave.

Once again, he was the only remaining wielder of the Dark Hado on the planet…

A faint smile curled across Akuma's lips.

"But of course. I, alone, am destined for the heavens."

His Dark Hado spread to fill the cave, deeper even than the natural darkness.

The trip to Africa had been a bust.

It had been nighttime when Elena fought the mystery man, so she hadn't gotten a good look at his face.

Chun-Li now sped across the Hong Kong nightscape.

The cell phone on the dashboard rang, and she picked up the call via her earpiece.

A familiar voice…

"Long time no speak."

"Too true, Guile."

"We found the man."

"You mean the enemy? Or your old friend?"

"The latter."

Chun-Li felt a stab to her heart at Guile's cool reply.

"Where should we meet?"

"I'm already in Hong Kong."

"Good…"

Chun-Li envisioned a map of the city and remembered the usual spot before stepping down on the accelerator, hard.

"Are you prepared to depart?" spoke the girl's father from the doorway.

"I am."

Elena zipped up the bag filled with her bare essentials and turned around with a smile.

"This could be goodbye for quite some time."

"That is fine. We always have the wind, after all" she replied.

"May the wind that graces our home here find you wherever your battles may take you."

"Yes…"

The girl stood and shouldered the bag.

"I'll be back!"

"More, please !"

The sumo wrestler's mouth was still stuffed full with pizza, so the restaurant's other customers stared with mild shock.

Honda's stomach already contained three pizzas, five plates worth of pasta, and the contents of a pair of two-liter seltzer bottles.

"Still hungry over here…"

He passed the time waiting for the next pizza to finish baking by picking bits of salami from his teeth with a fork.

Genoa, Italy.

Honda was in town looking for a famous fortuneteller, though he wasn't exactly hoping to have his palm read.

"This woman's supposed to be strong beyond words…"

The freshly arrived pizza rose in his thick fingers.

"Should be fun."

Dumbfounded looks all around as the pizza disappeared in a flash.

"Good to see you…"

A woman stepped from the sports car, and Guile's greeting to its driver rang out in the night.

Chun-Li's bounded over to him with a swift gait.

"It's been a while."

"Mhm."

The soldier removed his sunglasses, scratched his chest, and leaned against the guardrail.

They could see the entirety of Hong Kong's so-called million-dollar nightscape from atop the hill; the famous spot was bustling with tourists and local couples there for the romantic view.

Hoping to blend into the crowd, Chun-Li and Guile leaned over the railing and took in the sight.

The soldier broke the silence without turning to his beautiful, Chinese companion.

"The intel I've got comes from the best of the best on my side of the world. Slim chance it's wrong."

"So was it really Charlie?"

"Yep. He's dead."

"I see…"

Silence took over until Guile spoke again.

"That said, I say we make sure it's him with our own eyes."

They were talking, of course, about Chun-Li's supposedly deceased friend.

Had she really hoped for a different answer?

Still…

Guile was determined to see for himself, and Chun-Li was ready to know the truth.

"Honey, that nurse just gave me this, for you."

The still bedridden Ken took the crinkled paper from Eliza. It could only be a letter, as neatly folded as it was, but there was neither address nor return address printed anywhere.

"Where'd the nurse get it?"

"Whoever she got it from just said to make sure you received it."

"Gotcha."

Ken unfolded the paper.

"Th-this is…"

"Your friend has awakened, and he awaits your next reunion."

Distinctly clumsy brushstrokes. Ones Ken recognized.

"M-master… He's really alive?"

Ken cast his eyes towards the large window of his white hospital room. A pair of blackbirds soared across the clear sky.

"So you've come back to us, Ryu…"

"Please, eat more, traveler."

"I-I'm already stuffed to the gills, like I said!"

Bits of curry shot from Hakan's mouth as he shouted at Dhalsim, who extended a silver plate and wore a sour look.

"The tandoori chicken is ready, dear."

"Just leave it here, Sari."

"Very well."

A pleasant exchange between husband and wife. Dhalsim shot a grin at Sari, prompting her to disappear back into the kitchen.

The ascetic placed his plate on the floor and picked up the one his wife had just carried in.

"Try the chicken, traveler…"

"I keep telling yeh I'm full to bursting!"

Curry oozed from Hakan's nose and mouth, and he fell to the floor, defeated.

"C-come on, gimme a break already…"

The last thing Hakan saw, as his consciousness faded, was the married couple. Both husband and wife wore wry smiles.

"Sure doesn't smell like much."

"Enough of that. Just taste it. I daresay even *you* will fall in love with the blend."

Balrog took a sip from the white porcelain, egged on by Dudley. As the pleasantly warm tea entered his mouth, the fragrance of the sweet leaves hit his nose.

"Well? A peerless taste, is it not? Among all beverages, Darjeeling is positively unrivaled."

Balrog scowled at Dudley and his bold declaration.

"Really? It didn't suit you, then?"

"W-well…"

The red boxer set his teacup down.

"In that case…"

Dudley picked up a bottle of amber liquid and poured a shot into Balrog's cup.

"That's a bit of top shelf brandy. It doesn't do much for me, but perhaps you'll find it improves things."

Ignoring Dudley completely, Balrog made a grab for the bottle itself.

"Here we go. You've found the drink for me."

The blue boxer looked on with a sigh as Balrog took a swig of the brandy.

"I don't suppose we'll ever quite see eye-to-eye…"

Sagat dragged his mangled body through the streets.

The incessant raindrops steamed and returned to the sky where they pelted his scorching skin.

Though his flesh was beaten and torn, his mind was clear.

"Can't let it end just yet…"

Until the day he faced Ryu in combat once more, Sagat wouldn't let himself die.

"You'd better be ready for me."

The voice he shot out with at the darkness before him was surprisingly cheery and full of hope.

"I see… So he managed to flee."

"Apologies, sir."

Bison stared absentmindedly at his subordinate, who now bowed his head low.

"Never mind about Sagat. What of the test subject?"

"All is proceeding smoothly."

"Find as many fighters to face him as you can. Our data needs to be comprehensive."

"Understood, sir."

"Now go."

With a robotic bow, the subordinate left the room.

Bison stood from his chair and turned.

The window behind his desk was fully repaired, as if the fight against Sagat a few hours ago had never happened.

With the cityscape before him, a wicked smile rose on the dictator's face.

"Let the nightmare begin…"

As if shaken by Bison's words to no one in particular, the heavens split in a flash of lightning.

"Did I really awaken, or…?"

Ryu narrowed his eyes against a blast of wind but continued to look ahead.

Nothing but wasteland.

Did the opponent he sought really await him at the end of his journey?

There was no guarantee either way, but still he went on. He had to, because to live is to doubt.

Those who march forward while still doubting are those who embody true strength.

His master had taught him that much.

In that case, was this whole episode just another part of his path towards strength?

In that sense, could he really condone own his recent actions? How he bloodied so many opponents, crushed his friend and rival, and raised an impudent fist against his master?

The slate couldn't be wiped clean, at any rate.

So…

Ryu wondered what, if anything, he *could* do, foolish though he imagined himself to be.

"Hey, mister!"

A young-sounding voice, from behind.

Ryu turned to see a boy of about five, baked black by the sun, with tousled hair, a running nose, and cracking, white lips. The purity in his eyes shone clear, even through the violent winds.

"It's just a lotta desert over that way. You're gonna die, dressed like that."

"Really?"

After shooting a smile at the concerned child, Ryu kept walking.

"Hey! I said you're gonna die!"

The young voice turned angry, but still Ryu didn't stop.

He couldn't afford to die, and he wasn't planning on it.

"Why go? Whaddya think is on the other side, anyways?"

Ryu kept moving, silent.

"What're you even going out there to do, mister?"

The fighter slowed to a stop and looked at the boy over his shoulder.

"Find someone stronger than me."

AFTERWORD

Back during middle school, I used to cut my more tiresome classes and slip away to an arcade called "White" near school.

One day, even though school was still in session, the dimly-lit place was packed with uniformed middle and high-schoolers, standing room only.

They weren't playing any of the usual games. Instead, they were all transfixed on the newest arrival- two sets of versus-style cabinets (making four in total).

Nobody there at the time knew the significance of the new game, but make no mistake—we were all witnesses to gaming history in the making. *SF2*.

Everyone preferred that abbreviation over the full title, and on that day, every kid in that arcade was glued to those *SF2* screens. I was always enthusiastic about *finding someone stronger than me*, and sure enough, strong players walked through the doors of White day after day.

Fast-forward, 25 years later...

I'm older than old.

Over the hill.

I've found my way in life, but...

Now I'm bewildered again.

I look past the blank word-processing document on my computer monitor, over at another screen. The PS4's newest title is on display.

Street Fighter V…

And it's like I'm right back there, 25 years ago. Nothing's changed. Well, maybe that's not quite true. My favorite game has gotten even purer. More extreme. More complicated.

Everything I could've wished for!

Honestly, I'm glad that I feel comfortable proudly declaring that I like the things I like, at my age.

And I love *Street Fighter.*

Basically, I was on cloud nine the entire time I was writing this book. I drew on the images of battle ingrained in my brain from all those past matches and poured them all into the writing, being sure to leave nothing unsaid. Nothing makes me happier than imagining all the readers out there getting to picture the same fierce battles between Ryu and friends that have stuck with me all these years.

In closing, I'd like to give my deepest thanks to CAPCOM, for putting this project together, and to Mr. Yusuke Murata, who took time out of his busy schedule as a serialized manga artist to contribute some incredible illustrations to this book.

Takashi Yano

AFTERWORD

The world was introduced to *SF2* right around when I started middle school. From the first time I laid eyes on it, I knew it was no ordinary game.

People now might not recall, but when it came out in 1991, it was rare to see pixel art characters with quite so much charm to them.

Thanks to the technical limitations of most games at the time, your average on-screen character was little more than an icon or representational symbol; the developers would ask gamers to check out the illustrations on the packaging or in the instruction manuals if they wanted a more complete picture.

That all changed with *SF2*, which had these expertly crafted, larger-than-life characters, bouncing around on the screen. You could practically feel them breathing as they pulsed up and down in their "ready" stances. That alone was enough to distinguish it from other games, but beyond that, each and every character was also bursting with personality and little idiosyncrasies. Sure, they were "cool," but each was also funny enough that I remember laughing out loud at the sight of them.

"What's with this soldier's wacky haircut?"

"Check out this chick's thunder thighs!"

"The green beastman is spinning around and shooting lightning!"

"Look at that pro wrestler's moves!"

"The Indian guy is stretching his arms and legs and breathing fire!"

We're all familiar with the cast at this point, but at the time, their sheer uniqueness was a sight to behold.

I wasn't even the one playing at first (I didn't have much pocket change, so until we got a Super Famicom, I was relegated to the sidelines at the arcade, watching my older brother play), but it was all awesome enough to make me wonder, "Maybe videogames are even cooler than manga and anime?"

Plenty of other players and non-players alike were feeling the same thing, I bet.

Starting with *SF2*, the artwork of Capcom's design studio began to have serious influence on Japan's manga art as a whole.

Broadly speaking, more realistic, dramatic stories in the style of American comics became the norm, with characters having detailed musculature. *Heavier* art, with more intense lines. It was around then that Mr. Katsuhiro Otomo created his realistic style that achieved plenty with fewer lines.

People balked at the idea of losing the beautiful ladies and cool dudes of traditional, stylized manga in switching to a more realistic look. They thought it couldn't be done. But then along came Capcom, which showed us that having characters with proper anatomy didn't mean sacrificing the stylish highlights of manga as we knew them.

I'm well aware of the influence it's had on my own art, given that I was growing up right around the time of Capcom's artistic renaissance. In hindsight, *SFII* was a blessing in disguise for the effects it had on my work.

In that sense, it makes me so happy to be able to give something back, in the form of my involvement with this project.

I'm grateful to all the readers enjoying this book, Mr. Takashi Yano, editor Junichi Hashimoto- the one who brought me this awesome project, everyone involved with the *Street Fighter* series, and my own big brother.

Yusuke Murata

CONCEPT BY: CAPCOM

A studio that's given birth to a number video-game series that have won popularity both in Japan and abroad. Among the studio's most well-known series are *Street Fighter*, *Resident Evil*, *Ghosts 'n Goblins*, *Mega Man*, *Sengoku BASARA*, *Monster Hunter*, and *Ace Attorney*.

AUTHOR: TAKASHI YANO

Novelist who won the 21st Annual Subaru Newcomer Prize for Literature with his 2008 work, *Jashu Kidan*. He made his formal debut the following year with a revised version of the same work, *Jashu* (Shueisha). Since then, he's come out with original stories such as *Masakado* (PHP INTERFACE) and *Ran* (Kodansha) while also working on novelizations of videogames and manga, including *Sengoku Basara 3: Date Masamune's Chapter* (Kodansha) and *Naruto: Shikamaru's Story* (Shueisha).

ARTIST: YUSUKE MURATA

Manga artist whose debut work- 1995's one-shot manga, *Partner*- won the 122nd Hop Step Award. His most prolific series are *Eyeshield 21* and *One Punch Man* (both, Shueisha), but he's also done plenty of illustration work for CAPCOM series such as *Street Fighter* and *Mega Man*.

SOUND EFFECTS

To best preserve the original artwork we've decided to leave the original sound effects on the manga pages of the books. Nearly all the sound effects are simple fight noises, but they are provided here translated for those who are interested.

RYU/AKUMA
PAGE 2
2.2 RUMBLE (goooo)
2.3 BOOM (don)

PAGE 3
3.1 STEP (za)
3.2 BOOM (don)
3.4 BOOM (don)

PAGE 4/5
4.1 BOOM (don)

PAGE 26
26.2 VOOM (gua)
26.4 BLAM (doguo)

PAGE 27
27.2 TMP (dan)
27.2 SPIN (gyururu)
27.3 FWOOM (bua)

CHUN-LI/ELENA
PAGE 49
49.1 KERWHAMWHAMWHAM
    (dogagaga)

PAGE 50
50.1 WHAP (bachii)
50.2 FWIP (fu)
50.3 TMP (ba)

PAGE 51
51.1 KERWHAMWHAMWHAM
    (gyugagaga)

GUILE/HONDA
PAGE 86
86.1 FWOOSH (babababa)

KEN/RYU
PAGE 152
152.3 HUMM (buuun)

DHALSIM/HAKAN
PAGE 145
145.1 WHOOSH (fuwaa)
145.3 AAA
145.4 FWISH (pyuuu)

PAGE 146
146.1 WHAM (gan)
146.2 SPIN SPIN SPIN
    (guru guru guru)
146.3 FWOOM (gyun)

PAGE 147
147.1 KERWHAMWHAMWHAM
    (kagyagyagya)

DUDLEY/BALROG
PAGE 165
165.1 SHK SHK (kyu kyu)
165.2 WHAM WHAM (dodon)

PAGE 167
167.1 KERWHAM (dogoo)

SAGAT/M.BISON
PAGE 201
201.2 WHAM (ga)
201.3 WHOOSH (kooon)

PAGE 202
202.1 TMP (to)
202.2 TENSE (gun)

PAGE 203
203.1 KERWHAM (doga)

GOUKEN/RYU
PAGE 227
227.1 FWOOM (vuo)
227.2 WHAM (don)

STREET FIGHTER

THE NOVEL

— WHERE STRENGTH LIES —

[STORY]
Takashi Yano

[ARTWORK]
Yusuke Murata

ENGLISH EDITION

ENGLISH TRANSLATION - CALEB D. COOK
PROOFREADING - MICHAEL GOLDSTEIN
BOOK LAYOUT & ADAPTATION - MATT MOYLAN

UDON STAFF
UDON CHIEF - ERIK KO
DIRECTOR OF PUBLISHING - MATT MOYLAN
SENIOR PRODUCER - LONG VO
VP OF SALES - JOHN SHABLESKI
PRODUCTION MANAGER - JANICE LEUNG
MARKETING MANAGER - JENNY MYUNG
JAPANESE LIASON - STEVEN CUMMINGS

CAPCOM:
JOHN DIAMONON,
NORIKO MATSUNAGA
SUSAN SUAREZ
BAO LE

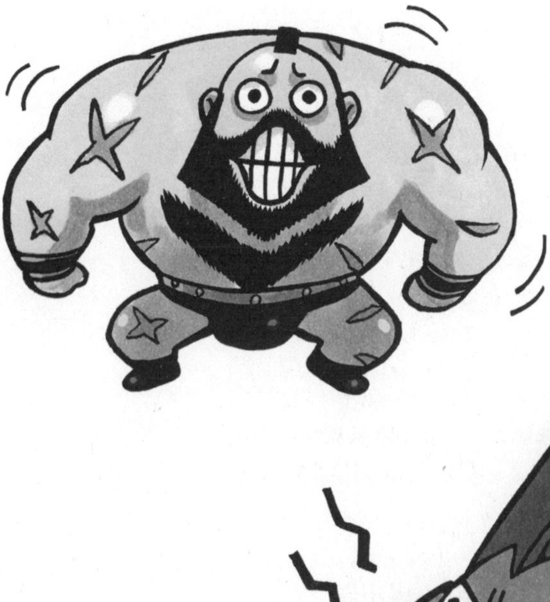

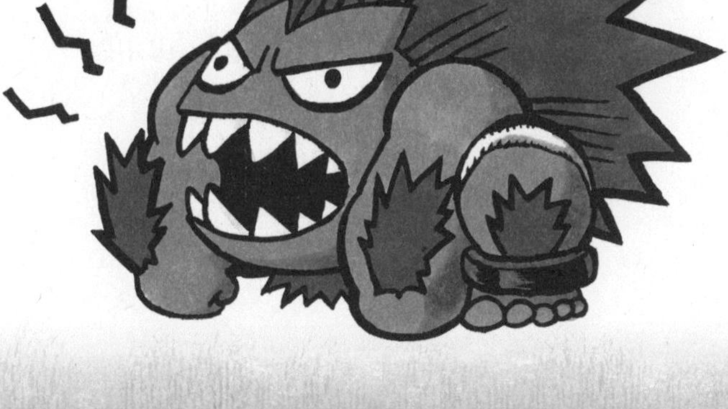

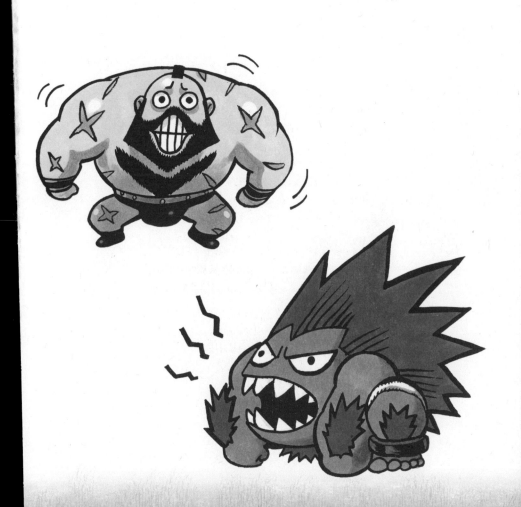

STREET FIGHTER
THE NOVEL
— WHERE STRENGTH LIES —

STREET FIGHTER: THE NOVEL

©Takashi Yano & Yusuke Murata 2016
©CAPCOM. Licensed for use by UDON Entertainment Corp.

Published by UDON Entertainment Corp.
118 Tower Hill Road, C1, PO Box 20008
Richmond Hill, Ontario, L4K 0K0, Canada

This book is a faithful translation of the book originally
released in Japan on APRIL 7, 2016, by PHP INTERFACE.

WWW.UDONENTERTAINMENT.COM

Softcover Edition:
ISBN-13: 978-1-77294-043-5
ISBN-10: 1-77294-043-7

First Printing: September 2018

Printed in Canada